Undisclosed

Desire 3

The Contracted Lovers

by Falon Gold

Text Naybery to 22828 to receive updates from Nayberry Publications.

~Prologue~
Twenty-three years ago, in Italy

"Camron, you don't have to respect anyone, but they do have to respect *you*, son. And if they refuse to, everyone has a price. Find it, then buy their loyalty, even if you have to take their money to get it. It won't be hard to do with the weaker people who—"

"Your poppa means those that have no money are weaker than those with money, Son, meaning us," Saleera Powers interrupts her husband, when she sees eight-year-old Camron's frown. "Their money is easy to access because they usually have very little and it's all in one place... if they have any at all," she adds condescendingly.

Like an island, Camron sits between his parents on a brown leather ottoman in the middle of the Italian tile in his father's study, mere feet from his parents' high-back, Victorian chairs. He's used to feeling isolated in his parents' presence and completely understands what Christophe Powers means by weaker people; he just doesn't know why his father said it. Yet, he'd sacrifice knowing the answer if it would get him in one of their laps or a hug from time to time.

Affection from his parents is as elusive as a pot of gold at the end of a rainbow. However, these kinds of talks come a dime a dozen around the Powers' mansion, where Christophe and Saleera don't talk *to* Camron, instead talk *at* him, bombarding him from both sides with their bigoted way of thinking.

Christophe laughs, humorlessly. "Right, love. People with no money have no power, Camron. They'll put up with just about anything from those who have both money and power. You already have them and can do what you want in this world to anyone because you're a Powers. That makes you better than everyone else who should bend at the knee and bend to your will. They will when you open your own branch of whatever business you choose in America someday. It's your duty to carry on the Powers' name in the corporate world, add to our influence in it, and succeed in everything you do, even if you have to walk all over someone else to do it. Never get your hands dirty with grunt work."

Camron's frown deepens. "What's grunt work, Poppa?"

Christophe leans forward. "Manual labor, Son, where you actually put your hands on the products you'll be using to make your life easier as an adult. That's beneath you. So is making someone else more money than you'll get out of any deal you strike. Always hire others less fortunate than you to do the grunt work. That's how the poor live. Off richer people's benevolence. Do you understand what I'm saying to you, Son?"

Camron nods.

Christophe looks over Camron's head, then raises his tumbler of whiskey from his bony knee to his mouth. His mouth is thin-lipped and cruelly made like his disposition, which he hopes to pass on to his children. So far, there's only Camron.

Saleera raises her glass of wine and gives an air toast to the ruining of their son.

In fourteen years, Saleera and Christophe Powers will turn a monster loose on Candleton, New York... and on Amari Spencer.

~Present Day Camron Powers~

Stepping from under the ceiling shower's rain head and body jet sprays before I'm ready to answer the ringing cell phone that's sitting on the marble countertop of the his-and-her sinks should be a crime. I don't need a view of the name on the screen to know it's Former Sheriff Blake Powers calling. Ever since he's taken it upon himself to rehabilitate me for Amari Spencer and enlist my help to plan his engagement party to Astrid Daniels, I can expect his call every morning. Somehow, he's managed to convince me that changing my ways is the only option I'll ever have to get what he has with Astrid: love, happy home, and a child. If I need to change most, okay *all* the ways I treat women and report to him each move I and his mother have made since she hijacked the planning of his engagement party from me, so be it. But Blake checking in with me daily is getting damn ridiculous.

I turn the water off, plod out of the fogged-up glass octagon to retrieve the phone, creating puddles on the bamboo flooring. I swipe a hand across the mirror. "Blake, your party is still being handled by Ashley, who finished up with the old-fashion mailing out of all the invites a month ago."

"That's not what I'm calling about this morning, Camron. Are you alone?"

Why in God's name does he need to know that? Unless something bad has happened that he needs me to keep confidential. God forbid. Enough shit went down when he was hurt during his stint as Sheriff, developing amnesia. I won't hear the end of Ashley's ranting if he decides not to take the helm of the Powers Royal Resort when it opens to the public in two weeks. It was much easier than I thought it would be to sway him to run the newest family business as CEO, essentially getting him back into the family fold. Ashley may have put me up to it, but Blake knows

I let her do it for my own selfish reasons and his growing family's right to be financially stable.

Most of all, I miss the cousinship we had years ago, before Blake put all the Powers in his rearview and didn't look back. From the time he was six, the Owens gave him something that the Powers couldn't or wouldn't: love. He gives the Owens his love and loyalty. Unfortunately, for me, I have no fucking idea what love or loyalty is for anyone other than the Powers. Nothing else besides ruthless business and survival tactics have been taught to me by my parents. Blake is determined to teach me what love and loyalty is for Amari's sake. If I don't let him, I could lose her, if I haven't already.

Unobtainable and unimpressed with my wealth, she's the opposite of my type. Bedding women is so much easier when they've targeted me. Amari targets whatever area I'm not in. I won't lie and say I've waited around for her to suddenly fall in love with me either. According to Blake, I'm an idiot for assuming she would because of who I am, a Powers, privileged, prestigious, powerful... You get my point.

Amari can barely stand to be in the same room with me. At this rate, I'll commit murder to get her to smile for me. She hasn't done that since I hired her.

"Camron, are you still there?" He's impatient as hell.

"Yes, I'm here and alone. What's going on, Blake?"

"Nothing. Just making sure you're not giving Amari any more reasons to hate you."

I wince. "She doesn't *hate* me, and I haven't dated anyone else in months. Trust me, my man parts are feeling the strain. I'm this close to locking her in the damn office and seducing her since I don't want anyone else."

"Yep, you're in love."

I scoff at my image. "It's not like she would notice though. She spends every available minute thinking she's hiding from me."

Crushing the phone between my shoulder and ear, I grab a towel off the chrome bracket over the toilet and wrap the thick cotton around my body.

"She hides because you're a jerk, Camron. You've got your work cut out for you there. Building a relationship with her is going to be the hardest thing you ever do, after she's been watching you screw around for years. First, you must earn her trust, which is why I asked if you were alone. Continue keeping the other women away. Amari falling in love with you will come later... hopefully." If I don't screw it up first is what he leaves unsaid.

If you ask me, I don't screw up at all. If I listen to Blake, that's what I've been doing since meeting Amari. Out of the two of us, he has to be right, because Amari wants nothing to do with me. No one in the Powers family has what he has with Astrid: mutual love and respect that's not gained from tearing somebody down and successful business dealings. Both love and respect pour off Blake and Astrid in suffocating waves when they're tuning out the whole world around them. It's worse when they're about to disappear into a bedroom together.

I'm tired of not having that with Amari, screwing up with her, and screwing around with women who mean nothing to me. For a few months now, I haven't been able to ignore that I want to settle down with only her. It started way before then, when I didn't recognize exactly what my heart wanted, nor was I ready to. Her heart doesn't want the same thing with me, period.

BJ starts to whimper in the background. Blake coos to his infant son, while making the racket that comes from fixing his one-month old's breakfast at his kitchen sink. I'd recognize the sounds from the making of a bottle in my sleep, after listening to him do it every morning for months.

"How different can love be from running a business?" I ask. "You spend hours with another person, convincing them to put their trust in you. I can do that standing on my head," I continue.

"You have no idea how different love and trust are. Trust is even harder to pull off, especially when a woman has already decided you're untrustworthy. I have a bad feeling you're about to learn the difference today. That's why I'm all up in your business this morning."

Being a sheriff has activated hunches that would've spared Blake a head injury during a burglary, if the owner of the hotel being raided had stayed out of the commotion. Now, Blake's a businessman like his parents wanted, and his feelings are being used to investigate my nonexistent love life.

I huff. "You and your feelings, Blake. You were not as subtle as you think you were the other mornings. You can fall back though. After I take Amari on a few trips, focus only on her for a change, and take her to bed, she'll love me back. What girl wouldn't, when I can give her everything she wants in and out of the bedroom?"

He scoffs. "So damn arrogant. Screwing her senseless and spending money on her isn't going to get it. She's not a gold digger and can deal with less drama from battery-operated boyfriends who women don't have to wonder about their whereabouts when they're not in the same room with it. It's what she *needs* that's going to give *you* the most problems."

"Man, what does that even mean?"

"Exactly, Camron! You don't know what it means because you don't know the first thing about loving anyone. That's your parents' fault, so I'll take pity on you and tell you. What Amari needs from you can't be placed in a box with a pretty bow on top and delivered or purchased from the corner market."

"I wouldn't go to the corner market anyway. Who knows where they get their goods from?"

Blake exhales heavily into the phone. "Oh my God. Who cares where they come from? And it doesn't matter because you don't go anywhere to get what she needs, Camron. You reach deep inside, pull out the best of you, and offer it to her no matter where you are. If you're sincere and she wants what you have to offer, she'll offer you the same. Now, the second step to getting mutual love and respect: she doesn't open a door or pull out her own chair ever."

I'm sure Malisa Owens' father taught him that because Blake's father sure as hell doesn't do any of that for Ashley. If Saleera doesn't open the door, she doesn't get in any building either.

"Give the best of me. Open doors for her. Everything I say off the top of my head is wrong. I got it." I really don't—reaching deep down isn't something I'm used to doing, as well as censoring what I say.

I'll conquer those battlefields for Amari though, even if it kills me. Now, what am I going to do about talking to her? Feel my way through it is going to have to do until I get the hang of loving someone.

The slow creaking of my office door two rooms over echoes softly through the quiet in the bedroom and bathroom.

Amari.

"Got to go, Blake. Amari's trying to sneak in with a contract that needs my attention. If I don't catch her, she'll drop it on my desk and run. She might actually hide somewhere other than the copier room this time, and it'll take more than a shout or a couple steps to find her."

Blake's healthy laughter punches me in the ear. "Best of luck to you, cousin. You're going to need it. Over and out."

At least someone is enjoying the difficulty I'm experiencing at Amari's hand. She's proving harder to pin down than the wind.

Chapter One
A few minutes earlier
~Amari~

Dreading, resenting, and hiding, all of which I'm doing right now between two file cabinets, is how I spend my work days at Powers Enterprises, and during business trips with my boss. The dread originates from wondering if I'll come to work one day and find him balls deep in a random woman in the corner office that we share, instead of behind the side wall that hides his bedroom and ensuite bathroom. Yes, he actually sleeps and bathes there to avoid getting up at the butt-crack of dawn for the forty-mile commute from his suburban mansion. He'd never get here on time with the horrendous morning traffic.

It's the other conveniences the secret room behind the wall provides that he doesn't take advantage of: blocking his kissing and fondling sessions with women at his desk from my sight. When he's in the middle of one, I have a horribly dependable knack for needing to get in the office. Walking in on him having sex is all that's left for him to do in front of me, and it's coming, sooner or later. I'm avoiding that for as long as I can.

Resentment for his highly inappropriate behavior in the workplace, how uncomfortable it makes me feel, and being too accustomed to the lifestyle that my job enables to quit has been growing since I accepted the position as his personal assistant over five years ago. The mistake of thinking I'd struck gold when I was called in to interview for the position, which I didn't apply for but stupidly accepted when he offered me an obscene amount of money yearly, would become apparent quickly.

Dumb enough to develop a crush on him at first sight before he said anything about money, I will never admit to out loud. Although, I have a damn good excuse for the short-term attraction I felt: Mr. Powers is gorgeous, beyond rich, has an Italian accent, and is brilliant when it comes to making money. What girl wouldn't go goo-goo eyed over him? Especially when tall, dark, and handsome is too lame of a description for him.

Inky-black eyelashes, dark, oval eyes. They stand out from chiseled facial features covered in smooth, olive skin. His deceptively lean build is assembled of muscles formed and maintained by daily martial arts workouts in the rec room complete with pool. On the top floor of the building is where he hones the air of a predator surrounding his hand-tailored suits, an unbreathable fog that women succumb to by the dozens, happily. Not me of course.

He doesn't walk but stalks wherever he goes. Renowned for his business acumen, he's often asked to do speaking engagements all over the world about his success in the real estate industry. Except, no one speaks about how he ran through personal assistants and women like a starving wolf does meat before I was hired. That's because anyone who has any knowledge of his actions can't discuss them openly. I signed a nondisclosure agreement too, before I realized why he needed it.

Only a few days in his employ passed before he showed me his true nature—a man whore who's impolite as hell. Thank God that he outed himself before I fell in love with him. Since then, I've spent most of my days ducking him in the copier room that's two doors down from his brothel... or uh, office, whenever I can. Although he wouldn't ever allow me to make the copier room my personal office, I sure as hell try, every day. Don't know why though. Other than it's as far as I can get from him while still in shouting distance, it doesn't do me any justice when his secretary, Sheryl Wright, can always track me down there whenever she needs to pass something off to him.

The regretful expression she wears every time she has to feed me to the lion in its den is why I consider her a friend. She can't help Mr. Powers is constantly buying up dirt cheap property globally, flipping it to make a hefty profit, so I don't take it personal when she shows up with something pertaining to his business that I have to take straight to him. However, coming out of the copier room for reasons other than going home for the day is just as much dreaded as finding him screwing somebody.

But, oh how I wish I had every right to lock the door before Sheryl starts the downward spiral of my day with the soft rapping of bluntly-shaped manicured nails on it. Then she barges in, in beautifully-cut skirt suits before I can tell her to go away. At least, she gives me some warning. Everyone else just walks in whenever they need to use the copy machine, which is their right. Doesn't mean I have to like it, especially not when it's Mr. Powers who's gotten down off his throne long enough to look for me himself. It's too bad that I don't have another place to hide after paperwork has landed on Sheryl's desk stationed right outside his office.

Instead of slipping the forms under the door for him to find, she slides them and her pity across the closest file cabinet's top to me. When I think about it, she'll probably get fired for making him bend over to pick them up, if she put them under his door. I even tried ducking down once after she knocked. She took the time to look for me between my iron havens. Now, I just beg her to take the freshly-typed contracts for another Powers' acquisition or payroll sheets to him herself, even though it's my job to stand between him and his other employees.

Whenever she gives in to my pleas, and that's not frequently, it doesn't do either of us any good. Mr. Powers makes her turn right back around, with instructions for her to bring me to him, too. I get a few more minutes of peace though, so the begging is worth it.

On the really bad days, when I rather face off with a spitting cobra than be here, because I know he's entertaining a woman, and Sheryl refuses to enter his inner sanctum, she starts giving suggestions about what I might find when I do. Bare asses are usually included in her description. I haven't seen one yet, but she always gets my middle-finger for her jokes. Then she laughs her ass off, while I slink toward his office.

In about ten minutes, my and her routine will begin. For now, it isn't a concern—I got to work thirty minutes early just to stand among the supply cabinets that are short enough for me to prop my elbows on top of. My back is holding up the speckled, cream-painted wall, bare feet crossed while I sip hazelnut espresso from my mug with *Bosses Suck* written on it. I'm mentally preparing for my Friday, a guarantee that my boss will have a scheduled liaison at his desk to kick off the weekend by three o'clock. A tropical island far away from Camron Powers and Candleton is calling my name when a tap at the door comes too damn early.

"Go away, Sheryl!" I yell before she strolls in.

It's the first time I don't have a throat full of hot coffee when she announces her arrival.

Her timing must be off today, I think to myself just as the door swings open.

Today's skirt suit consists of a fire-engine red, quarter-sleeve jacket with black trim. It hugs Sheryl's ample bosom and small waist and flares out at the bottom above her fitted skirt that respectfully stops at her knees.

No matter what pair of shoes she's wearing, I want them, even if they're spiked, black stilettos with red-bottoms that I'm not willing to pay the obscene amount of money that she spent. I couldn't afford the aching feet they'll give me anyway, since I'm not slim in all the places she is. I have fifteen pounds of extra padding on her, and it's all in one place, my ass. She's built like a skinny, but curvy, brickhouse with red hair spiraling down to her waist, and she's off-limits since she's married.

I'm sure my boss hates that and wishes he knew what her cupid-bow lips coated with glossy red lipstick felt like beneath his. He's tasted everyone else's in New York... except mine.

13

Yeah, that sounded petty. I promise I'm not. Mr. Powers isn't the man for me, and I only hate to see Sheryl's lips when they're tilted up in one corner with that ominous, sorrowful look that sits in her emerald green eyes.

Oh God, it's sitting there right now too. I already know I've lost the battle of who'll take their chances with entering his harem…I mean, his office before the workday has even begun.

I shake my head. "It's too early for this shit, Sheryl. I'm not officially on the clock yet." That complaint would carry more weight if I actually used a time sheet.

Still, I don't start work until nine. Every bit of reprieve I can grab before counts.

A princess-cut diamond solitaire and gold wedding band slices through the air. Paperwork glides across the gray, slick surface toward me, predictably.

"I'm sorry, Amari. I saw the light on under the door, and I need a favor from you this time. I have a mandatory safety meeting in five minutes in the other direction, or I wouldn't bother you this early. This contract is hot off the company's top lawyer's desk. Lance caught me on the way to the meeting. Mr. Powers could lose the waterfront property in Dubai if it isn't handled right away. Who knows whose head he'll chop off if someone gets in a bigger bid before the Sheik signs this paperwork? Save everyone's job here, including mine and my husband's, and get this to Mr. Powers right away. He may not even be up yet. If it's any consolation, the faster you get it there, the faster you can get out of there, and Saturday night's drinks are on me."

Damn the consolations, I just need ten more minutes of quiet time, but I can't refuse her. Resisting the urge to stomp my foot like a petulant child is hard. I go with the quiet tapping of my self-manicured toes on the plush carpet. It's either that, or scream.

"You know getting in and out of that man's office doesn't work that way, Sheryl. He'll want to know everything in this

14

contract without reading it himself. If I didn't know any better, I swear he likes to hear me read to him. Saturday night better be top shelf liquor, too. I'm going to need it. Next time I come in early, I'm sitting on the floor in the damn dark."

Now, why did I warn her of that?

Giggles rocket out of her mouth, making her slender shoulders shake, as her tiny feet spin toward the door. "You got it, love. Desmond says hello."

I harrumph, then snatch the papers up and slip my feet into the handmade, backless, flat mules I designed in college. "Give Desmond the finger for me. He's the one that found this future prime piece of real estate that needs urgent attention."

Damn her husband too, for doing his job of scouring countries for low-priced property that Powers Enterprises can snap up then turn into the place-to-be for the wealthy. Mr. Powers gives him bonuses after each purchase pays off.

"Desmond feels just as badly for you as I do, Amari. If he and I were Mr. Powers' favorite employee, we'd spare you this morning, love, but he's already trolling Europe for the next buy."

I suck air through my teeth. "If I didn't love you and Desmond, you'd be on your own with this one, but I'll have you both know Mr. Powers doesn't have a favorite employee, just favorite pieces of ass. Actually, he doesn't have a favorite one of those, either. He has *all* the ass in New York."

She points at me then her. "He hasn't had yours and mine, and he doesn't have a favorite because it would be his only, so he hasn't found the right one yet."

"He doesn't want mine, and that's fine, but yours is definitely enticing enough to get him off my back for a while so I *can* find my favorite. Now, that's a favor you can do me that I'll appreciate, even if Desmond will kill me for pimping out his wife. When Mr. Powers finds *his* favorite, God help the woman. No man should be able to get it up almost every day, Sheryl."

Am I whining right now? You can bet your last dollar I am. I'd like to sit at my desk instead of standing in here all the time to preserve my sanity.

"Oh yes, they should be able to get it up almost every day," she tosses over shoulder before walking out.

"You're biased, woman, married, and in love. Desmond is a blond God. Of course, you want to hump like rabbits with him."

"And you will want to, too, Amari, as soon as you find the right one," she comments while retreating.

"I won't find the right one hiding in here or in my apartment. Definitely not when Mr. Powers is dragging me across the globe." Sheryl is out of hearing range, so I'm talking to myself. "Damn, shouldn't traveling be a good thing?"

It isn't when it comes to going with Mr. Powers, even after the latest trip to Arrow, Colorado with him visiting his family for business purposes. Things will work out just the way he wanted, as usual for him. His successes are always a fiasco for me who sweats like a Hebrew slave in business attire, fetching flutes of champagne and serving lukewarm pâté for fresh bread slices, hors d'oeuvres, fruits, and cheese for his peers and family. This time, I had to haul it all out of a picnic basket that weighed a ton. *It felt like it did anyway.*

Did Mr. Powers assist with lugging it from one place to another with his chosen selections? Hell no. Would he risk his back to do it? For the answer, just double the first 'hell no.'

Being financially stable should be a good thing, too. It would be, if I wasn't sacrificing other important things to make the money, such as dating, which is always the last thing on my mind when I leave Mr. Powers' company. Once I'm home, I need to decompress immediately, with my feet up. I hate to leave again. Every morning is a struggle to get out of bed. I'm winning so far. One day, that streak is going to run out.

Mr. Powers' office antics drive me bat-guano crazy, and they're well known throughout Powers Enterprises, a Plexiglas tower of thirty-six floors. If he was a decent man, he'd be ashamed of his reputation. He isn't, but I am.

The monthly ten grand I make isn't nearly enough for all the shit I go through, hush-mouth money that I need if I want to earn a living. Or convince a bank to loan me more coins to start my own business someday. Maybe even help out my parents with health concerns, and continue saving for my retirement.

At this rate, five more years here will secure my nest egg that I can use for startup money if the bank says no, though the first rule of business is never use your own money. That is the only thing I managed to learn while working here. Learning corporate tactics and rules at the elbows of a successful magnate is the only reason why I took this job, but five minutes in Mr. Powers' company is enough to make me go mad.

I drag the length of the marble corridor. The distant click-clacking of Sheryl's heels veering in the opposite direction serves as theme music for the hopeless walking their last mile. Why in the hell don't I just quit?

For the millionth time, you need the money. Who else is going to pay you as much as he does until you're an entrepreneur?

No one, so I suck up my misery, halt at the office door that opens to the equivalent of the gas chamber, then rap my knuckles against it. Giving fair warning that I'm coming in. If luck is on my side, Mr. Powers and his date are fully dressed already. Sometimes, they're not.

Whatever state of dress they're in, it's not like he'll shove away whatever ditzy bombshell is wearing expensive highlights and little clothing. She'll become leftovers from last night's tryst with him. She just doesn't know it yet, probably standing within his powerful thighs that are pressed against the rim of his desk, thinking she'll get to see the inside of his bedroom again.

17

I'm not the one who's going to inform her that last night is a one-time endeavor. She'll find out the hard way soon enough. Everyone must take their licks for their bad decisions. Hopefully, he'll stop kissing her goodbye long enough to bid me entry.

Maybe, you should recommend putting a sock on the door when he's not alone.

It's probably a waste of breath, so why bother?

When no one answers my first knock, which is weird because getting no answer before I enter is becoming frequent, I do it again. Usually, I get a high-pitched griping sound from the latest 'her', if not his deep intonation of 'Come in, Amari' laced with Italian aphrodisiac.

No answer is good though—it means the office is empty and I won't want to bleach my eyes afterwards. It'll be even better for me if they're not through showering yet. The occasional opportunity for 'dropping the paperwork on his desk and running out' is a possibility today. I rarely get it, and I'm certainly taking it, even though my shoes with quarter-inch heels and no backs aren't meant for sprinting in. I'll take the chance of losing one if it helps me get away.

I breathe in deeply, then ease the lever on the door downward, cracking the wooden barrier wide enough to stick just my head around it. Peeking into the dim office with soft rays of morning light leaking in from behind his desk, the sliding wall to his hidden chamber is standing wide open. I've been finding it this way every morning for months now. That's unusual, too. When is the last time someone stayed the night with him?

Not your business, Amari. Getting in then getting out before he hears you is.

I set one foot on the lush, tan carpeting. Mr. Powers strolls out of the bedroom in a towel swathed around his hips, and that's all. It's not his bare ass, but damn close to it. Great, and not in a good way. Before another freshly-showered, half-covered body appears for anyone passing by to see, which will be humiliating only to me, I rush inside the room and slam the door closed behind me. With my back to it, I cross my arms over my thirty-six D-cups.

"I'm sick to death of this, Mr. Powers. If you have a date in there that spilled over into this morning, ask her to stay behind the wall until I've read through this contract with you for the Dubai property and scanned it into the computer to send to the present owner's attorney. And for God's sake, put some clothes on. Please!"

Cocking an eyebrow and dipping his head sends tendrils of wet black hair falling onto his brow. He brushes them backwards slowly, a move worthy of a photo shoot, while giving me a black, penetrating stare.

"Sick of what, Amari? And there's no—"

"I'm sick of the disrespect. It never stops with you."

And something has to give—it was always going to be my tolerance for the harsh environment I'm forced to endure. Today, that happens to be the definition if his pecs, arms, and the visible, thin line of hair that scales the middle of his abs, vanishing into the towel. Good God!

He twists at the waist, looking around the room for the person that I'm talking to disrespectfully.

"Oh, I'm talking to you, Mr. Powers."

Even if it costs me my job, I've earned the right to say what's on my mind, possibly getting fired for my troubles. Best thing he'll ever do for me. And I'll say exactly what's on my heart, ah, I meant my mind when I unglue the tip of my tongue from the roof of my suddenly bone-dry mouth. Anyone can guess why that happens every time I see a part of his body, and they'd be wrong. I know exactly where their mind would head, into the gutter, unless they're predicting my blood is drying up in my veins because of the boiling anger sweeping through me.

He trains his piercing black orbs on me again. A shiver wreaks havoc up my spine. I'm sure that happens whenever anyone is in the front sights of a predator, so I ignore it.

"No, you're not talking to me like that, Amari. And before you try it again, I advise you to check yourself before you say anything else."

"No can do. I'm going to wreck myself with saying even more, and you'll still be the only one that's going too far in here. This is not an office. It's a catwalk for you and your girlfriends. You parade them in and out of here like they're paying you and you have a bookie who needs his money now, or he's going to break both of your knees later. I can't go one more day of dealing with this. What employee spends as much time as possible in the copier room? Do you ever wonder why I do that?"

He raises one finger and opens his mouth to reply.

"No, you don't wonder," I cut him off. "Because you don't care how your actions affect me. It's downright painful to come to work every day and be treated like wallpaper, which wouldn't want to watch you with other women either if it had a choice. Oh, and you're bad-mannered. What boss walks around in a towel? You have no idea what please, thank you, and being a gentleman means. What real man let's a woman carry something too heavy for her? And by the way, I'm not supposed to have to give up almost every weekend to serve brunch to you and your family in other states or your colleagues in other countries. That's what caterers and their staff are for, so you're hindering someone else's ability to feed their family. But do you express your appreciation for robbing me of my weekends and other people of a paycheck? I'll answer that question for you, too. No."

His pupils shrink. "I don't rob anyone. I pay you extra for the weekends, Amari, so someone is getting a paycheck, even if it's not who *you* want it to be."

"Do you give me the option to turn the extra money down? No, and I'm going mentally insane slowly from the stresses of this job. Or in my case, I'm going insane while trying to stop *you* from driving me insane."

Suppose I had a love interest? Any man would've surely dumped me by now. I'd settle for getting my own business off the ground, but I haven't produced a sketch for a new shoe design in three years.

Mr. Powers sneers. "Who wants the option to turn down an extra three thousand dollars? My life is your life. If mine is running smoothly, yours is too."

"Everyone wants options. All money isn't good money. Your life only finances mine. They're not supposed to merge outside of this business, and I've accomplished nothing with the money I make. It's just sitting in the bank while I grow gray at twenty-six. No, I'm twenty-seven now. My freaking birthday was yesterday, and I *forgot* it."

I never expected him to remember or even know the date that's only special to anyone connected to the Spencer's. It wouldn't have hurt his business to let me enjoy my birthday with my family, who called and inadvertently reminded me of what day it was.

"When you work for me, Amari, there *are* no options. You work and make the money, and you'll have other birthdays."

Damn, he didn't even give me a 'Happy belated birthday, Amari. Take the rest of the day off.' I won't give him the satisfaction of knowing how much that stings.

"It's just like you to think some crap like that, Mr. Powers, but this isn't a sweatshop. Why don't I have vacation days I can take? There are no legal indentured servants anymore. It's like I'm a prostitute. You're my pimp or master, dictating when I quit working after normal business hours have concluded. Those are the hours you hired me for, remember? If you needed more, you

21

should've said so during my interview. I'd have saved us from this conversation by turning down the position. Furthermore, birthdays are too important to forget. They're milestones to celebrate on *that* day, which is everyone's special day. Each one the marking of the continuation of life amongst people like you who would rather break those still in their right minds. I sure as hell shouldn't have forgotten *my* birthday, even if you didn't remember it."

He takes a step forward.

Well, that certainly can't be a good thing.

"I didn't forget your birthday, Amari, and you wouldn't have celebrated it with me anyway." Another step. "But I'm much better than a pimp and master. I don't require you to take off your clothes at all." Another step. "Or work the streets nor twenty-four hours a day for me." Another step. This is going very badly. "Nor do you sleep in a cold room beneath my stairs in inadequate housing for terrible pay." Dammit, he's getting too close. "I haven't ever asked you to clean my house."

He stops in front of me, eyes dropping to my mouth. I forget what breathing is. Have no idea why I'm suffocating, but one of us should back off. I don't mind being that person. Except, purging my system of the baggage I've gathered since taking this job from several feet away won't be as effective as doing it right in his face.

So, stand your ground, Amari, no matter how much you'd like to run.

"No, you don't ask all that of me, just compromise my morals with requiring me to be a voyeur in your sex life. Don't mistake me for a prude. The human body is a beautiful thing." God knows his is, and every other woman in New York knows it too.

Petty again.

Am not. Now, where was I? Oh, the human body.

"But I have no desire to see yours wrapped around someone else's at any given minute of the damn day. Who's to say with your 'thy is your king' attitude, you *won't* be demanding I take off my clothes or clean your house at some point? I sure can't say you won't do it because nothing else is off limits to you, and you don't pay me enough to buy my ethics. You don't have enough money." Not even with his billions.

He smiles. It's more of a contemptible leer with one side of his mouth raised.

"Oh, but I do have enough money to buy anything I want, Amari. Or did you forget that too?"

How could I forget that he comes from money when he's around? He wouldn't let me. He even smells like cash. Yeah, that's probably the soap or the cologne he wears, and it's mind-scrambling right now.

I take a baby step back. "Money doesn't rule everyone's world and give you the right to treat me how you deem fit."

"Actually, it does. Without it, no one has nothing, are nothing, will amount to nothing, and will be pushed around until they have enough money to push back."

Bullying people. Yep, that's pretty much what he's confessing to. Something inside me fractures—whatever it is that's breaking wanted better from him. I've accepted that I wasn't going to get it a long time ago. The part of me that's splitting in pieces should too.

As long as I'm a thousandnaire, I'll never mean anything to this man or be treated as a person with feelings by him and his family. They're even bigger snobs than he is. I have the misfortune of being in the same room with all of them every year, when they come together in Italy.

Their family reunion is a conference around a table at the parent company that started the Powers' global rise in... well, power. Each member that runs an umbrella company in the corporation reports their individual failure and successes at the meeting, as if they're still children bringing home report cards to their parents. Suddenly, Mr. Powers' behavior makes sense to me,

23

and only the good Lord knows why it does at this moment after all these years.

"Who specifically taught you that baloney about the meaning of money and what you're allowed to do because you have it, which you obviously fell hook, line, and sinker for, Mr. Powers? Enquiring minds want to know."

You sound like you're leading group therapy, Amari. You can't save this man from himself. It's the last thing he thinks he needs or wants for you, of all people, to attempt.

His demeanor morphs from smug to insulted. "It's not... *baloney*."

He sounds disgusted. I'm not certain if it's because he's tasted the mystery meat once, or he thinks the almighty dollar defines him. It's likely both that has his luscious lips stretched taut and the bridge of his aristocratic nose wrinkled.

"Oh, but it is baloney that you've been conned into believing. I feel sorry for you. All your money will never compare to the treasures that come from love, respect, and sharing your life with people who you'll happily give your life for in exchange for while they feel the same about you. Those treasures cost nothing, are priceless, aren't touchable. Yet, they touch you in places the most skilled of surgeons will never reach with a scalpel. Some people even kill for them. Yes, you're rich, Mr. Powers, but you're poor in all the ways it truly counts. Filling up their hearts with love is how people of every race in every country made it in this world before money became the root of all evil. Trust me, your family was underprivileged once. Someone in your family still is. So, no matter what gibberish someone has filled your head with about the superiority you think money gives you over others, you still put your pants on one leg at a time like everyone else. It's your view of your bank account that makes wealth so poisonous, and you can't take it with you when you're dead. You'll need something else to get you into heaven, if there is one. For your sake, I hope there isn't, or you're just… exactly what your women are when you're done with them. Ironic how that puts you on the same level as the trail of bodies you leave behind in your wake, isn't it?"

I pity the fools that he traipses in and out of here. He won't ever be the whole package for any of them, and frankly, it's the waste of a beautiful man that has so much potential to better those around him. Instead, he just thinks he's better.

And why do you give two shits, Amari?

Maybe I've gone completely nuts finally.

Fine, keep pretending you're crazy, but your purge is complete. Now, get the hell out of here before you're being fitted for a straight jacket.

"With that said, I quit," rips out of my mouth.

Our jaws go slack simultaneously. I've stunned us both. I didn't intend to throw in the towel on this job just yet. Evidently, my subconscious seems to know what's best for me, and that his office shenanigans will never end. Nor will he ever understand how his character makes me despise a man I admired while studying for my business doctorate, aspiring to copy his accomplishments after graduating college, which he came to speak at once.

I missed his speech, which I heard was awe-inspiring. Because of it, many of my peers have gone on to start successful businesses of their own. Yet, he sees me and anyone else as prey if we don't come from a dynasty formed four generations ago that backs us in every idiotic and genius move we make.

When today didn't start like all the others, I should've known something would go sideways, but what's done is done. I shove the contract in his chest. He catches my wrist against his skin burdened with scattered dewdrops. My mouth waters. Mini-bolts of lightning strike overly sensitive places within. Drenching rain soaks my underwear, and he's only touching my wrist. I'll be surprised if my thighs don't squeak when I walk. What the mother-loving hell? I've never felt any of that before.

You've never touched him before either.

I snatch my hand away, banging my knuckles on the door behind me. The pain isn't even an afterthought. I'm more afraid of what else he'll effect on me if I let him touch me any longer.

"You should rethink about what you've just said, Amari," he snarls, balling his hands into fists at his thighs, one crushing his phone in a white-knuckled grip. "You're throwing away a good job."

I sidestep toward the corner desk positioned diagonal to his that's facing the door. Then I swivel to him before backing away, refusing to give my back to him. Some people need to be watched with both eyes, and they're not all criminals.

"You wouldn't believe how many times a day I've thought about saying 'I quit' since I came to work for you. Should've done this sooner. You're not the only one who's been conned. You're not the man I thought you were, nor do you deserve anything you have, and you damn sure can't teach me anything from behind that wall. I thought you were the best at business. That's why I took this job. You've mastered something alright. I don't need lessons in that area though."

In reverse, it's a much longer hike to the glass wall opposite the solid one concealing his bedroom. Perhaps, it feels that way with him staring me down, eyes roaming over my off the rack, white dress with crisscrossing straps over my cleavage. I've never felt so old-fashioned and plain under anyone's gaze. Mr. Powers manages to make me feel this way every day when he shouldn't, undeserving of the worst of my emotions.

"Are you judging me, Amari?"

I almost laugh, and I would have if I didn't think he was judging me, finding me lacking.

"Why not? You're looking down your nose at me right now. Turnabout is fair play, right? Oh, that's right, you don't believe in fair play, just fair preying on those that don't have as much as you do." I bend at the knees and relieve the bottom drawer of my purse. "That's preying with an 'e' by the way."

"I know what you mean. I couldn't have graduated Stanford at the head of my class if I couldn't spell and read between the lines."

"Kudos for you. I graduated from a regular old university, and I still quit this job. I'd wish you a nice life, but you'll have that anyway with your lifestyle. It's all you need."

"Isn't that what everyone needs? My lifestyle."

I shake my head. "Most of us just want to receive the respect that we give to others. It isn't too much to ask for, believe it or not. You be amazed at who couldn't be persuaded to stand anywhere near your lifestyle, and who all just wants the money to make life more comfortable for their families. Some even would use it to make a real difference in the world. Unfortunately, it does take money to do what giving your time and heart can't. We both know what you do with your time. If that's all you want the flashbacks of your life to consist of before you kick the bucket, then your life here on earth has been well spent already. Congratulations."

I bet his unused heart is as dusty as an attic.

"I won't tolerate your smartassness, Amari."

"You won't have to for much longer. All I have to do is get my purse, and I'll be out of your hair. Thank you for your cooperation in advance."

It's a relief I didn't fill my desk up with personal knick-knacks. The less to carry away from here, the faster I can leave. The cactus plant loitering on the edge of the glass surface was here when I took possession of the desk, or I would take it with me. It's the only thing flourishing from this work environment and the endless sunlight that pours in from the floor to ceiling panels.

"You're not leaving me, Amari," he growls.

I get a mental picture of an animal about to go rabid. He can't want me to stay that bad.

"You can't stop me. We don't have an employee contract for you to enforce."

If he'd insisted on one, I'll be stuck in his employ like Malisa Owens was with Apollo Nordic-Ford. The situation turned out beautifully for her though; she's happily married to him and the mother of his two boys and a girl, though the ultrasound alleged it was three boys. Can't visualize Apollo scrambling for girly baby stuff, but he'd have done it happily. He's not an asshat like Mr. Powers is.

On the contrary, Apollo's an extremely nice billionaire that I met in Arrow when he dropped by the sheriff's station to check on Blake, who introduced Apollo to Mr. Powers and me. That is, after I served the contents of that damnable basket to Mr. Powers, Blake, and his girlfriend, Astrid.

If it wasn't for Blake and Astrid, I'd have stood at the back of the room like a waitress, waiting to clean up, while blending in with the wall. Instead, Astrid chitchatted with me while I stood as far back as I could from the small breakroom's table where they were seated, until Blake bought over a chair. There's no way I'll ever willingly share anything, even food, with Mr. Powers. However, I did enjoy swapping gossip with Astrid, who eased my homesickness and improved my mood before Malisa waddled in, to Apollo's disapproval. Apparently, she was supposed to be at home in their castle, with her feet up, heavily pregnant at the time, being waited on hand and foot.

A man's concern is something to look forward to when I find my favorite piece of ass, but the resemblance between Malisa and Astrid, who were both pregnant at the time, is freakishly freaky. I barely managed to not comment on it. Mr. Powers didn't hesitate to, creating an awkwardness that didn't depart until Malisa and Apollo left and Astrid struck up another conversation about the nursery she hoped to build for her baby boy. Mr. Powers can learn a thing or three hundred from the well-mannered people in Arrow, but I highly doubt if anyone can teach him any new tricks.

I walk toward him. He opens the door for me, his first chivalrous act that I've seen. Of course, it would be to show who he considers a lesser being the way out. Perfect.

"Fine, Amari," expels out of his gritted, pearly-white teeth. "Take the day off. Celebrate your birthday, but be back in the morning."

"Not in this lifetime, Mr. Powers. Thank you for opening the door for me."

For a moment, he just stares as if he's issuing a silent challenge as I approach him.

"You're welcome, and I'll see you tomorrow, Amari."

I smile up at him, then exit the room, retracing the path I take every evening to the elevator at the end of the corridor, with his eyes burrowing into my back. Only thirty-four floors to the lobby to go, seventy-eight paces to my Hyundai Accent parked in the underground garage.

It's liberating to be on this journey for the last time. Although, there's a conflicting heaviness in the bottom of my stomach. That's to be expected when I've tossed my livelihood in the dumpster. Nothing that getting another job won't cure though.

****

~Camron~

After Amari disappears into the elevator, I shut the back door and tread into my bedroom where I dial Blake's number. When he picks up, I sink down on the tousled bed linens, with my chest hollowed out like someone blew a hole in it. No, not someone. Amari.

"What happened, Camron?"

"Your steps backfired on me. She came in, tore into my ass about the woman that *isn't* here, then she quit. You'll be happy to know I opened the door she walked out of, while hoping she'd stay on this side of it." Why did I ever listen to Blake's advice? I practically let her walk out on me myself.

"Did you tell her that you didn't have a woman in there with you?"

"What part of 'tore into my ass' did you not hear? No, I couldn't get a word in. When I could, I was more concerned about her trying to leave me and convincing her that I'm not the monster she thinks I am."

Obviously, I didn't think she cared about what I did, as long as I paid her on time, sure she'd never want me. Now, I'm sure she'll never want me *because* of what I did, which are mistakes I stop making a while ago. I feel like I've been caught up and spanked. Hard! Everywhere!

"She's not yours, Camron, so she didn't leave you. She left the job."

"Feels the same to me. I got to get her back by any means necessary."

"No, not by any means necessary. That kind of thinking creates stalkers. And maybe she needed to quit. Or you'd still be tiptoeing around her. What *did* you say to her by the way?"

"Nothing that should've made her quit... I think."

"'You think' is double talk for everything you said to her was *wrong*."

"I might've repeated something that my father has said to me about a hundred times, and I told her to be back at work in the morning or she'll regret it."

I can hear, plain as day, Blake slapping his forehead.

"Good God. I'm surprised she didn't swing on your ass, fool. You basically threatened her, killed any chances you have with her before you had any, and you told her she amounted to the trash under the bottom of your shoe if you said anything that Christophe has told you. Step three, which should've been step one; never threaten or repeat anything your father or mother said to you to anyone else. Nor anything my parents say. It's all bullshit. Money doesn't make you more than anyone else or them lesser, unless you're talking about most of the people who have money, especially the Powers. They live on baser instincts and have no emotional connections, which makes them the poor ones." And animals who thrive on the 'survival of the fittest' rule.

Blake won't ever identify with that or completely embrace our family, even after agreeing to reenter the family just to make money with us. At this point, I can't blame him, especially not when according to him and Amari, my upbringing has left me lacking in a lot of departments. Right now, I just need to fill up the one for love.

Bless Blake for trying to help me by becoming to me what the Owens are to him: a link to the world where normal people are the ruling majority, money just a necessity to live in it. This makes me a minority and the ways of my world useless. I didn't think my wealth would ever fail to get me what I want, and maybe, Blake shouldn't be the one to teach me how to care for other's like he seems to have mastered.

But maybe, Amari should... on my territory.

"Camron, I can hear your brain working all the way here in Colorado. What are you scheming up?"

"She said something to that effect, too, about rich people. I need a plan to get her back. Yours isn't working."

"Whatever you're thinking of doing, Camron, don't!"

"Have to, cousin. She's not coming back to me on her own. I can feel it. I need to make some calls. You can monitor the situation if you want to. It's time you came for another visit anyway. The party's in a week."

I don't know why I enjoy my time with his family. He takes every chance to tell me how much of an ass I am to Amari. No one else would dare, save for him and Amari. And yet, I want them both in my life because it feels right to have them in it. Yep, I've lost my damn mind, over love no less. My father would be scandalized.

"Monitor what situation, Camron? You know what? I hate to ask what you're about to do. You'll probably incriminate me in a crime that your clout will get you out of doing the time for, so I'll repeat myself. Don't do it, Camron."

I grin for the first time in a month, looking forward to something since I don't know when, actually. Just because I smiled before today doesn't mean I was happy.

"Don't worry. I'm respecting Amari's decision to quit on me."

"Only because you have that contract to deal with, I bet. She has the right to quit, Camron."

I know that. A part of me just doesn't care. I can't make it either.

"Fuck the contract, Blake. Something else is at stake right now." My happiness and happily-ever-after, the only things that will fill the void in my chest. I want them both in the worst way now.

Even more since Amari grew the balls to kick me in mine. Watching her stand up to me is the hottest thing I've experienced... ever.

Feisty beneath her cool exterior. Who knew?

And dammit, I don't want anyone else to have it.

"With any other woman, I'd be glad to hear you say you have something at stake, Camron. It means you have genuine feelings for someone. The older Powers don't encourage that, but this is not any other woman you're dealing with. Amari doesn't play by rules that you do. She doesn't still need to learn when it comes to what matters the most in life. She already knows. I thought she and Astrid were going to cry when Apollo damn near carried Malisa back home and told her he'll be her personal butler until the triplets were born. He's setting the bar high for the rest of us."

"No such thing, Blake. I excel at everything I do."

"Because you don't play fair, Camron, or know when to give up. I swear if you do something stupid or illegal to get her back, I'll handcuff your ass myself and take you—"

"Yeah, yeah, to the woods and give me the 'do right by Amari, or this'll be where I lay' speech that you used to give to Malisa's boyfriends in school. We're too old for that, Blake." Always the protector, but Amari couldn't be safer with me.

Or she will be when I make her mine.

"No one is too old to be stranded in the forest to find their way back out again, while cuffed. I don't think you'd survive."

I find that extremely hilarious. "I've survived worse. You wouldn't arrest me anyway. You can't! You're not a cop anymore, remember?" Thank God for that.

"Break her heart, Camron," he says deadly serious, "and you'll find out the hard way what I can do. Right now, she has no idea who's coming after her, so she needs a shield, because going after her is exactly what you're going to do, isn't it?"

I stop laughing. "I don't want to break her heart. That'll be counterproductive when I need it *and* her. Never wanted anything or anyone like this. It's killing me that she's not near right now. I don't know what to do with the emptiness I feel."

"That empty feeling has a name. It's called consequences and repercussions. You've had them coming for a long time, cousin. You can't really treat people how you want to and expect for it not to come back eventually. Not everyone is going to just fall at your feet, Camron. You'll have to put in work this time, and it takes time for women like Amari to warm up to you. You'll have to show her you can be a better man who's willing to wait for her affections, and then cherish them."

"Done, done, and done, Blake. I'll give her the best of my world, while she walks me through hers in the meantime."

"Yeah, that sounds good in theory, but you're saying it, so no I'm still not feeling good about whatever the hell you got planned for her. Don't do it, Camron."

"If it doesn't work, I'll let her go, for good." I hope I can anyway. "Show up at my house two days from now. I'll tell you what I'm up to, and I'll have the jet on standby at Arrow's airport today. Whenever you guys can get away, just ask for my pilot Nathan Hamilton at check-in. The clerks will have instructions to call him for you, if he's not there looking for you. You need to see what Ashley has planned for Astrid's party and approve her engagement ring anyway."

"And check on Amari."

"You'll probably actually be checking on me. I'm not sure she isn't going to kill me after this."

"Camron! I swear if-"

"Blake, I heard you the first time. I... I love you, cousin." I don't know why I suddenly want to say that to him, never have before.

34

I guess I thought he always just knew it, and I need the practice. Or maybe Amari's totally going to murder me, and I should be telling everyone how I feel about them while I can.

"I love you too, cousin," he mimics softly. "I don't think we've ever said that to each other."

"Powers don't say it period, remember? It's time we changed the dynamics in this family, by bringing in people who actually know what real happiness is." I sure as hell don't.

"Yeah, no, I don't like how I feel after you say that either, Camron. You'll go over and beyond the call of duty to get this family on whatever path you think it should be on." Absolutely.

I chuckle low into the mouthpiece. "Bye, Blake."

"Bye, Camron. Astrid, we got to start packing!" he yells out without hanging up. "And bring your badge! Camron is up to some shit! It's about to hit the fan! Amari is in the middle of it!"

"Babes, Amari is resilient," she shouts back. "She lasted five years in your family's world. Much longer than me. I was ready to run after meeting Camron, and besides New York isn't my jurisdiction!"

"No, it's going to be mine! Hey, sweetheart," he finishes in his gentler voice.

Oh God, they're about to kiss.

Riots of laughter explode from Astrid. "I don't think my badge works that way for a former Sheriff out of Colorado in New York, or anywhere else on this earth for that matter. And hello to you, too."

"We'll see about that, woman."

"The Powers men are something—"

As interesting as the conversation they're having is, I cut the connection to make the first of many calls to call in quite a few favors. It looks like I'm going to have to play hardball with Ms. Amari Spencer before she becomes Mrs. Amari Powers. Hardball, I can do with one hand tied behind my back.

Chapter Two
~Amari~

Home sweet home is the third floor of my apartment building that I found the same day I interviewed for my job with Powers Enterprises. I haven't been here at this time of day in never, other than the weekends or sick days. Those are so few and far apart that they don't even count.

I lock the front entrance, then follow the walkway of off-white, ceramic blocks to the short countertop that borders it. Dropping my purse down on it, taking care not to bump the canisters and the plants spilling out of their pots, I descend three wide steps into my sunken living room.

For a moment, I stand behind the oversized couch with attached chaise, smiling, and letting the sun wash over me as it streams through huge, undressed windows from across the room. I'm depriving some of the houseplants of the light, but it's worth it. I feel lighter than I have in years. My job had become like a weight around my neck that I've offloaded once and for all.

Peacefulness closes around me, squeezing out the bad energy lingering from my argument with Mr. Powers. This place has always been my refuge for as long as I've known him. I needed one when all his faults and bad tendencies started to manifest. It's fortunate for me that he's never been here to taint my home. He wouldn't come anyway. It's only fifteen hundred square feet with two bedrooms and one and a half baths. Anything that doesn't boast excessive and elegant is beneath him. Here, he'll develop a case of claustrophobia quickly.

For the first time, I'm glad that Mr. Powers is uppity. I don't have to worry about him showing up here, but he'll still have to bear the burden of feeding his superiors and picking up his own dry-cleaning until he finds another victim to do it. The next personal assistant will have no clue as to what they're getting themselves into. Not my problem though. I need to worry more about replacing my job soon.

You should probably look for that in the next state, too.

The sooner, and the further away I get from Candleton, the better. I'll get right on that after I eat something.

At the top of the stairs, I enter the rectangular kitchen. At the far end is a simple, white refrigerator. In it, I find the essentials for a working, single, black female: eggs, cheese, butter, milk, two-day old pizza, and half a six-pack of bottled water. If I want an omelet, I'm set. I'd rather celebrate quitting my job with a real meal, which means a run to...

Oh wait, I can *stroll* to the corner grocery store and down its aisles today, not jog there before it closes just to shop in a rush for everything I'm out of. Getting back in the car and finding parking all over again would cost me time I wouldn't have if I'd worked all day.

It's often I get home too late to catch the small grocer open, because I've waited around for Mr. Powers' choice of takeout to arrive; gourmet meals that always have to be cooked right before delivery. Then I have to settle for a bottle of water before falling into my bed face first. Most times, I'm too exhausted to eat and nauseous after spreading out the takeout on a small dining-table in the bedroom at the office for two. Mr. Powers doesn't dine alone regularly.

And you've still got him and his repulsive ways at the brain.

Dammit! My gut roils.

Well, stop thinking about him. He's no longer a part of your world, Amari.

Right. So why is that giving me acute indigestion when I detest the ground he walks on?

When at least one reason doesn't come to me, and the roiling stops, a yearning for my mother's spaghetti recipe and a salad manifests. I'm not up for making anything out of scratch today though.

But you should go visit your family tomorrow.

It's been six months since I've seen my parents, my brother, and his wife, and I won't have anything else to do.

Grabbing my purse and keys, I backtrack out the door, then amble down the block to the store where I peruse the shelves, dropping random ingredients in my cart. Enjoying the simple shopping trip, I drive the groceries to the register line with an older lady stocking tins of cat food on the belt. If I don't start dating soon, that'll be me.

I make a pact with myself to mingle as much as I can outside the house from here on out, after a lazy night at home. While I unload my buggy, the cashier, a white guy, who's fresh out of his teens in a short-sleeve dress shirt and red apron, grins at me. I haven't seen him here before, but it's almost afternoon and I haven't been in the store this early. Hell, I'm not sure who works here in the evening.

"I don't think I've ever seen you smile before," he says when I lean over the rim of the cart to reach for a canned spaghetti sauce.

I straighten up to drop it on the belt. "I haven't had a reason to..." I glance at his nametag. "...Jimmy. I haven't seen you here before, have I?"

He snickers and rings up the first of my supplies. "I've worked here for two years while I attend college, but you're usually in a hurry when you come in, so I won't take offense."

I let the threads of the conversation drop, to retrieve my matching wallet from my generic purse, which has no money in it. According to my mother, I need to keep cash and a fresh pair of panties on me for emergencies. I try to at least keep the money on me.

Jimmy gives me my total. I swipe my bank card and wait for him to give me two hundred dollars cashback.

Sweeping the plastic bags up into my hands, I nod at him before exiting the store. I'd take my time going home, basking in the warm temperature and the clear, sunny day, but my arms are already sagging under the strain of my purchases.

After speaking to the doorman at the sliding doors of my building and refusing his help, I rush into the elevator. In my kitchen, I release the bags to the countertop, kick off my shoes, and turn on the plasma screen television mounted to the wall between the windows of the living area. My headspace is clear as I get right down to cooking.

You should've brought some wine.

Would have, but I'm a lightweight who wants to get up early enough to beat the afternoon traffic to Winchester. One glass would make me sleep 'til then. As soon as I fill a plate with my meal, my cell phone shrills in my purse. I answer on my way to the couch.

"Hey, Mama."

"Hey sweetheart," Cecilia Spencer chirps back. "I thought I'd get your voicemail."

I laugh, then dump the plate on my glass coffee table. "Not today."

"You sound... *happy*, Amari. What's going on?" Her suspicion isn't unusual.

Normally, I'm venting about working for Powers Enterprises by now.

"Nothing's going on, and I like it. You should too, Mama."

"Well, I would if I knew why. That boss of yours has you busy and madder than a wet hen by now."

"He's no longer my boss!" I squeal. *"I quit an hour ago!"*

She chuckles. "If you sound this good, I guess you should've quit a long time ago."

I pinch the phone between my shoulder and ear, forking food into my mouth. "My thoughts exactly. How is everyone?"

"Well, your father is still here and his heart condition isn't getting any worse, so I'm grateful for that. Oh, and your brother is going to be a father. Gabriela's pregnant."

My fork clatters into the plate. "I'm going to be an auntie?"

I love children. If I ever meet the right man, I'll love my own so much more.

"Yes, you are, Amari, and I'm going to be a grandmother." Her tinkling laughter fills the receiver. She is overjoyed about her first grandchild.

God knows she's harassed her children enough about giving her some for years. I can't because I don't have what Brandon has with Gabriela. I won't, if I don't get out into the dating world.

"How far along is she? How does Brandon feel?"

"He walks around with his chest puffed out like he hung the damn moon. Gabriela is six weeks and sick every afternoon. Don't know why they call it morning sickness. Must've been a man who thought of that name for it. Anyway, she and Brandon told me and Mitchum today. Now, I'm telling you. When are you coming up? Mitchum and I haven't seen our baby girl since Easter."

"I miss you both too, Mama."

"Good, now come up tomorrow," she demands. "Seeing you a few days after your birthday is better than not seeing you at all."

I scoff, as if I hadn't planned the trip as a surprise anyway. "Fine, Mama. You talked me into it."

"Good. We'll have some of your favorite foods when you get here. Are you staying overnight?"

I mull that over. I hadn't thought about spending the night, mainly because I wanted to join Candleton's nightlife as soon as possible. Waiting one more day to make my mother happy won't hurt anything. I'll just have to get up in time Friday morning to avoid the heavy morning traffic.

"Okay, I'll stay until Friday."

"Glad to hear it, Amari. Now, I have to go make your bed up and let your father know you're coming and that he needs to go to the store. Oh, I need to make a list, or he'll come back the way he went."

"Empty-handed!" we chant together.

"Alright, Amari. Call me before you leave so I'm here when you arrive. I love you, baby girl."

"Love you too, Mama. Give my love to everyone else. Bye."

After hanging up, the day and night pass just how I want them to, free of anything consisting of work. Every now and again, during the break in the television shows, Mr. Powers slips into my thoughts. My middle curdles. I prompt myself to stop thinking about him, then stick to that advice rigidly. Then comes the next break for commercials.

Fortunately, I drift off to sleep, until red dots appearing behind my eyelids forces me to open them to the morning ball of fire in the sky that's causing them. I pop up from the suede upholstery of my sofa, then load the dishwasher with last night's dishes. After taking a leisure shower, washing away the last of Powers Enterprise, I stand, examining the woman in the mirror in front of the single-sink beneath a mirror topped with a trio of large light bulbs.

Today is the first day of the rest of your life, Amari. Make it count for something.

With a nod, I strip the common ponytail from the back of my head and begin a morning routine that I have every intention of keeping up. Thirty minutes tick away before I'm satisfied with my hair flowing like a wavy curtain down my back and a thin layer of foundation that makes me look airbrushed. I coat the gift of long eyelashes from my mother with mascara, the duplicate set of her lips with gloss, and unplug the curling irons that I'll take with me on my trip.

41

In the top of the small closet at the foot of the bed, I locate a fake Burberry duffel bag. As I pull it down, the doorbell sounds off. I freeze, wondering who would be visiting me. Sheryl is at work already, probably wondering where I am. I don't know any of my neighbors well enough to do more than speak in passing in the hallways. I haven't had time for getting to know many people in Candleton while working for Powers Enterprises.

The bell chimes again, stirring me into action. I toss the bag on the bed, snatch a satiny, black housecoat from a hanger, and pull it on while moving for the front door. The damn bell rings again.

"*I'm coming!*" I shout. "Keep your shirt on."

Through the peephole, I get a distorted view of my visitor. I can tell it's a man who's tall, staring down the hallway, with black hair, and that's all. All I need to make my stomach drop.

"Who is it?" I ask warily.

"Camron Powers! Is Amari Spencer in?"

Air whooshes out of me. I was so hoping it was another tall, black-haired man. He's not supposed to *be* here. We have nothing else to say to one another, besides whether I should pick it up my last check at the human resource department or wait for it to arrive in the mail.

I drop my forehead against the door. I wanted my first day to go well as the new Amari, well, the Amari I used to be when I still had time to comb my hair and wear attractive clothes. The last time that happened, I was in college, when Mr. Powers wasn't mucking up a perfectly good day.

And he won't again. This is just a hiccup in the rest of your life. Now, answer the door.

I fling it open. "What can I do for you, Mr. Powers?"

His mouth falls open as if I surprised him. He rakes his eyes over me. When warmth rushes up from my bare toes to my chest, I grow disturbed. A cold draft wraps around my legs where the robe stops midthigh. I should've put on more clothes, like a jogging suit. Why is he looking at me like that anyway?

"Mr. Powers," I call through clamped lips.

His attention snaps up to my face then he grins. "Hello, Amari."

I instantly loathe his syrupy tone that he uses with the women he finesses out of their underwear. I get queasy on top of a weird swirling low in my belly that shoots tendrils into my core, caressing it. I refuse to examine what that sensation means, clench my legs together, and hold firm to the nauseousness taking root within me.

Be nice, Amari.

"Hello, Mr. Powers. What do you want? I'm busy. *You* shouldn't be here." I pronounce the words slowly so he catches the underlying message that he's not welcomed to darken my doorway again.

"I want you, Amari. Are you going to invite me in?" he asks casually.

"No, you don't, and no, I won't. Please leave." I step back to close the door.

He slaps it with his palm. "Wait, Amari. You need your job, so come back to work, or did you forget I promised that you'd regret quitting? I meant it. You won't work in this town again if you don't."

He smiles. It doesn't reach his eyes, where his usual transparent arrogance is sitting.

He thinks he has you over a barrel.

I nod, then grin back. "I'm glad you meant it. You and your harem are soon to be a case for the Center for Disease Control to investigate. I don't want to catch anything you've contracted that'll probably spread throughout the city. Blackballing me will put a *healthy* distance between me and it, and you and I, so go right ahead. Do your worst. You're good at it. No need in stopping now."

His threats are a guarantee that we'll never see each other again. What can he do to me besides blackball me with the other high-profile companies in this city? Though none will pay me as well as Powers Enterprise does, I've already applied with them all and rejected what amounts to a minimum wage offer to switch companies. Mr. Powers' influence with the other business owners in Candleton will be just the push I need to move back home where the people who love me live. I'll get to start my own business finally, doing what I'm passionate about; designing shoes. I'll probably have to sell them online anonymously to evade Mr. Powers long reach and ruining of my business. Do I think he'll sabotage it if he ever gets wind of who owns it? In a heartbeat. He's as ruthless, maybe more so, as the next businessman.

My stomach tumbles around. I ignore that too. One day, I'll ask myself why he affects that part of me so much. Today is not that day, because his smirk is transforming to pursed lips enveloped in sheer, quiet fury.

His Italian loafers step into my personal space. "You think you're better than me, don't you, Amari?" His low tone heaps an unnatural dose of intimidation on me.

I thought I was done with feeling like that after my first year of working for him.

"Mr. Powers, it's you who thinks you're better than me. Why don't you go back to the women with the same frame of mind as you and leave me alone?"

"Amari, I couldn't leave you alone even if I wanted to. For one, you keep my life running smoothly. For two, I don't know if I can find someone who'll do it as well as you. Now come do the job I pay you so well for and stop this."

Is there a 'for three?'

I confess that he just stroked the hell out of my ego, but it's not enough.

"Mr. Powers, there is one person who can do my job better than me. You. It's your life. Coming back to Powers Enterprises would be subjecting myself to Chinese water torture." Wearing me down until my mind leaves for more peaceful pastures.

"Amari," he summons softly, his dark pupils simmering with anger.

For once, it's not me who's frustrated when I can't get what I need out of our working relationship.

The tables have turned at last.

I realize I'm giggling cheerfully under my breath when his chest begins to puff out in jerky movements only inches from my face. It's sort of hypnotizing to watch his double-breasted, pinstriped suit breathe.

"Mr. Powers, you make it seem like it's painful to realize you can't have your way all the time. Most adults have figured that out by five years old, you know?"

"Amari, I'll ask again. *Please* come to work right now or face the consequences."

I let my breath out, tired of the dialog now. "You killed the point of saying 'please' with 'face the consequences.' You don't ask. You demand. I have the God-given right by the God above you, not the one you think you are by the way, to say no. Goodbye, Mr. Powers."

I try to shut the door again.

He pushes again. "I'm serious. Come back to work."

"Or?"

"Or I'll make your life a living hell." His warnings are becoming dangerously close to ominous.

I've never seen him act out violently, but usually things go his way. I don't know what he'll will do if pushed far enough, especially since it seems he isn't going to leave until he gets what he wants. Well, he can't have me.

"Mr. Powers, I'm not asking you to leave. I'm *telling* you to, or I'll call the cops. I don't have to work for you. You should start making a list of things that don't mesh with what you choose to believe so you can keep up. Here's another one. Nor do I want to be the crowd you crave to watch you fondle women like the promiscuous teenager you are in a grown man's body. Do yourself a favor. Seek professional help for that. It can't be coming from any place good inside you."

His eyes and mouth widen again.

The poor thing is shocked again.

Truly amazed that I find him lacking as well, I bet.

"Are you saying I have issues, Amari?"

"I'm saying you're twisted. Issues would mean your way of thinking can be reversed. You've been carrying on like an arrogant prick for far too long for that, but maybe you could be reprogrammed into a much nicer, saner man."

The fury in his face intensifies, ripples off him, and nearly suffocates me.

"No one speaks to me like that. I'm *not* crazy. What happened to giving respect to receive it?"

"You've never respected me, and I'm surely not about to give you any more without getting some back first."

He looks away, swallows deeply, and then puts me back in his crosshairs. "Look, I'm sorry for whatever you've had to endure while working for me. I was wrong. What if I make certain promises to you like I won't date at the office anymore? I've stopped doing that by the way, months ago, but you didn't notice it. And I respect you. You have to come back to work for me to prove it."

He can't pay me to believe that, even when he sounds sincere.

But you want to after that apology.

Shut up, conscience.

"Too late, Mr. Powers. Besides, I wouldn't do my best as your PA anymore and your life would not run smoothly again. Lucky for you, I'm already gone. I'm staying that way. No need to change who you are for me now."

"Too late," he whispers.

His cryptic statement catches me off guard. I almost ask what does he mean by it, except I suspect he's just saying what he thinks I want to hear.

You do want to hear it.

I said *shut* up, conscience.

"Look. You have to go, so do I." I'm not talking about just getting going to Winchester either, but possibly moving to another apartment after this meeting.

There's memories of him infecting my doorway now. I wouldn't enter it again without remembering him standing here. Yeah, no I don't want to know why I would be doing that either.

"I'm not going, Amari, until you come back to me."

Come back to him? Did he not hear me?

"Yes, you *are* going, or… I'll… scream this building down," I warn, with every intention of doing it.

His hand slides down the door as a leer crosses his lips. "You have no idea who I am, do you?" There he is, the old Mr. Powers.

"Oh, I know exactly who and what you are."

"Then you know exactly what I'm capable of."

I wouldn't be amazed if he makes damn sure I don't work anywhere in any of the states now.

Always wanted to go to Canada.

I'm determined to find a silver lining in the thunderclouds that Mr. Powers will rain down on my head with. So, I'll get wet. That's better than working for him.

"Fine. Make me pay for doing absolutely nothing to you and everything for you except the one thing that matters the most."

He cocks his head. "And what's that?"

"Make you human. It's not possible. You're a goddamn animal through and through." I stand up on my tiptoes to peer over his shoulder at the door behind him. "*Mrs. Harrison, please call the cops! I'm being bothered by a man who likes to harass and fondle women!*"

I don't know my neighbor's name or if a Mrs. Harrison actually lives on my floor, but I don't have to, to show him I mean business. I'm not his prey or anybody's victim. However, I did screw up when I didn't speak up sooner about his behavior in the office and didn't leave before things got this far gone. Now, he's riding me to resume my position as third party to the games he plays, or wants to play. Either way, it's not fair to me.

He glances back at the apartment across the hall, then spears through me with hard eyes meant to inflict the maximum amount of damage. He's five years late and a dollar short on that too.

So, you admit he hurt you when he brought the first woman to his office?

No, he didn't.

Liar!

"You'll pay for that, Amari."

"You've hinted that I'll be doing that already. Starting to repeat yourself. I think that's a sign of dementia onset. You should call a psychiatrist now. Psychologists can't write prescriptions." And he needs a shitload of them.

He glares at me harder, then steps even closer until I almost inhale the paisley tie adorning his navy-blue dress shirt. I have to crook my neck back to look him directly in the face. I think I'm supposed to be intimidated by his nearness. The time has passed for that, and I just don't see him physically attacking me.

"You haven't seen the last of me, Amari."

His face dips, lips set down on my cheek. Then they're gone. Flames blast through me. I shudder… from fear, or at least that's what I'm going to convince myself is invading my spine and licking at my insides.

You're just going to lie to yourself, huh?

Yep, and shit, he needs to go now before I want to come.

Too late.

"Mrs. Harrison, are the cops coming yet? If not, call them again! This man refuses to leave! He's threatening to make me pay for quitting my job! His name is Camron Powers! If anything happens to me, he's the culprit!" Then I smile. "You should leave now. If I so much as trip down the steps leading into my living room, you'll get blamed for it."

He snorts ungentlemanly in my face, before his gaze lands on my mouth. One side of his lifts. He turns and walks away. I stare at his back side, having gotten the last word in again with the almighty Camron Powers. I should feel like a damn champ after facing the devil in battle and winning. It's more like I've been buried under six feet of dirt while watching him retreat. A victory in battle doesn't guarantee a triumph in war. Mr. Powers isn't going to let these defeats go. He doesn't work that way.

****

~Camron~

Walking away from Amari dressed in less than half the material she wears to work is damn near impossible. I can hardly squash the urge to look back at her.

And I thought giving up on my parents showing me they at least cared about me was hard.

With Amari, it's impossible. But nothing is harder than I am right now, or compares to how much I ache in my chest when leaving her behind before she gets me arrested. I should be angry with her about it. The old Camron would be. She has the upper hand. Feels more like foreplay to the new me emerging, albeit gradually. The more she struggles against me, the more I need to know what makes her tick after I get her in my arms for life. I'm going to find out why she's different from every other woman, and no one will stop me. Not even Amari.

I excavate my phone being jabbed by the pointed edge of the tent in my slacks that's been constant for months. I'd rather torture myself with the pain my erection causes then allow a woman other than Amari to satisfy me. Second best just isn't going to cut it for me anymore. Second best is what all the other women who have passed through my world have been for me since saw Amari, which was long before I hired her.

Dredging up my call list, I find the last number I dialed.

My top computer analyst picks up his extension. "Yeah, boss."

At the lift, I press the button for the ground floor of Amari's building. "Deon, hack the system."

"Shit... uh, sorry about the curse word, boss, but I was hoping you were joking when you called me this morning about that. You're sure you want me to do this?" Damn right.

"You want to get paid the extra five grand, Deon?"

He sighs heavily. "Alright. Give me two minutes. I'll text you when it's done."

Money, the ultimate motivator, works damn near every time.

"Thank you."

"Ah... you're... welcome," he stammers. He has a bad habit of tugging on his tie when he's nervous, too.

God, I hope he's not getting cold feet now.

"What's the problem, Deon?" I stride inside the elevator.

"You've never said 'thank you' before to me... and I probably shouldn't be mentioning that to you. Idiot!"

What does everyone consider me as? A Neanderthal? Probably.

"Everyone can change, Deon."

I can imagine him wiping sweat from his forehead, wondering if his job is at risk and if he'll have to go back to the rough streets he was born on just because he spoke openly to me. He knows me well. Any other time, he *would* be fired.

"Most people don't choose to change though, boss."

"I'm not most people. Don't forget to cover your tracks. Bye."

The elevator's doors spread wide, letting me out. I might as well call Blake now. He's going to be highly ticked off when I tell him that I reverted to my old self, threatening Amari when I didn't get my way and going through with my promise to make her come back to me by any means necessary. I'll need to calm the storm that'll kick up inside him when he finds out what I've done. It'll be much worse and unmanageable if he finds out from Amari.

I can't put it pass her to tell him as soon as she sees him. It doesn't help me that he's a former sheriff out of Colorado, his soon-to-be-wife filling in the position. As of now, the steps I've taken to bring Amari to me are unlawful. I highly doubt that Blake won't go through with his plan to arrest me for any one of them either.

His line rings three times, possibly on the other, completing business for the resort. When he finally picks up, I pass by Amari's doorman who tips his hat to me for the generous tip I left him to make sure no one leaves a parking ticket on my car.

"Camron," he says in a monotone.

"Are you sitting down?"

I cross the sidewalk, approaching the car double-parked in front of the building, with the sun beating down on my head. I feel it's weight, not the heat. I'll stay chilled until Amari is mine.

"What did you do?"

"What I said I would—get her back by any means necessary. The stakes are higher now, though. If you want the details, get your ass to Candleton."

The line goes dead silent. I expect him to be hollering at me, at the top of his lungs after that indirect admission of my bad acts. Since he isn't, he's stroking his jaw, considering my actions. I wait for him to recover, while I start the engine of the black Ashton Martin.

"Camron, I'm not even going to get mad with you for doing whatever you've done. You're about to learn that you catch more flies with honey than the vinegar you've been serving up to women. When it comes to those who make men better versions of themselves, you're going to fail... epically."

"Are you calling me sour, *Blake*?" I prefer his yelling much more than his insults.

"So is everyone else that you treat badly, *Camron*."

"I didn't treat her badly. I just visited her place and asked her to come back to work. I told her I'd change for her."

"And she didn't believe you." That is not a question.

"Which is why I had to do what I had to."

"You didn't have to, Camron. You chose to, which is why whatever you've done is going to backfire in your face."

"We'll see about that."

52

"You certainly will. I might as well continue your lessons in learning to deal with the public who's not star struck by you. Step Four; you don't forget special days such as birthdays or anniversaries... ever."

"*Fuck!*" I yell like Blake should have.

When the soundproof interior of the car tosses my shout back at me, I lower my voice. "Now, you tell me, Blake. Amari's birthday was two days ago. I told her to celebrate it yesterday, since she was obviously pissed at me about making her forget it, and be back at work today. When she didn't show up for work or call in, I went to her place to bring her back. I'm learning it's bad for me when she's angry. She basically screamed I was a pervert to everyone on her floor."

Blake snickers. "Damn straight, it's bad for you. Did you at least wish her happy belated birthday while you were there?"

"No," I answer reluctantly, guessing that was the wrong thing to do. "She wouldn't even let me in."

A hail of laughter breaks from Blake. "Because you're an idiot, Camron."

I grind my teeth. "You may not remember but Powers don't celebrate birthdays."

His mirth cools. "I did forget some of things the Powers don't do, just to get out of making someone happier than themselves, like showing affections. I'm more concerned with what they *will* do. Sorry about that. Okay, you make it up to her. It won't be the same as doing something on her actual birthday, but she won't forget the effort. Might not do you any good at this point, but she'll definitely remember you tried."

"Is this where I find something to put in a box with a pretty bow on top?"

"Oh yes, preferably over dinner. I don't know if that's an option for you at this point, but you can still reach down inside you and offer her something that you can't buy. Still might not do you any good, but it's worth it."

"Shit! What if it's not? If she doesn't see I'm trying, and fall in love with me, I don't know what I'm going to do."

"Then you walk away, Camron. There's nothing else to do, and I can only hold you down and tell you what to do and not do until you feel better."

"Okay, what else is there?" At this point, I'm damn desperate, even after the tactics I've initiated.

Amari has you by the gonads, man.

"I'm assuming you're going to try to make up for missing and dissing her birthday. Don't have your secretary pick out Amari's gift. Spending time to find what you think she likes goes over well if she hasn't mentioned what she wants and you don't already know. It's the thought that counts to women... mostly. If she doesn't like your choice, offer to take it back and get what she wants. She doesn't have to be grateful for something she doesn't want or need. It's rare for them to throw jewelry back at you... or flowers... unless you've made them mad first. Save the trips to exotic locations for after you've slept with a woman, or she'll think her body is what you're after. No one wants to be used, rich or poor. Well, most people don't. There's exceptions to every rule, and you seem more than lucky in finding those that fit that category and settle for your short attention span."

"It's not short when it comes to Amari," I defend, "which isn't doing me any good."

"Repercussions and consequences for your past, Camron. Deal with them in silence until they stop dealing with you. Oh, cars and more expensive places to live have to wait until you know her better, too."

"When did women get so complicated?"

"When you chose to go after one that isn't shallow. They're looking for something in a significant other that what they can't

54

provide for themselves. I know you pay your people well, even if you do nothing else right, so Amari doesn't need you flashing your money in her face when she has her own, just *your* good manners and behavior right now."

"I did manage to kiss her cheek before she threatened to call the cops on me," I boast. I don't know why I think that's improvement with her either, but I do.

He barks more laughter in my ear, shredding the little progress I think I've made. "You don't steal kisses unless she's staring at you with puppy eyes."

"Puppy what?"

"Eyes, man. She'll look hypnotized, and probably be staring at your mouth or deep into *your* eyes. You'll know the look when you see it. You'll feel it, and can't help kissing her. If she slaps you, stop then give her some space. She's still not ready, but you'll have given her something to think about… that's if it's a good kiss for her."

"I can take a slap. She didn't slap me though, and I'm a damn good kisser, Blake."

"I'm sure you are after all the practice you've had, but it's not going to help you until she wants your *mouth* on hers, which she may not after watching you kiss other women with yours."

I huff, and brake for a red light, two miles away from my building. "Blake, it was more convenient to date at the office than drive all the way home to do it every night, or I'd have ogled Amari's body like a pervert every day. That certainly would've made her uncomfortable and she would've quit on me sooner."

I should stop defending my past. He never sees anything I've done as rational.

"How well did dating others instead of her work out for you, Camron?"

"It didn't. I apologized for it to Amari. Maybe she didn't understand what I was apologizing for."

"No apology can fix what you've done every day in front of her. You still look like a sexual deviant to her, and she's not going to be happy that you thought you were picking the lesser of two evils either. You should've picked her first, but I don't think she's not attracted to you, or she wouldn't mention or care one way or the other about what you do with other women. You damn sure wouldn't have gotten your lips anywhere near her. Right now, she's probably having a severe case of principles and pride. You have to wait until they let her feel her attraction for you. They won't ever let her be just another body in your bed like your other… dates."

For the first time, I feel the need to pray. It'll start something like this: Jesus, what have I done?

"So, what are my chances with her in your opinion, Blake?"

"Next to none," he says way too fast for my liking, but he's right.

I can sense it.

"I'm not giving up on her."

"Camron, I don't know if I could respect if you did, when you seem to love her so much, but you can't manipulate her into your bed."

"No, just my life, where she should be. She shouldn't have stolen my heart. I can tell it's gone because it feels like there's nothing in my chest. My life is nothing without her in it. Even when she's hiding from me most of the time, I know she's near, but I'm not content with that anymore. I need her *with* me, Blake."

"Trust me, I understand. Six months without Astrid was hell on earth. When she came back, things got worse before they got better for us, but she'd missed me and could barely keep her hands off me. So, I had something to look forward to while she learned to trust me again. Sometimes, walking away is the best thing for everyone. It gives old hurts time to heal. Fresh bad memories develop a haze. Clarity of feelings happen. I couldn't tell her I

56

loved her and would be what she needed in a man fast enough. When I did, she didn't want to believe it, but I backed off every time she needed me to when I came on too strong. You'll have to do the same, even when it feels like you're ripping what's left in your chest out. Amari has every right to turn down whatever it is of yours that you want her to have."

"That's everything, Blake."

"I know, but you don't want to be on the other end of a restraining order either."

"I won't."

"Oh, there's a judge that'll grant one for her. You can't have them all in your pocket."

"I do, in this city. Most of them are my investors who are friends with the rest, but she won't get the chance to request an order of anything against me anyway."

"You covered all your bases, huh?"

"Yep. You'd be amazed at what a private investigator who performs miracles when doing background checks, a good keyboard warrior, and a topnotch lawyer on payroll who can type a hundred words per minute can do."

"I already know. I worked in law enforcement, remember?"

"How can I forget? You won't let me."

"Nope, Camron, I'm not. If I find proof of the hacking you've had done into Amari's life, I'll have your ass arrested for it, too. I still have pull with law enforcement."

And can influence his woman who carries a real badge to do what he can't. He didn't need his blood family behind him to get the power he has either.

"I believe you, Blake, but you won't find anything. I keep around only the best."

"For as long as they let you keep them around, Camron. That's what you have to get through your thick skull."

With anyone else, I could. Just not Amari. Not now anyway.

"Maybe I will after she's run over me with the car I intend to give her, and kills me. Her Hyundai can't be safe."

"A compact car is certainly enough to stop you on this demented track you're determined to go down. I'll be sure to speak at your funeral."

"You might as well start the eulogy now. I'm dying inside without her."

"Slowly."

"God, yes." I wrench my tie loose and sling it onto the passenger seat of my car.

Blake sniggers. "You'll be fine even if she doesn't fall for you, cousin."

"Doesn't feel like it."

"I know it doesn't now, but you will. You got me and my family to support you."

The rest of the Powers wouldn't even try to understand why I care so much for her, or why it's getting worse the more I'm in Amari's company. Hell, I don't get the latter either. I swear the woman is a spell-casting witch.

"Can you come sooner than two days then, Blake? Amari is going to come gunning for me the minute she realizes what I've done. She has a temper I didn't know anything about. I should've called in some bodyguards first thing this morning."

Blake howls his hilarity into the phone. I remove it from my ear until he's done.

"Sorry, Camron. I'm not laughing at you but with you. Use some of those martial arts you've been practicing since birth to defend yourself, and nope, I can't come any sooner. The resort's construction crew is missing in action again. I've been taking bids all day from others and starting a lawsuit against the one I'm about to fire for breach of contract. They'll never work in this state again... *Oh God*, I sound like a true Powers already." Ashley may be converting her son anyway, and he's panicking.

It's my turn to laugh at his expense. "Repercussions and consequences for leaving me alone with my parents by myself. They ruined me."

"And now you know why I didn't stick around every chance I got to break *out* of my childhood home."

"You should've took me with you. You know… I think I resent you for leaving me."

If he had taken me, a ring would already be on Amari's finger by now, my son or daughter in her, except Blake was only six when he met the Owens in Colorado. He couldn't take *himself* anywhere, let alone let me tag along all the way from Italy.

"You don't really blame me, Camron."

"No, I don't, but I do blame myself for being gullible."

"You were a child. How were you going to stop them from filling your mind with what amounts to hatred for everyone not in a certain tax bracket? I'd be a Stepford replica of our family, too, if it wasn't for the Owens showing me better. My parents put in as much effort as yours did to influence me with their nonsense."

"I can't get away from what my parents taught me. It was so easy to fall back into my old ways with Amari."

"Your old ways didn't develop overnight. They won't go away that soon either. I'm not going to give up on you neither, Camron, so I have to tell you that it's possible to find someone else to love as much as you do Amari."

"I don't think so. I'd have found her by now."

"You only think that because you've been through so many women. There's a hell of a lot more out here."

"I've been through enough to should have found at least one who can make me feel a tenth of the things Amari does. She's it for me."

"And I won't be the one to try and convince you otherwise, Camron. I found my girl, and I'm keeping her, no matter what anybody says, even if I have to sleep outside the house until she feels sorry enough to let me back in it."

Images of that play before my eyes. "I want pictures of that."

"Oh hell no. I'm not even going to tell you about it until she gives in to me or we both give up on the other completely."

"So, you understand why I'm doing what I must to keep Amari?"

"I understand, just don't approve. You could do more harm than good to you both."

"I'm going to take that chance, Blake."

He sighs. "Every man must make his decisions and live with the regrets if there're any, Camron."

"I will."

"You're going to, trust me. Now, my other line is beeping. I need to go, but I'll get to New York as soon as I can."

"Bye, Blake. Let me know if you need any more weight to throw around for the resort."

"That's a guarantee. See you later." I hope he does.

What I've done to Amari could make today my last if she goes postal when she finds me at the office later. And she's coming in hot.

****

~Amari~

After Mr. Powers vanishes, I shut the door back then lean against it, allowing my emotions and snippets of my last quarrel with him to run unchecked through me, along with the weird catch in my gut still present from his inspection of my body—he saw something he liked.

And you're pleased about it.

Well, yeah! It's hurt more to realize your well has run dry after you've found someone attractive just when you've lost them for good. I'm glad to be the instrument that teaches him everything in this world isn't for his taking.

Bull hockey. You wouldn't be picking apart his words if you weren't thrilled about him finding you good-looking enough to stare at, finally. You'd just be glad he's gone, and you're anything but that.

Jesus, who's side is my conscience on? If I wanted to admit I still found him attractive after everything he's put me through, well, I'd just admit it to myself.

You just did.

Well... yeah... *but* I won't become a part of the masses he's slept with and thrown away, like he didn't find what he was looking for in them.

I can't find fault with that reasoning.

Happy I've found some harmony with myself again, I heave myself forward to finish preparing to leave. If I procrastinate any longer, the forty-five-minute trip will be two hours. I hate to drive as it is. Most of the other motorists are just as hazardous to my health as Mr. Powers is, turning their vehicles into two-ton weapons. He only needs his words and actions, which weigh more, and could leave me a shell of a person if they cut too deeply.

That's the very reason why I filed away whatever it is that draws me to him in the first place.

It takes twenty minutes to pack and garb myself in black, skinny jeans with bleached stains, matching cropped vest, and a white, waist-length, high neck blouse. Around my neck, I drape a thin gold chain with a charm molded into my first initial. It falls into the sink, the rounded end spread too far apart to lock the hook into place. After meddling with both ends, I fasten it back around my body. It stays put.

While putting on white leather boots, I try to recall the last time I dressed casually or had time to admire my slim waist, perky breasts, and way too curvy hips in the mirror hung across from my bed above the dresser.

Too bad Camron hasn't seen you this pretty since the day he hired you.

Things might not have turned out any differently though. I was given a flashing warning that he didn't carry himself like regular people when he called me a week later, at eight-thirty in the morning, and told me to show up for work by nine or I was fired. I ignored the sign, ecstatic to have a job right out of school, and I've been rushing to it almost every morning ever since, in whatever outfit I lay my eyes on first. I shop like that too. Don't have time to browse usually. No more of that.

I grin at my reflection, haul my overnight bag over my shoulder, and seize my purse and keys from the kitchen countertop. When I walk into the hallway, a gray-haired lady in yellow cardigan and slacks joins me, the same neighbor I was commanding to call the cops. I gauge her age around seventy. She smiles up at me on our path to the elevator. I palm the door pockets, so she can slowly walk in.

"Thank you, neighbor. We haven't met before, have we?" she asks with a wide smile.

After pressing the button for the underground car garage, I slide in behind her already facing the reflective silver panels.

"No, we haven't met. I've been too busy to meet anyone. How are you?"

She peers over her shoulder. "Well, slow down a little. Life will pass you by if you keep moving through it at the speed of the rat race, and I'm fine."

I nod respectfully to the wise woman.

"I don't want to get in your business, but I heard you shouting for a Mrs. Harrison to call the police on the gentleman who seemed to be bothering you. I didn't know if you really wanted the cops or not since no one by Mrs. Harrison lives on our floor. But I waited by the door with the phone in my hand just in case he got *out* of hand, and I should admit that I came out when you did so I could talk to you about it and introduce myself. If you ever need to call on a real person for real help, you just call my name. We single ladies need to stick together." She turns sideways, and extends her hand to me, with a warm smile. "I'm Lucinda Mason and I live across the hall."

She reaches my shoulder, so she had to be standing on a chair to watch the entertainment Mr. Powers provided for her peephole. I take her short fingers in mine. They're warm like her smile, and perhaps her heart. I need a kind, nosy neighbor with Mr. Powers running around free.

"Hi, Miss Mason. I'm Amari Spencer. He's my ex-boss who's trying to get me to return to the hellhole he calls his business. I said no. He thinks otherwise. Next time, call the cops. He's not a good man."

She snickers quietly, releasing my hand. "Call me Lucinda. Are you sure that's all he wanted?"

I hope she doesn't think I've already slept with him. Her grin takes on a sly quality.

She does think that. Oh, hell no!

My hand begins waving around, as if I'm directing air traffic. All I want is to steer *her* in the right direction.

"Hey, there's never been anything but a working relationship between us. He just needs me to be at the helm of his life while he dates other people freely in front of me. I gave myself the axe yesterday. Now, he has to be an adult and run his own life. He's not feeling that, as you could hear."

She takes both of my flailing hands into hers. "I perfectly understand that, Amari, but he wasn't checking you out for nothing. That visit wasn't all about your job either. Trust me."

"He thinks I'm furniture and a voyeur. He's a bigot and a pig, and that's just two of his endearing traits."

She chokes on air before freeing a husky giggle. "Most men are pigs until the right woman comes along and straightens them out. These days, sometimes, the right *man* has to come along. Whatever. I'm not judging."

"Believe me, Lucinda, when I say there isn't a woman, man, or psychiatrist in this world who can straighten that man out. His ways are set in stone," I reply dryly as the doors slide open, trickling light into the dimly-lit garage.

Gently, I pull my hands from hers. "It was nice meeting you. Introduce yourself again soon."

"I will, sweet girl." She lifts her gnarled fingers to cover the door pockets. "And watch out for Camron Powers. He's well known in this city. Rarely does a man like your boss let a beautiful girl like you go without a fight. You can trust me on that too."

I'm sure that I can trust her on a lot of things. This just isn't one of them, even when she couldn't have gotten to the age she is without fielding most of what life throws at everyone. Sure Mr. Powers wants me to make his existence orderly, just not straighten him out, particularly not romantically.

****

~Camron~

Sitting at my desk with the contract from this morning crumpled in my fists, I stare out of the glass wall without seeing Candleton's skyline. The mirage of Amari shimmers on the pane. So, I'm seeing what I want to see. That doesn't make me a candidate for schizophrenia when it's not a good daydream and solely based on reality. She's just as furious as she will be when she learns what I've done, but when she shows up here, she'll have to let me explain why. I simply want to get to know her through and through, not destroy her good name. It's squeaky clean.

"Who could pull that off in this day and age anyway?" I scoff. "Should've known she'd be able to."

Oddly, I'm proud of her for it. She's more prone to do the right thing than I am, which is why I'm convinced she can teach me a thing or two about life, and I'm going make sure she does... one way or the other, while I take things slow with her.

Chapter Three
~Amari~

I nod at Lucinda and walk onto the concrete lot. She holds the elevator doors open until I reach my car. When I drive out of my assigned space, she drops her hands. I wave while creeping by. When the doors close, I pick up speed. Suddenly, I'm not in a hurry to get home. My family's going to demand the details of why I left my job. I'm not relishing the telling of what bought me to such an extreme choice.

At the first gas station I see, I stop to fill up. Could get used to having time on my hands. Hopefully, I won't find another employer to swallow it up like Power Enterprises did.

I get out at the pump and breeze into store, looking for a healthy snack to finish up my drive. A bag of chips and soda is what I haul to the counter where a grizzled, scowling, pale old man stands behind the register in overalls. I get the nagging feeling he doesn't like for black women to enter his store. Then the chime above the entrance resonates through the franchise. Glimpsing back at a haggard-looking blonde with black roots, she carries two small children on each of her hips inside. His head swivels to her, and his scowl deepens. Okay, I take it back—he doesn't like for *anyone* to come into his store.

I deposit my stuff on the counter before him and tug free my credit card from its slot in my wallet. "Forty on pump one, please."

He scans my purchases, swipes my card, and then glowers at the machine. "It's declined, ma'am." That's not right. I never pay late or go over my limit.

Now irritated, I shift my weight from one foot to the other. Today is supposed to go better than this.

"I haven't used this card thirty times since I got it four years ago. Swipe it again."

"Fine," he fires back, blowing tobacco breath in my face. Then he gives me the card along with a scrap of paper. "It's declined *again*."

One glimpse at the slip confirms what he's told me twice.

I panic. "I haven't maxed out this card!"

"Ma'am, even if that's true, there are identity thieves who'll do that for you without even removing your card from your purse. Give me another card or cash. It's up to you."

Suspicious, something tells me to go with cash, not my bank card. It's attached to my credit card account. If a crook has gotten to it, how hard can it be to get to my banking info since the internet lets anyone into your business? What if I hadn't withdrawn the cash yesterday for moments like these?

I unearth two twenties and a five out of my wallet. After tossing the change in the bottom of my purse, I pump the gas and eyeball my cell phone on the passenger seat. Shoving the gas pump back into its compartment, I drop into the car and call up my credit card company. When the automated system asks for my info, I punch it in as fast as I can, and request a customer rep.

"How may I help you today, Ms. Spencer?"

"You can tell me why a card I use sparingly like I'm supposed to is maxed out."

"It isn't maxed out, ma'am. You cancelled it online and had your account flagged for identity theft. Any fraudulent claims, we take seriously, and will prosecute whoever opened this account under a false name."

My blood runs cold. My credit limit hasn't been jacked. I've been hacked.

"Fraudulent! I'm Amari Spencer. I've always been me. There's nothing fraudulent about that or my account that I've had for years. I didn't cancel my card or make a fraudulent claim. There is no suspicious activity on this account. And if it is, it isn't on *my* end."

"I'm sorry, ma'am. There's nothing I can do until we can prove who opened this account and who closed it."

"You can track the IP address to whoever stole my information and cancelled this account. Why would they steal my info to not buy things, just take my financial stability from me instead?"

"Ma'am, I've never heard of something like this happening either, but we had to honor your request to close the account and open a case."

"Well, close the case and open the account back up then. I didn't do this."

"Before we can reinstate your credit privileges and issue you a new card, you need to prove who you are."

"I need to prove who *I am*?" The range of my voice rises with my rage. "*No, you need to prove who's pretending to be me!*"

"It's required by law for you to send in documents so we can clear up the matter, or we can prosecute *you* to the fullest extent of the law."

"What? I haven't done anything wrong!"

"We didn't either, ma'am, and I'm sorry if someone has misrepresented themselves as you online, but you need to get those documents to us as soon as possible. The company is required by law to investigate the matter thoroughly since terrorists are using every institution available to funnel money to their organizations."

Haranguing the customer rep for doing her job isn't going to make her be any more accommodating to me.

"You think I'm a terrorist?" I ask with a calm I don't feel.

"Someone does, or they're making sure you appear as one."

"Who? I haven't made anyone that angry with me."

Yes, you have.

But would Mr. Powers launch retaliation of this magnitude to keep his promise of making me pay, by robbing me of my ability to pay for anything? Maybe even cost me my freedom.

Being his personal assistant is not this damn serious.

Or is it to him? I won't find out sitting here halfway between my home and my parents.'

"I don't know who's this angry with you, Ms. Spencer. You have one week to send the documents to me. I'll reinstate your ability to upload documents to your account, but that's all I can do at this point."

"I can do a lot more from my end. I think I know who did this."

"If you can prove they did it, we'll give them over to the authorities."

"Thank you." I hang up and peel out of the store's yard.

When I arrive in downtown Candleton, traffic is still light and moving at a fast pace. I can't be grateful for it. I'm too busy being afraid that two hundred and ninety-seven grand is gone from my savings account, six thousand from checking. If it was him who did this to me, he would've went after it all, and there's no point in calling my bank. A waking nightmare is what today is turning out to be.

Before I stumble upon anymore of Mr. Powers' criminal activities, I need him to fix what he's already done to me, and make him promise to never cross my path again. How could anyone do something this crazy?

I guess you'll find out when you get to his office.

A mile away from Powers Enterprises, a cop wearing aviator shades passes by. He glances at me from his partially-rolled down window. For all I know, there's a warrant out for my arrest, and he's going to recognize my car and flip his sirens on any second now. It's not as if the customer rep would've told me they were already pressing charges. Terroristic acts are the most hated crime in this state right now, the judges throwing the book at anyone who dares to break those laws, and getting terrorists off the streets is a priority.

I grip the steering wheel until my caramel knuckles turn white. By the time the cruiser disappears from my rearview, I'm even more convinced of Mr. Powers' guilt. It's no coincidence this is happening to me right after his threat. I deliberate on the notion of seeing if his money is as vulnerable as mine is. Destitution won't sit well with the elite status he enjoys so much. I'm not a tit-for-tat kind of girl, however, choosing to believe in an honest day's work, integrity, and karma.

I can't wait for that bitch to get her hands on him.

Finally, I arrive at the yellow bar barricading the entrance onto Powers' premises. Positioned in between the in and out lanes, a guard shack spits out Grady, who's overweight, heavily-tanned, and smiling. There's no returning the simple greeting, too numb from the explosive rage that built during my drive. I'll unleash it on Mr. Powers, if he hasn't revoked my access to the building already.

"Amari, why aren't you here working? Are you sick?" He makes it seem painful to lower himself down off the curb, halting at my window.

"No, ah, I'm late, Grady." Uneasy with lying, the backlash for it comes back too soon for my tastes.

Grady should know I'm no longer an employee by now, and will probably be asking me to drive the U-turn around his station right about now.

"Go right on in. Mr. Powers is probably having a fit that you're not already up there. He drove out of here like a bat out of hell this morning. Came back even faster. He usually takes great care with that car, so stay on his good side and have a good day, Amari."

"You too, Grady."

He disappears into the shack. The bar rises. If only he knew just how far I've traveled across Mr. Powers' 'bad side' today, and him mine.

I ease forward, park quickly in the first vacant space underground, and scramble to get the badge out of my purse for the elevator. Then I run for it. Once inside, it moves too damn slowly upwards, doesn't open fast enough for me when it stops. I bang on the doors until it opens a millisecond later.

Outside Mr. Powers' office, I bang on that door too, causing several heads to peep out of their workplaces. I rather feed the gossip mill, even when pissed to the highest point of pisstivity, than get an eyeful of anyone's bare ass in his office. However, he'll let his current date go long enough to reinstate my financial status, or I'll create a ruckus that'll have the national news camped out on his property until he does. He can have me escorted away afterwards.

He flings the door open. The palm of my hand almost smacks him in the face. I lower it to my side as a fist, which I will use on him if he doesn't fix what he's broken.

He has the audacity to smile while stepping aside. "Come right in, Amari, although I wasn't welcomed into your home. I don't mind showing you how to be hospitable."

I storm pass him. "You probably can spell hospitable, Mr. Powers, but you sure as hell don't know the first thing about it."

I look for extra bodies that must leave. No one is cowering at my vacated desk yet. All the walls are in place. We're alone. That's new, well, not quite. It has been awhile since he's had someone in here.

Who gives a flying flip? He stole from you.

He closes the door deliberately slow, then swivels to face me on genuine, black leather loafers from his home country that cost a fortune.

"Why did you do it, Mr. Powers?" I seethe and shake.

He knots his hands in front of him and widens his stance in front of the only way out of here. "Sweetheart—"

"*Sweetheart!* No one treats people they call by that name like you've treated me. You had my card cancelled. Reported me as an identity thief. God knows what else you've done. All for what? So, you can molest other women in front of me? What about that is so appealing to you? Never mind. I don't want to know. What I do want is absolutely nothing to do with you. So please, for Pete's sake, give me my money back and let. Me. Go."

"No," he says simply.

Pure hell breaks loose within me. My hands raise themselves in the air and make a choking gesture near his neck.

"Why? You don't even like me! I'm nothing to you!"

He eyes my hands that'll cheerfully kill him if I think it'll get my money back.

"That's not true, Amari. I—"

"Yes. It. Is. I've been nothing but décor around here, and there's someone you can hire who doesn't want a life outside work and can stomach your dating habits that are disgusting... just like *you* are." I want to hit him where it hurts, devastating him, like he's doing to me.

It's doubtful if my pitiful punches will indent his shirt, even less his ethics, so I yell so more. "I'm not your property! You're not my owner! Your money gives you privileges over material things! Not people, jackass! And here's a piece of advice: if you like being watched during intimate moments, go to a BDSM club where it's acceptable!"

His shoulders lift almost to his ears, chest expanding and collapsing as if he's breathing fire. Immediately, I regret my insults and losing all rationality. This isn't the way to get what I want out of people like him, so I turn my palms out, signaling for a truce.

"Look, Mr. Powers. I don't want to work here. I feel physically ill sometimes when I get off. If you persist with trying to get me back as your PA, you'll be jeopardizing your company. I have no loyalty to it, or you. Please undo whatever it is you did to my credit and return all my money. It's all I have," I plead to his compassionate side, just not sure if he has one.

"No, Amari," he murmurs.

I'm right—he doesn't have compassion and I'm flat broke since he didn't deny emptying *all* my accounts. Can't be swayed to put back what he stole without me returning to work for him. That pushes me past my breaking point. Crazed, I capture two handfuls of my hair and pull, spinning in aimless circles, trapped by a man who's impossible to deal with.

"Stop, Amari, and listen to me. I want you here because I—"

"Because you think you should have what you want!' I scream, and whirl around to him. "Because you're self-centered and no one else's wants, feelings, and needs matter to you. Does that sound about right, Mr. Powers?"

He sighs. "You're not going to let me explain why I did it, are you?"

"Explain? Hell no, you can't explain. You had no right to do it period. Nothing you say will justify what you've done."

"Nothing?"

"Nothing!"

"Fine, have it your way then… and I'm keeping your money." This isn't how this visit is supposed to go.

Feeling as if I'm in a tunnel, I gravitate toward the sunlight that's warming my backside, mumbling under my breath, "I don't know why I came here, thinking I could reason with the same insatiable monster who's punishing me for exercising my rights to not be driven insane. I've really gone nuts." And totally spiraling.

Nothing left to do but hit rock bottom now.

Hands grip my shoulders and twirl me around to face him. His expression is a mask of fury. Good. He's as angry as I am, and he probably wants to do something violent too. Right now, I'm only hurting my scalp. Assaulting him probably won't get me back what's mine either, so I prepare to wait him out. Hopefully, he'll see things my way, and soon. He becomes blurry first. I realize my hopelessness is building up in my eyes and coursing down my cheeks, teetering on the edge of my despair, which he might find a way to take from me too. Well, he can't have it.

You should stop it from leaking from your face then.

I swipe the tears away and blanket the worse of my emotions. It's difficult, but I'm stubborn, even while I'm a certifiable basket case.

His expression dulls. "Amari," he calls too softly, as if he's worried about me.

I sniffle. "No! You don't get to pretend you care about me. You're incapable of acknowledging I'm in the room, even less my feelings. I'm calling the cops and telling them everything you've done to me."

"What have I done, Amari?" he asks too damn nonchalantly.

"You sick bastard! You know what you've done. How could you? I've never asked for anything from you, and if you think I'll sit behind that desk meekly after you've treated me like this, you have another thing coming."

His head shifts to the side, appearing meek when he's anything but. "You didn't say what I've done."

"I did! You ruined me. The credit card company is going to prosecute me after a week, if not already. I didn't dare call my bank. They're probably about to do the same thing. I came straight here stupidly, hoping you'd straighten this out because you had a conscience somewhere."

"You can't prove *I* took anything from you."

"Yeah, no one will suspect you when you're the only one who's promised to make me pay for quitting on an A-1 jerk, and now I'm barely legal in the state I was born in," I spit. Just being run out of New York on a rail by him must've been too much to hope for.

74

"My point is that you need evidence, sweetheart." Point made, and there isn't one to calling the cops. This case will be deemed a 'he said, she said' complaint and filed at the back of the precinct's database.

"Stop calling me sweetheart," I spew. "Of course, you paid someone else to damage my finances for you. That's what you do: get someone else to do your dirty work so you have time to get your hands and mouth filthy on the women you've met on the street. Or maybe they're all call girls. I don't know. I don't care. Just leave me alone."

"You've mentioned the other women a lot today, Amari. Are you jealous of them?"

My mouth opens and closes, as I marvel at his nerve to ask me such a question when it has nothing to do with what he's done. Eventually, I rediscover the function to speak. "Jealous! Are you out of your ever-loving mind? You are toxic, and you probably have every sexually transmitted disease known to man. A few they don't know about."

He grins. "Then prove it."

"Prove what?" The abrupt change of subject is mind-boggling, and he better not be talking about what I think he is.

"Prove you're not jealous of the women I get my hands and mouth dirty on... no, you said filthy." And there it is.

My stomach begins to eat on itself. "Why? Obviously, you're not really interested in me if you can sleep with others right under my nose. I'm definitely not interested in you for the same reason, so I have nothing to prove. Not to someone that stole from me."

"And I'll give it back to you if you prove you're not jealous of me spending time with other women."

I flinch. I don't want to think about what he does with the other women at all. "Again, I ask what does that have to do with my money?"

He shrugs. "Nothing. I'm just a businessman seizing the opportunity to satisfy the insatiable monster you called me."

The verbal abuse is coming back to haunt me, but it's the only defense I have in this clusterfuck, and I have many more derogatory names where those came from. "I don't care what you want! You don't count as a man whore in a Brooks Brothers suit to me, and this is all about what *I* want right now!"

The clicking of his tongue, chastising me for the insult, grates on my nerves. I can't help the rant filling up my chest and then tumbling out of my mouth. I have every right to be furious—I've been shanghaied and left penniless. Of course, he'll never comprehend that. He's a billionaire, the wall around his wealth undoubtedly like Fort Knox.

"Amari, stop the name-calling, or our time together will be full of strife… for you," he warns in a decadent tone, prompting thoughts of warm chocolate dripping off a ripe strawberry onto my flesh.

I don't even know what that feels like, so why the hell am I imaging it? Especially now of all times. Oh yes, it was so stupid to come here.

"I'm calling the cops. I can't prove what you've done, but I sure as hell can lead them in the right direction. Wait, what do mean by our time together? This is the last time I'll ever be in the same room as you."

"The time you'll spend showing me that you're not jealous."

Disbelief plops down in my chest, forcing me to lean back to bear its weight.

"Why on this earth would I do that? I. Hate. You."

I blink once and find my chin tilted against the silky material of his tie. He's conquered the pitiful three feet of my personal space so damn quickly someone should add more inches for my sake. His nearness is swallowing up my senses, compelling me to inhale the very essence of him. And fogging up my head.

76

My mouth droops open. His hand lifts, fingering a curl flopping around my cheek. A tingling explodes under my skin. I forget to breathe, which is better than sucking in whatever chemical he's giving off, drowning me.

Losing the ability to think clearly allows something else to take over. It wants me to get closer to him, as if that's possible. Well hell, I'm developing Stockholm syndrome, or something like it already, and he hasn't even told me what he plans to do with me next. Any minute now, I'll be drooling.

Then you better get angry again.

I snap my lips closed then take a step back. "Don't touch me, Mr. Powers."

My hair slips from his fingers. He shoves them all in his pockets.

"You know, Amari, I read somewhere that there's a thin line between love and hate."

"It's a good thing I'm planted firmly on the side of hate, well away from the border, isn't it?" Now, I just need to convince him and my body of that. It's betraying me for him.

What is wrong with me?

Hard up for…

Don't you dare.

…sex.

"Being firmly rooted on one side of that line may be good for you, Amari. Not at all for me, but I can work with that. Do you hate me enough to lose everything you've worked for?"

"Losing and being taken from are two very different things."

"Semantics, sweetheart, and you didn't answer my question."

I point a finger in his face. "You wouldn't think the details didn't matter if it was *your* money that had been stolen."

"Then take it back." He looks down at the digit almost poking him in the nose, and his eyes cross up.

I'd laugh, but I've totally crossed the line over into looney-bin land, where humor is a distant memory. "How the hell am I going to do that? I don't know where you *put* it."

His gaze finds mine again. "In a safe place, like my home, where you'll live for three months to prove you'll never love me."

My hand drops like a lead weight to my side.

I gape at him dumbly. "Love you?" I thought this conversation was about my jealousy. I mean proving I'm not afflicted with it.

You can't keep your own issues straight. How are you going to manage his in close quarters?

I'm not, if I'm truly honest with myself, which means I can't guarantee I won't come out the other side of three months loving him fully... or that'll he won't break my heart during our time together. Shit!

And you'll be knee-deep in it, whether you accept his deal or toss it back in his face.

His home is the perfect place to isolate me, a breeding ground for brainwashing and spirit-breaking. No good comes from loving a man who likes variety. I'll be a fool to let him sequester me anywhere where everything I feel for him will blossom, especially when he'll get tired of me. I'll be broken. The money just isn't worth the damage he'll do. Besides, I can always make more money.

Somewhere.

"You can go to hell by yourself on Blanchard Row, Mr. Powers. I'm not moving there to prove anything to your toddler-sized brain. Why would I when you've already demonstrated how much of a cad you are to me and everyone else you've dated?"

His lips crook at one corner and eyelashes wilt, creating half-moons on his cheekbones. "Then your parent's money will go the same route as yours. Poof. Gone."

He's done his homework and found my weakest spots. I'm not going to outsmart him when I don't have the details of his life or the power he wields. Therefore, no threat I use will be big enough. I'm caught on his hook, dangling, helpless.

My nails bite into the heels of my hand. Every ounce of strength I have is used to bottle up the frustration rising like a tidal wave and the urge to scream and cry, leaving me with no energy to speak coherently. Even insulting him won't make me feel any better at this rate. But there is one thing I can do.

"Don't do this," I beg, willing to get down on my knees if it'll help my case. "Please! My father is sick."

He swallows deeply. "I know he has congenital heart failure. With the right doctors, he could have the experimental surgery that could correct it, but he won't because he and your mother are on fixed income. Even if she went back to being a general manager at the local power plant and return to coaching college football, her and his salary combined won't cover a million-dollar hospital stay. No bank will ever loan them that amount of money. Do you have any idea what the minimum payment on a million dollars is even at the lowest interest rate? I do."

I've done my own legwork on my father's condition too. And why isn't Mr. Powers taking the opportunity to be smug about having the advantage? He's got me bent backwards, but he actually seems sorry for me.

"Yes, I know how much," I say quietly, and start to pace in a tiny circle. "I have every intention of getting the money, as soon as I start my own business."

Tuning him out, I think hard but come up with nothing to undo his sham.

"Can your niece or nephew on the way wait to eat while you get a business off the ground with no capital of your own?"

Even Brandon's family isn't safe from him.

"You're coming after everyone I love," I state needlessly.

He nods. "You have a grandparent still alive on both sides too, but I won't go after anyone if you move to Blanchard Row and prove to the toddler-sized brain inside this insatiable monster that you'll never love me."

"You'll just come after *me*. I feel so much better now." No, the sarcasm maligning my tone isn't helping my predicament, but it's either express myself in some way or spontaneously combust from all the emotions tangling together, manufacturing a time-sensitive bomb inside me.

That's when I will punch him.

"Yes, Amari. Just you. You said I didn't have enough money to buy your ethics, so I took your money instead, but I'll put it back and undo the fraudulent claim. I won't even make you work here. Although, I'll miss your eyerolling before you disappear into the copier room."

I whirl around to him. "You knew I hated watching you with other women, and yet you kept bringing them in here anyway?"

"Is that a confession of your jealousy, Amari?"

He's confessed everything finally too. Would've been helpful if you'd recorded it for evidence against him.

Not having proof of everything he's done to me is the least of my worries. The nauseousness flopping around my midsection is amplifying. I grab for my throat where it's building. Need to leave, but I can't go without everything I've worked for and stopped him from robbing my family blind too.

"No, it's not a confession, but I think I'm going to be sick, so let's cut to the chase. People like you want what they can't have very badly. So, if it's sex you want from me, it's done. Right here. Right now. Want to molest me in front of other people? Done. Call someone. I'll wait. Want me to watch you molest someone else? Done. Call anyone. Everyone you know is fine. I'll even come back to work. Just leave my family out of this."

"No. No. No. No. And *no*."

I'm completely thrown by his intense refusal. "Jesus! Even the insatiable finds gratification at some point, and I have nothing else to give you."

"Yes, you do."

"What is it then?"

"I'll tell you in time."

"You can tell me now."

"No."

My surrender, it's all he wants and will take. All I have left.

"Fine. I'll move with you on Blanchard Row."

I have no real clue of what I'm signing up. It's best if he doesn't tell me until the last minute, because backing out of whatever deal he's building up to will be a solution that I'll take.

He inhales deeply then just stares. I don't get a contented smile from his lips or even a triumphant expression in his eyes like I expect now that he's gotten his way.

That's because he's still unhappy.

I open my hands wide on each side of me. "What more do you want from me? If you're still allowed to sleep with other women, why aren't you happy about it?"

His thick eyebrows pull inward. "This is not about sleeping with other women. It's about you, only you… and me, and meeting your family as your man."

He grows two heads, or at least that's how I'm looking at him as if he has.

"You didn't say anything about meeting my family. You're asking me to lie to them about us. Why would you want to go anywhere near them?"

"Because I want to, and I can, and I haven't told you everything I want."

He'll get it all as long as he has what doesn't belong to him, and he's knows it. Now, he's grinning, but my family will be this deal's undoing.

"They'll see right through you, Mr. Powers. Right to what you're making me do." The words grind through my teeth clamped shut to keep my fury contained.

"You won't tell them anything but what I approve for you to say, Amari. You'll act as my woman to the best of your abilities at every moment of the day."

What the hell? Nuh huh! Not happening.

"Approve? Who the hell do you think you are? Don't bother to answer. I'll tell you who you are. Someone who will never know my love after this. Anything I ever felt for you just went right out the damn window."

There's no actual window in here, so it must be on the floor.
Shut. Up. Conscience.

Mr. Powers pinches the bridge of his nose. "Are you done? Can we talk terms now? Or you can leave without your money and your good name?"

I loathe how he casually offers up what is rightfully mine to me. "How do I know at the end of the three months I still won't end up in jail for your stupid machinations of my credit?"

"You won't get arrested because as soon as you sign the contract—"

"Contract!" I screech. "You had this planned all along!" How far is he willing to go to own me lock, stock, and barrel that he's got me spread-eagle over?

You're about to find out.

"…that I had drawn up, I'll have your money put back in both of your bank accounts and your credit restored," he finishes as if I never interrupted him. "But you won't have access to any of it. You'll give up your identity for real and be solely my girlfriend, dependent on me. You'll do everything I say, when I say, however. I. Say."

Breaking down, that's what I do with each word that he utters. I'm back to being his employee, only there's a goddamn contract involved now. Shrewd businessman in everything he does, legit and underhanded.

"And if I refuse you anything you ask even if it's beyond the reasonable?" I know the answer, just procrastinating, trying to decide if what he has in mind for me is worse than being the reason those I love are rendered bankrupt.

It isn't, but whatever he does will be humiliating, degrading, and the systematic splintering of my soul as long as I'm at his mercy, which he doesn't have. At least not for me, but I'll protect my heart at all costs.

"Refuse me, and the deal is null and void. Your money disappears along with your family's."

I look away from the bane of my existence in front of me. My emotions tornado within. Then my knees buckle. I'm going down. I stumble backwards then slump to the ground, determined not to even graze his sleeve on the way down. And then, the tears come, wave after wave racking my body. He squats down. I can't see him through the sheen of waterworks but can sense his every move like there's a link materializing between us. More like a ball and chain.

A hand glides down my arm, shocking me. I lunge sideways from the live wire, because his touch almost hurts. I should be dodging it because I'm repulsed by him. Well, I'm not, and I detest myself for it. How can my body want him even when we both know he's just on this side of depraved?

"Don't touch me," I croak.

"Amari, I'll do a lot of touching of you over the next three months."

"Not until I've signed the contract."

"We can do that right now. But remember, if your family even suspects this deal between us, you lose everything."

"This feels like a backwards prenup, except I'll get my own money back before the relationship starts."

"Yes, and this contract is tight and binding, so you need to adhere to its every term or face the consequences."

A wail seeps out of my throat before I start mopping at my face. "I think it's too late for the consequences. They started when I started working here, but I get the feeling that the trauma is only just beginning." Then I get to my feet. "Can I use your bathroom?"

Might as well clean myself up and start as I mean to go on… emotionless. My feelings are traitors around him.

He drills into the top of my head for what seems like hours with a penetrating stare, possibly waiting for me to look up. I can't face him, don't want to plummet again from being on the wrong end of his ruthlessness. Dragged back into his world only hours into the journey of rediscovering happy Amari that's already being rerouted by none other than Camron Powers, my self-appointed tormentor.

"You know where it is, Amari."

Of course, I do. I've had countless cleaning services restore it and the bedroom to their former glory. I didn't work today, so I don't know what I'm going to find when I press the button behind the brass statue on the custom-built bookshelf.

The wall slides away, and the nausea morphs into self-stacking Lego blocks. I really don't want to go in here, but I sincerely hope that the bathroom has been cleaned enough for me to vomit in.

The office door opens in my side view before I step over the threshold of the hidden bedroom. Lance Armstrong, one of several Powers Enterprises' lawyers, enters. I glare at the custom, king-sized bed with leather headboard in the oversized space, his home away from home that's seen more action than a Michael Jai White movie. My insides stir, sickness doubling in strength. I'll ask myself why that's happening after I'm done racing over the iron-gray carpet to the darkened doorway on my left.

The rising bile floods my throat, taking my breath away. I slap a hand over my mouth, feet pounding the walkway between the his-and-her sinks and jacuzzi. Then I fall down to my knees in from of the porcelain God being lorded over by the state-of-the-art shower stall. Fortunately, I don't have to lift the seat up to part with last night's dinner. I wouldn't have risked touching it.

At some point, I'm going to have to sit down and have a good talk with myself. I need to face head-on all the questions I left unanswered for years… mainly the one that pertains to wanting to hurl every time I encounter evidence of Mr. Powers' liaisons. It's not normal. Yes, he undeniably sickens me. But enough to make me actually sick?

"Camron, are you sure this is a good idea?" Lance asks from the bedroom, which is too damn close. "She seems…well, ill by the whole situation. I can't say I blame her. What kind of man makes a woman give up her life to be with him?"

Why didn't I think to ask that? Right, I have other pressing problems.

Another bout of sickness clogs my ears up before Mr. Powers replies.

The lights come on. Instantly, I know who's braving my purging in the dark.

"Go. Away," I get out before another onslaught overtakes me.

The crystal knob on the closest sink turns on without a squeak, before a cool cloth is held firmly to my forehead. I snatch it off, tossing it behind me. It gives off a whacking noise as it collides with the basin of the jacuzzi, the only satisfiable hitting that's going to go on with him in the room.

He heaves air into his lungs above me. I couldn't care less that's he's irritated by my childishness, or that he's trying to take care of me. I have my own heaving issues, which stop abruptly, allowing me to tip backwards to the floor on my butt and catch my breath. Why is he trying to take care of me anyway? He never wanted to before.

"Amari, let me help you to the bed."

Waves of revulsion punch me in the abdomen. "Never will I ever sit on that bed, playboy."

"The linen is clean."

"Don't care. Nastiest bed in the city."

"Which I'll take you on first instead of the one on Blanchard Row if you don't go back to acting like an adult." Which means we'll be having sex on it one day, technically more satisfiable hitting... for him.

I wish I could contest that announcement, but it's not worth the aftermath that won't fall on only me. Still, he's going to learn to compromise today.

"I will not go anywhere near that bed until I get a tetanus shot and bubble wrap for the mattress, and you've provided a clean bill of health after your next checkup. I know you've been with over half of the women in this state alone... if not all of them."

"Not one of them ever mattered to me, Amari, and I never slept with anyone unprotected."

"Wrong. They all matter. At least to them and their families, they do."

I can't get his words 'not one of them ever mattered to me' out of my head. Where is this man's heart? If he truly has one, why is he trying to stick me on the black side of it with everyone else?

I scramble to my feet, rush to the running water, and scoop some into my mouth, rinsing it out, praying it washes away the new ripples of revulsion for him.

"Fine, Amari. They matter, just not like you do. When the newest update of my medical records posts online with everyone else's, then I'll have you in every way I can think of." That's a promise if I ever heard one from his mouth.

"Yeah, I'm sure you will, lover, but you'll get tired of me eventually. Then I'll forget you ever existed."

I cry bull…

Shut up.

…shit.

"Don't count on it, Amari. Three months is a long time to be around someone. You might find I'm not as bad as you think I am." That's what I'm afraid of, along with the systematic reprogramming of me that he'll do.

It's not his fault you're half in love with him already.

Whose is it then? And who asked a part of me to be honest *with* me? There's nothing wrong with sticking my head in the sand concerning Mr. Powers. It's how I've endured his employ this long.

Barely living, sleeping alone…

Oh my God! Shut! Up!

I prop myself on the edge of the countertop with trembling hands, head hanging low. "I don't think you're bad, Mr. Powers. I knew you were when you were too stupid to hide the scores of women you've played with in here. So many more would do you just for the bragging rights. If you'd bypassed all of them just to waste your time on me, you're even more twisted than I thought."

My head swivels to him behind me. He's got a cruel twist to his lips, the very same egotistical expression inherited from his father that I was expecting when he crushed my first efforts to combat his manipulating.

"We'll see who's more twisted when I'm done with you, Amari."

I raise one hand above my head. "It'll be me for sure. Can I be alone now, please?"

He chuckles and moves toward Lance, who's waiting in the bedroom with the scent of uncomfortable wafting off his camel-colored Tom Ford suit like cologne. Both men vanish into the office, talking amongst themselves too low for me to hear. Minutes later, I retrace their steps to the client's side of his desk, where Lance perches on the edge one of two leather and silver-trimmed chairs.

Lance's unease will become a shared experience as he explains each clause of the contract to me. They're simple. Camron Powers and I are an exclusive couple with full benefits that he can reap wherever he desires, whenever, however, and I have to keep it all to myself. Whatever he tells me to do, I must do in a timely fashion. If I renege on the gag order or just one of his commands, I forfeit every penny any of the Spencer's and immediate relatives every saved.

I'm enslaved to Camron, and there isn't a damn thing I can do about it.

The question is why does he really want you so damn badly.

I must be the one that got away.

You offered yourself to him, so that's not it.

Then what is it?

He'll tell you in time.

Time with him will work against me.

If you know that, then you already know what not to do.

Fall in love with him completely. That's much easier said than done when your heart is stupid.

Then concentrate on just not falling in love… completely.

"This is an illegal document, Amari," Lance says suddenly, disrupting the nagging thoughts flitting through my head. "It won't hold up in a court of law."

"I know, Mr. Armstrong. But if I don't commit to it… to him, I might not get back everything of mine before I can prove he took anything from me in the first place, or he takes something else. I would take that chance, but my brother Brandon certainly can't support a growing family on nothing. My parents' savings have to last their lifetimes. My father's condition could make him keel over into his grave from the stress of losing their home, cars... their customary way of life."

It's astonishing how I got us all into this mess by simply looking for the root of Mr. Powers' success. I'll get us free of his grip come hell or high water. There's one silver lining in these thunderclouds hovering over the Spencer's though, the time limit. If there's a God in heaven, all my future scars will be on the inside after this ordeal is over.

Lance hands a Rosewood Executive pen worth hundreds of dollars to me. "Call me Lance. No need for formality when we're all in this circus together. Are you sure you want to do this, Amari? You don't have to sign this contract."

My head wrenches upward, looking for some indication that he may be able to rescue me from the ringleader of this circus. There's only sympathy swimming in the sad, green depths beneath a brunette, hundred-dollar haircut.

"Do you have three hundred grand, Mr. Armstrong?"

He shifts in his seat and side-eyes Mr. Powers, who winks and smiles.

The prick.

Lance breathes out heavily. "No. I'm prone to spend money sometimes faster than my check clears." And Mr. Powers knows Lance wouldn't be able to give me a handout or a hand out of this hole that he's has dug for me.

I'm going to have to shovel all the way to China, as he always intended.

"Then you can't help me, Lance, but thank you." I sign my name on the dotted line.

When my prison sentence is secured in black ink, I jack rabbit out of my seat.

"Wait!" Camron orders.

I palm the doorknob before stopping, craving to be on the other side of the barrier I should've never entered... ever. His presence emerges behind me, casting his shadow over me, and I should get used to being swallowed up by him right now.

"Our agreement goes into effect immediately. I'll pick you up at your apartment tomorrow at four. You take nothing with you from there but the clothes on your back. We'll go straight to your parents' home in Winchester, where you'll introduce me as yours. Call your parents and let them know we're coming tomorrow tonight for dinner, please."

Well, he didn't say I have to announce myself as his, so that's something.

Not much, but he used manners. Where did he buy them at I wonder?

"They're expecting me today, Mr. Powers."

"But not me. I'll be grateful if you'll all wait one more day. I trust you'll give them a heads up." Without actually giving them one about the true nature of our association.

"Yes."

"Yes, what?"

Hatred bubbles underneath the weight of his arrogance, superiority, and demand for obedience and respect that he isn't due that's pressing into my chest. "Yes, Mr. Powers."

"Amari, we're not colleagues anymore. Call me Camron."

Call him… I thought…

Just stop thinking at this point, and go with the flow. He's more confusing than a Rubik's cube.

And his request for less formality isn't unreasonable. Wouldn't have dreamed of calling him by his given name four years ago.

But you have dreamed about it.

Once.

Try in the triple digits.

Try shutting the hell up sometimes.

I glance back at him. "I can do that."

"Then say it," he whispers. "Please." Pleading.

"Camron," I murmur.

Using his first name feels too damn intimate while I'm looking at him. It's as if I'm crossing a line I never wanted to with him.

Oh, you wanted to. You just gave up on it a long time ago.

And now the boundaries I set are already distorting.

Imagine how fast they'll disappear when he's inside you.

I snatch the door open, petrified of what I can't control. With one foot outside out the office, I'm seized by the waist, tugged backwards into a hard body.

"You didn't let me say thank you," Camron whispers directly into my ear, too close for the flow of my blood to not screech to a halt in my veins.

Something much more terrifying takes its place, a pulsing within that pushes against places too sensitive to be ambushed. Heat waves undulate through me. Yet, I shiver. Strange.

His head dips, lips setting down on the side of my neck, the equivalent of getting smacked by a runaway train. On impact, I gasp loudly. Moisture pools within my thighs. I barely resist turning in his arms to kiss him earnestly. The power it takes to hold myself back compels a whimper from me.

Suddenly, he steps back, setting me adrift in the middle of unknown territory. His. "See you later, sweetheart. Go enjoy your day."

How could I after this morning's disaster and the storm brewing and thrashing around inside me? With hardly any money in my purse?

Don't have the answer to either of those questions. Haven't been this broke since college, but you need to get it together. You're loitering. Can't afford to break even a minor traffic law right now.

"O-okay," I stammer then stagger into the hallway, as if I've been drinking since sunup.

Why did he have to put his mouth on me?
Felt damn good to me.
Too good.

****

~Camron~

Again, it's hell to let Amari go anywhere without me, but Blake's advice comes to mind in ghostly chains rattling around my skull: give her space. She's still willing to believe the worst of me, even less ready for me to tell her why I destroyed her credit and maimed her good name temporarily. Unwilling to even *trust* me. And I'm worried about her. She appears unstable while sauntering for the elevator in skin-tight jeans that mold to the half-moons of her ass like she melted down and poured herself into them.

I let her out of my sight only when she disappears into the lift, then I pivot to Lance approaching me. It's written all over his face that he's still concerned about the arrangement with Amari—he wanted no parts of it. Just witnessing could cost him his right to practice law, ever. He didn't hesitate to inform me of that, loudly.

Unlike Deon, bribing Lance didn't pan out. He swapped the much-needed extra payday in exchange for speaking his mind, starting with what he thinks of me. Apparently, I need a long stint in an insane asylum for conjuring up the idea of entangling Amari in a contracted relationship. I think he called me a savage too. Normally, I wouldn't care, but Blake says I should and that Amari hates me because I don't. Lance even warned me that he'd help Amari if she asked for it. Thank God, he burns through money like a fire-alarm blaze, and she doesn't.

"Camron—"

"Save it, Lance. I have to go."

He squints at me. "Go? What about the Dubai contract? The contract in my hand?" He waves it at me.

"Tear them both up."

"Do what?"

Don't have time for this.

Exhaling, I do something rare: make time. "I said—"

"I heard you. I just don't know why you went through so much to obtain both deals only to tear them up." Then his eyes bulge out of his head. "Ohhhh!"

Who asked him to figure out anything?

"Anything concerning the matters of my heart is above your pay grade, Lance."

He grins. "I see. Alright. I didn't want to wheel and deal with the Dubai lawyer anyway. I can barely understand a thing the man says."

I snort and turn around. "Cool. I'm gone for the day."

"Can I ask where you're going?"

I stop to. "If you must know, I have to see my doctor. Need to confirm that my body's not crawling with something, and then call in reinforcements. There's a store I need to buy out. Apparently, I have several birthdays to make up for. Although, my efforts will probably be deemed useless."

Suddenly, Lance looks as if he needs the nearest bathroom. "Crawling? Yeah, I can't help you there, but I wouldn't be so quick to think whatever you do is useless. I heard Amari's reaction to your stolen smooch, and no one pants like that unless they're affected by the one doing the stealing."

I hope that's not all she lets me steal.

"Bye, Lance, and thank you for your help."

"You're welcome, Camron. I'll walk out with you... and good luck with Amari."

"I'm going to need it."

Chapter Four
~Amari~

I arrive at the apartment in one piece. My emotional state doesn't. It's all over the place now that Camron has worn off. He'll probably be pissed when he learns I sent a quick text, asking my mother to set one more place at the table for a friend tomorrow. She's disappointed in the change of plans and that I didn't just call, but understands it's more sensible to wait than make two trips to Winchester. Fortunately, she's not fond of texting. I avoid the third degree, not ready to lie to her face just yet about what Camron really is to me, even if he'll penalize me for not following his instructions.

The serenity in my home doesn't calm me for the first time, while I rack my brain for ways to get ahead of his maneuverings with my finances. The only peace I discover comes from wearing a path in every room's carpet, wringing my hands like washed clothes that won't release the water. It's impossible to eat, relax, or adjust to abandoning everything I know to be ensnared like a wild animal in the gilded cage of Camron's house. It's where I'll be waiting to be led to the slaughter by the strings of my own heart.

Can't bear to think about how far astray that organ will go if given half a chance, or if Camron sneaks me from behind with more affections that I haven't braced for. Evidently, I haven't erected enough walls or lines between us yet, so I vow to be indifferent to him until I have. Then, I point my focus elsewhere: my struggle with bowing down to him until the proof that he's a blackmailing cutthroat is in my hand before the three months are up.

Now that I don't have to respect Camron as my boss, instinct will demand I push back every time he commands me to do something, or bail on him altogether, ultimately my family too. Since he's goes out of town on business trips regularly, and I'm not

95

his PA any longer, I should have enough space to uncover at least one loophole in his conditions. It would be much easier to take the contract to the cops as proof of his thievery... if I had a copy of it.

Why didn't you ask for one, idiot?

In my defense, it's hard to plot on someone when my world is being turned upside down and I need to get far away from the madness.

It's hard for you to plot at all.

Hopefully, searching through other people's belongings is a different matter.

If I'm lucky, Camron will be gone even more frequently from home. Or I'll locate the original document quickly. If it's not locked away safely in the Powers Enterprises building that I no longer have access to.

Insurmountable obstacles crop up in each plan I concoct, each disappointment shredding my faith in beating Camron at his own game. It's rigged, so I can't play it with him on equal footing *or* lose.

You'll just have to come out somewhere in between, with your mind and heart intact.

I just can't see how yet, not as long as my body reacts to every skin-to-skin contact he instigates.

The hours rebel against becoming a part of the past. Repeatedly, I catch myself memorizing the formation of my furniture. When it's too dark in the apartment for that, I watch the neon green hands circle the clock below the multi-fruit strips of wallpaper in the kitchen, from the couch. Night comes gradually then hangs around.

No, you're just really, really slow about accepting your fate, Amari.

And my new position in Camron's life too.

If you would, you'd be asleep by now.

Rather be awake, thank you very much.

Eventually, the new day beats the darkness back to mere shadows in every corner. When it's down to ten minutes before four, I'm exhausted and tempted to resurrect old Amari, who wears cheap, dress clothes, glasses for reading, and a ponytail. Camron might just make me change just because he can, wanting me at my best. In the bathroom, I wash up, brush my teeth and hair, snubbing the makeup I'll be unable to repair it if I start to cry again.

Yeah, you'll probably do lots of that.

The doorbell chiming interrupts my gaping into the mirror at the woman permanently cringing. She had an identity yesterday, a future. Feels like a lifetime has passed since then. Camron will be delighted to tell me who I am now, which he will, and it's infuriating that I have to open my door so he can.

When it swings wide to his gorgeous, smiling mug, he looks absolutely stunning in a casual Polo shirt and jeans, even genuinely happy... at my expense—all it took was the signing away of the rights and privileges to live my life as I see fit. That's even more maddening.

"It's a shame God wasted all that beauty on a pervert," I spew.

His joy slips into a dirty frown.

That's enough pettiness, Amari. More than you have something at stake here.

"Let. Me. In. Amari." His tone is hard and clipped, and only the devil knows why I hear a double meaning in it. The devil as in Camron. If there is a hidden message in his voice, I choose to overlook it. It'll be to my detriment if I don't.

I move to the side, letting him violate the other side of the only shelter I had from him. I want to shove him right back out of it when he starts to peruse my humble decorations that are nothing like the sleek, white and chrome museum he rarely sets foot in on Blanchard Row. Taking in the living room from the top stair, his inspection makes me examine my apartment too.

I'm not looking for what could make it better though, wouldn't change a thing about the stark, white walls or the single tan one that stands out and matches the couch perfectly. The plants hanging from the ceiling and the floor pedestals loaded down with more creeping vines bring the outdoors inside, providing its own colors. Healthy, potted palm trees show off like peacocks from the corners housing armchairs, miniature glass tables, and crystal reading lamps.

Camron ambles down the staircase, stopping in front of the gas fireplace below the mounted television to scrutinize the framed family snapshots on the mantel. It's not long before he strolls to one of the windows hidden behind closed blinds. I leave them shut when I'm traveling. Couldn't bring myself to open them when I got back yesterday. Would've had to close them right back today.

It would've felt as if I was letting the sun pour into my soul, lighting up the places blackened by Camron's extortion, only so he could come and block the healing rays.

That kind of torment, I can do without, rather stay in the dark until the sunshine is eternal.

He thumbs the leaf of a floating Devil's Ivy. "What are you going to do about your plants?"

"They'll die of course," I respond hoarsely.

They're the closest I've gotten to having children, reduced to collateral damage to his rule of 'take nothing with me.'

"You could have someone come feed them," he suggests logically, with his back turned.

I swipe away a lone teardrop. "I would, but that'll be one more person you're forcing me to lie to about why I won't be home to do it myself. No, thank you."

He frowns. "What lies? We'll be together, living together. A couple in every way."

"Bullshit! No real couple needs a contract to be together. Prenups, I get, but you have some nerve to be concerned about my plants after what you strong-armed me into yesterday. Do me a favor and don't convince yourself this deal is real. I only agreed to it to keep you from destroying my family through me. The plants are the least of my worries. Yours too from now on."

Camron knits his fingers behind his back. The plant becomes interesting to him again. "Giving up your life for your family's well-being," he breathes. "It must make you feel all self-righteous to practice what you preach."

His memory is like an elephant's.

"I'm no damn martyr, Camron. Any sacrifice I make for them is because of you."

And then, his hard gaze is gouging my face. "Amari, I'm not your enemy."

He's that and more, a formidable opponent. Unbeatable.

"Says the man holding indentured slavery over my head," I comment dryly.

And you're going to lose much more to him than you ever intended to.

Stupid conscience always has something to add, as if I don't have enough shit to deal with already, like dinner with Camron at my parents' table.

"Can we get this charade on the road please? The fastest we get to my family's house and outright lie to them, the faster we can leave."

He looks off into the kitchen. "No. I'd like a tour of your apartment now."

Good Lord!

"There's no need for that. It's not like we're going to live here, which isn't anywhere near the scale of the places you're used to."

"No," he says softly. "It's better. I can breathe in here. The other places are too polluted with the owner's self-importance."

I balk, not sure I heard him right, or want him familiarizing himself with my apartment, contaminating it with *his* ego.

He fans an open palm toward the dim hallway connected to the walkway I'm standing on, determined to have a walkthrough. Since I'm not getting out of it, wearily, I swivel on my heels. He quickly takes the stairs, to form a single file line behind me. We move toward the bedrooms. Halfway, I pause and push open the doors on each side of us and flip the light switches.

"This is the guest room to our right. Bathroom on the left. Both are decorated in mauve and hunter green, and this tour is so damn cheesy."

He chuckles quietly behind me, while inspecting the small rooms.

I move forward, expecting him to follow when he's ready. It's not like he can get lost in my apartment, even with his eyes closed.

In the master bedroom, twice as spacious as the guest's, I break beside the nightstand next to the real oak queen bed under a thick, floral comforter and a mountain of colored throw pillows. Matching tall armoire and dresser sit against the adjacent walls. My stiff posture displays in the mirrored doors of my closet sandwiched by the ensuite bathroom and armoire. I dislike the fatigue wrinkling the space between my eyebrows, so I stare at him as he catches up, finally. Couldn't have been anything that fascinating about the guestroom and half bath to take him minutes to move on.

I point toward the bathroom that gave me a few moments of blissful ignorance from his vendetta yesterday. There isn't anything I wouldn't do to go back in time.

"That's another bathroom decorated in purple, lavender, and peach, same as this room, which is the master's and the end of the tour."

He smirks. "You haven't shown me the kitchen yet."

"I'll describe it to you on the way out the front door."

He cocks an eyebrow. "Are you refusing me?"

Yeah, he's so going to milk his time with me for all it's worth. *And then some.*

I charge past him to the last stop, where I plop down on a barstool hidden neatly under the low counter. "There's nothing spectacular about the long row of white cabinets and farm sinks against the back wall, or the fridge on the right, nor the stove on the left. You'll find nothing interesting on the other end of the room either but a little alcove behind the wooden doors for the washer and dryer. An ordinary kitchen for an extra ordinary woman."

"I'll be the judge of that."

"I'm sure you will," I mumble, while swiveling on my seat to stare off into the living area.

In my peripheral, he takes long observations of the wall fruit plaques and decorative pictures, then vanishes within the shuttered doors of the laundry room. If I didn't know better, I swear he was taking notes. For what? Who the hell knows? But it shouldn't take him long.

I prop my foot on the bottom rung of my chair, elbows on the countertop, chin in my hand to wait. Utterly bored. Can't leave here fast enough. Should be vice versa, but Camron has a way of flipping everything on its head.

The next ninety days are going to be trial by fire. Nobody has to tell me that I'm not going to come out unscathed or be the same afterwards. Not sure if that's a good or bad thing though. To figure out which it'll be, I'll need to turn myself inside out. At least I'll have lots of time on my hands for self-evaluating, but I'm not looking forward to it.

"Amari," collides with the hazy edges of my awareness, startling the hell out of me.

I lurch back to reality. My hand smacks the flat surface, as I jerk toward the voice. An empty, ceramic canister springboards up then tips toward the backend of the countertop.

Camron, who's standing a hair's length away, saves the cookie jar from tumbling onto the walkway, while I gawk up at him, mainly at his mouth. Those lips have caused me enough trouble for the next year, and yet, I can't stop eyeing them.

"Sorry for scaring you, Amari."

His deep voice, closeness, and another rare, random apology from him should be more than enough to keep me alert, but they're more like wind machines blowing my senses wide open.

My God, I want him… in the worst way.

Took you long enough to admit it.

"Amari."

"Yeah."

"Can I kiss you?"

The odd question drives me right out of my daze. Isn't he supposed to take what he wants from me?

"Why are you asking, Camron?"

"Because I want to."

He leans toward me slowly, giving me the impression that he's waiting for me to shoot him down. I would if I could. The unidentified part of me that's takes over when he's too damn close won't let me reject him. I surge forward, as if I'm starving for him. Our mouths collide. The heavens meet the earth.

Kissing him is an unwise thing to do—I was always going to find this out the hard way. Too late to undo my mistake. Tongues are already exploring warm nooks and crannies, when they're not tangling together. He sips from the tip of mine, withdrawing something that I need, replacing it with something I want. I'm not sure if it's a fair trade, but I'm positive his lips shouldn't be this soft. Intoxicating. This damn demanding. Lifting me off my stool.

That's not his lips, fool. It's his hands.

Hard arms encase my waist and the bottom of my butt, maneuvering me into vertically straddling his erection. It's wide. Long. Fitting within my thighs like a glove to hand.

Just right. Take advantage.

I hook my white, ankle boots behind him then wind my hips against his, satisfying the yearning in my core briefly. He groans. We revolve toward the living room. I cave against his chest, fingers circling around his neck for balance while I attack, then reattack his mouth. Already addicted to the essence of him—I knew I would be if I was ever where I've wanted to be, except, I wanted his arms around me years ago. Now, they're the most dangerous place in the world.

Only because you want to be horizontal while in them.

Want. I should contemplate why my inner voice didn't use that word in its past tense form, but I don't care. Too busy craving Camron more than my next breath, more than I did when I first met him. The day of our first kiss isn't supposed to have dawned. For all I know, I could be dreaming that's he's here right now. I've done that before, but there are a few annoyances keeping me firmly rooted in reality, prohibiting me from getting closer to him. My tan jeans and sleeveless, lacy blouse with attached bra take up needed space like chaperones, and there's a relentless buzzing beneath my leg.

When he softly lays me down on the couch, depositing a knee beside me on the cushion, I shut down the kiss reluctantly. "What *is* that, Camron?"

"My phone, sweetheart," he replies gruffly, with glazed eyes.

He looks high. I'm more than pleased that it was me who put that expression on his face. I shouldn't be though, not with the shit show he's pulled me into, but nothing else is making sense right now. Why should my unwelcomed desire to make love with him be any easier to decipher?

"I should answer it, or it won't stop, and it's important, baby." His fingers extract the device from his front pocket. "Did you get them, Bailey?"

Who the hell is Bailey?

Better be his chauffeur.

I begin to shamelessly eavesdrop on his call he's taking with a half-smile. He's definitely talking to someone he gets along with quite well. Then the unmistakable husky giggle from a woman resonates out of his earpiece. My arousal dries up like the desert, chest hollowing out again.

I shove at his with both hands until he's on his feet and I scramble off the sofa, angry more with myself than him.

Why the hell am I mad with him at all? He's just being who he's always been, himself. I've gotten what I deserve for backsliding on the pact I made while still working for him: never let Camron Powers get to me or my heart.

You didn't specify your body though.

And that's my fault. Lesson learned.

I speed-walk up the stairs.

"Amari," he growls. "Bailey, let me call you back," he says to my back. "That call isn't what you think it was about, Amari."

It wasn't the chauffeur either.

"You don't have to explain, Camron. Technically, you're only mine on paper. Bailey was probably on the scene before I was, so she's earned first dibs at you."

Camron has already taught me the hard way that I'm not into sharing. His touch will make me forget she exists in his world. I don't think he'll forget her or not answer her call the next time it interrupts us either, and that hurts, much less than it will if I let myself fall for him completely.

"Can we go now?" I seize my keys from beside the canister he saved, their jagged edges stabbing the skin inside my closed fist.

The pain doesn't compare to what's blooming in my chest cavity.

Leaving my purse on the countertop before going out goes against every feminine habit I have, but I abandon it all the same.

He marches past me, silently. "As soon as you put the keys back, Amari, we'll go."

No wonder he didn't push to explain who Bailey is. He's gearing up for another battle.

"They're just keys, Camron, and I can't lock the door without them."

"I'll have your landlord lock the door."

"And leave my stuff in here for anyone to walk in and take?"

He's got to be kidding me.

He doesn't look like it.

A blank mask adorns his feature. "We're not going to leave the door wide open, and you can try trusting me, Amari, or lose everything anyway. Your choice."

An eerie calm layers his tone, as if he's not demanding I choose between losing my possessions and my family losing sleep over their future. How am I supposed to trust him when he puts me in constant bent-over positions? The decision I have to make is a no-brainer though, and Camron has found a way to be even more despicable to me. I won't forget how he operates again.

Beyond enraged, I pitch the keys clear across the apartment. They somersault off the rim of the fireplace then botch the landing on the fragile top of the coffee table, scratching it up as they skate across it to the floor.

Cutting off your nose to spite your face, huh?

Better than me trying to slap him into next week, and my things will possibly be ransacked or missing before I come back for them anyway.

Twice in one day, I barge past him, going out the door this time while struggling to keep my temper at a manageable height. I burst through the opened elevator being vacated by more of my neighbors, with my world still wobbling on its axis.

Camron knuckles the button for the lobby before taking his place beside me. It would be more appropriate if he stood in front of me. Side by side means we care for one another. That is not the case when I'm being made to feel subordinate and toyed with at every turn.

"Tell me about your family, Amari."

Emotional overload is choking me while I'm concentrating fully on not giving him a front row seat to me cracking up. Everything that matters to me will be gone in a matter of months. Not just my belongings either, if I'm not careful.

The lit number panel blinking out with each floor we descend becomes fascinating. A non-shining example of every light in me that will blow out each day I'm with him.

"Amari."

He doesn't know when to shut up either.

"Why should I tell you anything? It's not like you give a damn about them. I can live without the chitchat."

"Are you refusing me?"

If you keep this attitude up, he's going to be asking that a lot, and you're going to be crying a lot. A match made in hell. Everybody will pay the price for it eventually, so suck it up, stop trying to buck his system built around you, and giving him reasons to void the contract. Material things can be replaced.

Got it.

After swallowing the lump in my throat, I share the bare bones of my family's structure in an automated drone. Enough of that voice, and he'll let me go with time served for good behavior. My monologue is over way before he waves the male chauffeur back into the limousine's driver's seat, then opens the rear door for me. Installed dim-watt bulbs guide me to the front of the cabin. Luckily for me, Camron parks his rump at the back.

I shift sideways toward a heavily-tinted window then let cold detachment overtake me, voluntarily dying inside to exist pain-free. We merge with traffic. Camron tosses the first of harmless inquiries into the awkward atmosphere, usually requiring one-worded responses, or I fit the answer into one that sounds like absolute nonsense. Doesn't deter him from his objective to get to know me though. I'm not buying his sudden curiosity in my favorite color or movie. We're not a damn couple transitioning into the next phase of our relationship. Yet, getting our stories straight before he meets the parents is wise, so I cooperate... mostly.

The journey turns into an eternity in the snail-like traffic that I'd hoped to avoid. I doze off, until my head bobs to the side too far, wrenching me awake to Camron watching me sleep.

I mumble, "Stare much?" then draw my knees up to my chest.

You just had to say something rude, didn't you?

We're at a standstill in a sea of cars, only halfway to Winchester. Dusk has settled in.

"Amari."

"What?"

"Turn around."

A pet who does tricks. I can do this. Could do without his black eyes biting into the side of my face while I sink to a new low though. I place my spine along the plush, velvet seat embroidered with his initials, content with my view of the other drivers.

"Look at me, Amari."

Slowly, I angle my head in his direction.

His neck bows to the left. "This won't work if you're not much nicer to me."

"You didn't put a niceness section in your contract, just sex, secrecy, and obedience."

His face hardens. That is *so* not good.

107

"Niceness was implied but have it your way. Take off your clothes, and I expect you to keep the details to yourself of what we're about to do."

"We're going to do it right here... like right now."

Seriously! Our first time together will be in the back of a vehicle?

A limousine actually... with plenty of room for different positions.

No dinner date before or foreplay. I'm falling below his routine courting-ritual.

"Camron—"

"Undress, sweetheart."

Maybe if I just stare at him wide-eyed, he'll change his mind.

"Need help, Amari?"

I say nothing. He bends at the waist then crabwalks his way across the interior. Instead of coming off like a clown, he resembles an exotic, white panther on the prowl. He's so damn hot to watch something pools in the very center of me.

That'll be your will to reject him liquefying.

I stiffen my spine. The air sizzles and sparks when he reaches my side then retakes his seat next to me. His fingertips trace the twisted chain at my neck, electrocuting me when the pads of fingers slip onto the patches of skin visible through my shirt. The physical reactions he provokes are going to be the death of me. If I sit quiet as the dead, perhaps he won't recall I'm still fully dressed.

"Who gave you this necklace?"

"A man."

His eyes fly up to mine. I can't tell what he's thinking with his fist clasped around the charm, his knuckles blistering my cleavage.

"Is he your lover?"

"No. It doesn't matter who he was."

His brow boosts up to his hairline. "Was. An ex. Did you love him?"

This man has a one-track mind.

"No, I *didn't* love him, Camron, because I still do."

He flinches as if I struck him. The thin chain comes apart, wilting around his wrist.

"Shit! I'm sorry, Amari."

"It's fine, Camron. The clasp was acting up this morning. Just give it back."

I grab for it. It's all I have left of what's mine.

He swings his hand behind him. I lunge for it, getting one knee over his lap before the sudden seizing of the nape of my neck redirects me towards Camron's chest rather than past it. I clutch his shoulders to catch my balance. It's not necessary, since he has me firmly supported and eye to eye with him. He's too damn strong. My decision to omit some of the facts about who the necklace came from is coming back to bite me in the ass.

This is why I don't lie often. The backlash is always... *always* too swift.

"Give it back, Camron," I ask nicely, calmly, as much as I want to splinter into a thousand pieces. What else is he going to take from me?

You don't want to know.

"There's not a snowball's chance in hell of you getting it before the next twelve weeks are up, Amari. And that comes with conditions too."

Remember to be emotionless.

I swallow down my rising temper. "Why?"

"It's disrespectful to wear another man's gift around your current one." So is slightly manhandling me and answering one of his girlfriend's calls in my company, but I'm not treating his transgressions as crimes.

Wrong. That's why you didn't tell him who the necklace is really from.

I may have wanted to make him jealous... but I'm not confirming that. Rather sacrifice the necklace than own up to the fib I've let him believe. It won't matter in time.

In the meantime, he outweighs me by brute strength and eight inches of height, so when I receive the gift back is out of my hands anyway, but I want out of his.

"Then keep the necklace and just let me go."

He eyeballs the scraps of metal. I can't contain the anger any longer or stop myself from pushing off his body. He hauls me forwards, my arms crumpling at the elbow between us.

"Let me go!" I shriek.

"Finally, a reaction from you, Amari. I was getting worried."

Wait. What?

"You *provoked* me? So, you really don't want to have sex?"

Why am I not relieved?

Refuse to answer that, Amari, because it will incriminate you.

"Yes, I provoked you." His grip relaxes as I kneel frozen, shocked at his confession. "There's no point to this if you don't feel anything, Amari, and any heterosexual man in his right mind would want to have sex with you."

"Then why the dramatics to make me to feel something? Just so you can hurt me in three months' time when you dump me? Are you *that* determined to get back at me for quitting?"

"One question at a time, sweetheart. This isn't about you quitting, or dumping you ever."

Could've fooled me, and he did if he's being honest, which means he lied earlier.

Pot meet kettle.

"Then what is this about, Camron? Tell me the truth."

"Getting you to..." he trails off, looks away, rethinking his answer, then retrains his stare on me. "Getting you to like me at least a little, Amari, among a few other minor things."

That can't be all there is to this war he's waging.

110

"Camron, you tore my life apart to get me to *like* you, among a few other *minor* things!" I parrot, quite disturbed.

Just liking him is major. Only God knows what else he wants from me.

"No," he murmurs. "I did it to get your attention for the most part."

My attention. The man is nuts, and I'm cooped up in a limo with him. I start to tremble, overloading on pure rage.

His insanity is not why you're pissed.

If there're other reasons, I'm not into learning them right now. Not when he's rearranged my life to suit him. I recognize a slim chance to be let out of the jam I'm in, and I'm taking it.

"Okay, you got my attention. Now, call this whole thing off."

"No, Amari. I haven't gotten what I wanted the most. You wouldn't ever believe what all I'm willing to do or give to get it. Enough to bite your damn neck hard to leave my teeth imprint for every man to see you're taken now."

Oh, okay.

"I believe you, Camron, but I'm yours for a little while only, and you sound like you're desperate. For what, I don't understand. I've given up everything you asked me to. I have nothing else but the necklace at this point."

"Not true, Amari, and you're not ready to give me what I want, but I'll wait."

The impulse to strangle him rears its beautiful head. I almost succumb to it, but he won't be able to talk.

"Wait for what, Camron?"

"For when you're ready."

His evasiveness is exasperating.

"Are you going to tell me *anything* I can comprehend?"

"No, you're not ready, but I will make a deal with you. Let me kiss you for however long I want to, and I'll get the clasp on the necklace repaired tomorrow."

He's got a lot of nerve wanting me to trust him after all he's done.

More like making you do it, but what choice do you have?

None.

I simmer down. "Okay."

"Okay what?"

"I'll kiss you for however long you want." Won't be a hardship for me.

He's a damn good kisser.

Down comes another wall.

God, I hope not.

****

~Camron~

I want to believe Amari is kissing me angrily because she wants to, her fingers walking through my hair while small moans reverberate in her throat. All signs of her starting to understand I'm not as bad as she thinks I am, that's if I was into deluding myself and I hadn't stripped her of everything she owns, which is why she'll do anything I ask to get the necklace back. And why I'm regretting pressuring her into the arrangement, just as Blake promised I would. She seems more pissed now than when I proposed the deal.

I rather she wanted me because it's her choice, and I would love tossing this damn necklace out the window, but even a crash dummy can see she needs something of her old life to hold onto badly. It's like her new life with me depends on it, so I'll give it back after a few modifications to it. My existence hinges on getting her to love and depend on me before the three months are up. I'll do whatever it takes to make that happen.

Her occasional return in affections are worth the turbulence we're both experiencing. It's peaceful moments like these when she's pulling me to her by fistfuls of my shirt, devouring my mouth, and grinding on my hard-on that won't allow me to own up to the tearing up of the contract. If I do, she'll clear out of the limo in a heartbeat and hitchhike in any direction that leads away from me.

Yes, I'm going to have to tell her... one day... when the ice around her heart isn't as massive as glaciers.

Yes, I know my actions put them there. The consequences and repercussions are still boomeranging. I'm smart enough to relish, while I can, the masterful slow glide of her mouth over mine, nipping at my bottom lip and scrambling my brains. I drink in whatever she's willing to give me of herself.

The car begins to move. I don't think she's noticed.

My hands drop the necklace on the seat, to roam over her, homing in on her chest and declining to move any further. Pebbled nubs nudge my palms from behind a solid, slim band of fabric encasing her breasts. I roll her nipples between my thumbs and index fingers. She gasps then bucks above me, head falling back, fingers cupping my head. She's so much more than beautiful like this, and not holding up her end of the bargain.

"Don't stop kissing me, Amari."

She's welcome to consume me whole, but her top has to go first.

"Camron, I can't do anything when you're doing that to me."

"New deal then, sweetheart. I taste test."

Her head drops, eyes begin to burn right through me. I wait for her to decide.

Finally, she murmurs, "Works for me."

I tug the hem of her shirt from her pants. She jerks the delicate material away, arches her back, and shimmies out of her top. I suckle a bare nipple. She sways forward uncontrollably, suffocating me with her breasts. I'm not trying to die before I've gotten what I want, no, *need* from her. Lowering her down to the seat then switching to my knees is purely for survival.

I alternate between the identical dark berries. She whines her approval and backbends, heaving the twin peak further into my mouth. Her third sweet spot for sure, the column of her neck the first. I'm collecting them like stamps to be cherished and manipulated for her maximum pleasure... for as long as she lets me.

Her nails scour the expensive upholstery over her head and beside her. I dive toward her navel, tonguing it. Her stomach ripples. She opens then closes her eyes again. Then her limbs soar in different directions. Knees up, framing my waist. Arms down, so her fingers can pinion my ears tightly to my head. So damn responsive. Feasting on her is better than a five-course meal. How am I supposed to ever give this up?

That's what plan B's are for.

I don't want one.

Stubborn.

Indeed.

Removing her jeans is a grand production. The material fights back, by sticking like glue to her hour-glass figure. When I curse under my breath, Amari giggles.

"I got it, Camron."

They glide right off for her and land on the floor in a heap.

I give the denim the evil eye. "Should've stated 'skirts only' in the deal."

She snorts. "Maybe you should have."

Completely nude at last, she's relaxes on her back again. Waiting for me in a comfort zone that I never thought she'd reach so soon, if ever, with me. She may not stay there for long. The one thing I am is realistic, so I commit every one of her curves to memory, trace them with my fingers, stopping at the trimmed hair at the apex of her thighs. When I skim through her jet-black nest of curls, she jolts upright, as if lightning struck her, balling my fingers in hers.

"Camron, not there. Please."

Sweet spot number four.

"I've leave it alone… for now."

I gently push her back down then lie parallel with the long seat, to lick, bite, and suck her heat, savoring her flavor. It's all mine now. Wrangling climax after climax from her is almost too easy. When she's begging for me to stop, and my ears are ringing from being beat repeatedly by the inside of her legs scissoring around my head, I lightly pass the taste of her onto her lips. She's too worn out to participate in anything else. Exactly how I want her to be.

Redressing her body is complicated however. She's limp, no help whatsoever. Eventually, I get the job done, with her observing my every move from beneath heavy eyelids. I reorganize her body across mine, settling her into the fetal position. Surprised when she nestles into my chest instead of demanding her space. If she doesn't mention it, I'm not either. But what is she thinking about?

"What about you, Camron?"

That's what.

I twirl a silken strand of her hair around my finger. "What about me, baby?"

"You didn't get yours."

"I did when you got yours, and I can wait."

She blinks, confused. Adorable. Visions of a little girl with Amari's face and caramel-coloring looking at me in the same way flash in my head. I find myself wanting to talk to Amari about children, but we're not there yet. She's tired.

"I got a checkup yesterday, Amari, so tonight we'll make love in a real bed where I can learn more secrets of your body. For now, sleep. You didn't last night, and you're fighting it now."

She yawns. "How do you know?"

"Because I know when you're tired." I massage the wrinkles between her glossy eyes with my thumb. "It always shows right here, sweetheart, which doesn't happen before five usually. These crinkles have been here since I came to your apartment."

A sleepy grin trespasses over her mouth. "I didn't know you knew that about me."

How could such a small bit of insignificant knowledge make her smile like that?

Must be significant to her.

Well, in that case. "I know lots of things about you."

Her eyes drift closed then open one more time before staying shut. "I am tired, almost too tired to move to the other seat."

"And you're not going to. I'm not passing up a chance to hold you."

"Camron," she starts drowsily but never finishes.

Clearly, she has more questions. I would too if someone has done a complete turnaround on me, but her need for sleep wins out first. I'm almost glad of it. We aren't going head to head if she's passed out. Neither can we make love.

I'm still pondering if one tradeoff is better than the other when my phone vibrates in my pocket again. How hard is it to get a little peace and quiet to stare at the woman I love?

"Yes, Blake."

"Checking in."

"On Amari, I guess."

"Yes, Amari, Camron," he snaps. "You're a grown ass man. Why would I check on you? Where is she by the way?"

"Asleep in my arms."

Am I gloating? Hell yes.

"What did you do to her, Camron?"

"I didn't drug her to get her in my car, if that's what you're thinking. I did give her a sample of my mouth."

"Just a sample, Camron? And yeah, I think you needed a drug for that too. That lady hates the ground you walk on."

"Maybe not as much as you thought." As we both thought. "Although, for a moment, I thought she was going to choke the shit out of me when she came to my office yesterday morning."

Blake sputters, "Ch-choke you! What did you do?"

"No, you don't get those details until you're in New York. Besides, I don't know who's listening to my phone calls. The American government is notorious for that crap."

"Geez, man! How many laws did you break to get to her?"

"None over the phone. Talk to me face to face tomorrow."

He roars with laughter. "She should've strangled you. You're an idiot."

"Well, I'm trying to be less of one."

"Good. That's all I ask of you."

"Wrong. You asked me to help plan your engagement party, and therefore deal with your mother. It's the same as dealing with mine. Impossible."

"You let Ashley take over the party preparations, Camron. Not me." He's never going to let me live that down.

"Things could've been worse. I could've let *my* mother take over, nimrod. Saleera would've planned the event in Italy, and had us all hopping a plane for a weekend stay there instead of the other way around."

"Have you told Amari when she hopped on your radar? What you want from her?" The light bantering back and forth takes a turn for the dark side.

"No, Blake, I haven't. She's not ready for that, barely tolerating my touch as it is."

"Just because you think she's not ready doesn't mean you continue to keep secrets, Camron. You have too many concerning her. I've been down this road. Put everything on the table before someone else does with a twist that makes you look so bad you can't come back from it. Let her make up her own mind about being with you before you cause a rift between you two with your tricks that can't be undone." The latter isn't a *rift* I'm willing to take.

"I hear you, Blake."

"I know that much, but you haven't been listening, cousin."

"That's not true." Just taking my time about implementing the changes I should've made years ago.

"You wouldn't still be hiding shit from Amari right now if you had, or have her sinking or swimming. I'm not entirely sure what you've done, but I know it's got her life at a standstill. You're a Powers through and through, and they thrive on plotting and scheming and watching people squirm."

"The last thing I want is Amari squirming, well, not fully-clothed anyway, and I've already undone everything I did to her, but I will ease her into my demons one at a time, starting tonight at her parents. Happy now?"

Mewling kittens let loose in the background.

"No, I'm not happy." He never is when I do things my way.

"I'm sure you're not happy, Blake, especially with that racket around you. Where are you at? An animal shelter?"

"Worse! I'm in Malisa's and Apollo's nursery, which looks more like a military barrack for the two-month-old triplets who woke up while I was changing BJ's diaper in here. There are cribs everywhere. The triplets started to cry in them. Apparently, they do everything together. BJ joined in the chaos. Now, everybody is wet, hungry, and raising hell. I'm up here by myself. The women are on the other side of the mansion, ooohing and ahhhing over Malisa's finished sunroom on the first floor."

I have to put in work to not laugh out loud at his dilemma and wake up Amari. At least, my envy of his predicament is a quiet sentiment. I've wanted my own family for years with the right woman. Now, I need to make things right with her, earn her trust and her heart, then make her mine. It doesn't have to happen in that order though.

"Blake, go get backup. I'll call you later, and you're much luckier than you know."

"Backup sounds like a master plan, and I know I'm surrounded by God's gifts that doesn't come with a volume button. You will be too one day. Bye, Camron."

No sooner does he hang up Bailey calls back.

Chapter Five
~Amari~

I cruise into consciousness overly warm and curled up between a rock-hard pillar at my spine and a hard barrier pressing into my cheek. I was in this spot before I went to sleep too, which means I'm still in Camron's lap.

"Got any shaving cream, Dad?" someone whispers behind me, only to burst out laughing.

"Not any for you to waste in Amari's hand so she'll slap herself with it, Brandon," my father drawls from the same area as my brother, the prankster.

Conditioned to keep my back to the wall when he's around, I pop upright.

I'm surprised you didn't do that the minute you realized where you were.

So, I'm off my game right now. Bite me.

"Whoa, sweetheart." Camron strokes down my arm soothingly. "There's no fire."

"Oh, there will be if Brandon catches me slipping. I've got the singe marks on my Pretty Princess vanity table to prove it. How long have we been in Winchester? The last thing I remember is..."

Camron putting your ass to sleep in the car.

I'm definitely going to keep that between him and I. The letting down of more of my guard around him goes to my grave. Couldn't help allowing him in. Foreplay with him is like walking in a mine field, stepping on every bomb buried, leaving me in pieces to put back however he wants to.

That wasn't the foreplay that did that.

Maybe not, but why was he determined to hold me afterwards? As if I'm precious to him?

Why are you still in his lap, as if you don't want to move?

Because... there's nowhere else I'd rather be, and that would be me stupidly developing more feelings for him, but I've stuffed that genie back in the lamp before. I'll just have a fatter demon to cram inside this time, right after I deal with my family. What the hell was Camron thinking carrying me inside like he's my lover when he's a stranger? How am I going to clear up the text reporting him as my friend?

I should've told Camron about it. What has he told my family already? We hadn't synced our stories enough for him to be entertaining them by himself yet. Rectifying that right now is a must while everyone that I don't care to lie to can't see my mouth move.

When I look at Camron, with the brown wood door enclosed by long windows with tan sheer scarfs and curtains as his backdrop, he's wearing a carefree grin. And it's hypnotic. I relent to it, forgetting the reason why I was looking at him. Recalling I haven't seen him smile like this since he hired me. A woman would be more than fortunate to wake up to that every morning.

It won't be the first time you thought that.

I'm not going any further down that road.

Coward.

I need to concentrate on untangling the web of deceit I've spun.

Camron squeezes my thigh resting along his stomach. "What's that smile for, sweetheart?"

No, not the terms of endearment in front of the relatives!

I mouth silently, '*Stop talking right now, Camron*', then slither to an empty space beside him on the crocodile-green, wraparound sofa that's freestanding in the middle of the living area.

"So, the princess is awake, finally," Brandon quips, using the age-old nickname I loathed from eight-years-old until the day he went away to college.

It's attached to childhood memories that I'm fond of now, not so much when I still wore princess costumes and a crown. Play things that I'll spend more time chasing Brandon for than actually wearing after school. He was merciless in snatching then squirreling them away in places I couldn't reach.

I point an accusing finger at him as he sits beside my father, Mitchum, on the other side of a dark wood coffee table, in matching reclining armchairs.

Brandon's a younger version of my father's dark complexion, muscular build, and clean-shaven face. Only Brandon wears a Caesar cut with waves tempered by a razor-edged hairline. Daddy's receded years ago, so he sports a shiny, bald head.

"You're still a bully, Brandon. I swear all you did was make me cry before you left for college in California."

Camron's thumb runs along the seam of my jeans squished between our legs. "It must've been fun having an older sibling."

All my blood rushes south to pump savagely in the core of me. Jesus! I scoot further down the couch.

"Anything but fun, Camron," I croak then fan myself viciously with one hand.

He casts a frown my way.

I buck my eyes at him. "What? It's hot in here."

Camron winks.

Brandon scoffs. "Really, princess? If I'm a bully, why did you cry the whole time at the airport before I left for Cal U?"

I shoot him a mean scrunching of my nose and mouth. "I had to pretend you'd be missed. That's my job as your sister, or you would've never left, and stop calling me princess."

Deviousness swamps his face. "Would you rather I call you sweetheart?"

Smartass.

Daddy cants his head in a quizzical manner. Well, shit! Here comes the third degree and my mother strutting through the backside of the room from an arched doorway. It intersects with a hallway running dead center of the house, leading to three bedrooms spread out unevenly on each side of the brown-bricked house. Brandon and I co-habited on the left, the master bedroom taking up the whole right wing. I was very unlucky for sixteen years with Brandon as a noisy, unclean neighbor that I shared a bathroom with. Wouldn't change it for the world. Not going to tell him that though. I'll never hear the end of it.

Camron stands up, extending a hand to me. I take it until I'm on my feet, then drop it like it's scorching hot. One of his eyebrows dive upwards.

"*Hey, Mama!*" I say a little too high-pitched.

Damn nerves.

Six inches shorter than me, she weaves her way around the men's seats and end tables laden with overweight lamps surrounding the chairs. "Give me a hug, baby girl."

Her warm, tight embrace never changes. Always bear hugs me like she hasn't seen me in years and won't again. These cuddles have gotten me through all the rough periods during school—two were disastrous relationships. A three-year high school affair with my first love that ended in infidelity on his behalf right before I went to college, the other my first boyfriend dumping me in eighth grade when I wouldn't sleep with him. The last hurt more than the first. I really had no clue about love back then.

You do now though, don't you?

For the love of all things holy, shut the hell up.

My mother reverses out of my hold to inspect me from head to toe, her shoulders a little thicker than the last time I saw her in her normal blouse with vibrant tones, slacks in the same solid hue as the overriding shade of fuchsia pink in her shirt. With her love for color, this woman should've never been curbed in a puke-green uniform at the local car-manufacturing plant before retiring to watch over my father's health.

She grins brighter than the muted rays of the lamps beside each of the guys. "Amari, you had poor Camron carry you in here like you're a queen or something. When did you two get together? I thought you were single."

"That's what I thought too," my father adds.

Double shit—they were waiting for me to wake up before questioning us.

I smoosh one side of her jet-black bob out of a bottle behind her ear. "Well, ah, I was, Mama. How long have we been here?"

Camron drapes an arm over my shoulder. "About ten minutes. We've been together for only a day, Mrs. Spencer, though I've been in love with Amari for a few years now. When she quit working for me, I realized the best thing that happened to me was leaving and I couldn't live without her. She put off coming here yesterday so I could come too. I wanted to surprise you all."

Didn't I tell him to *stop* talking? He's doing the worse thing possible: laying on the lies too thick. I elbow him in the ribs. He grunts.

My mother narrows her eyes at me. "Oh, I'm surprised alright, Camron."

"Me too," my father and brother chant together.

Great. Now, they're all suspicious. Thank you, Camron, for drawing all three Spencer's to my business. Brandon will meddle just because he can, and my parents will utilize the perk that comes with their twenty-eight-year marriage and giving birth to children—helicopter parenting.

Triple shit!

My mother crosses her hands in front of her. "I don't know about the two behind me, but I'm shocked she brought you here, Camron. Amari hasn't brought anyone home since high school. It's nice to finally meet you since I already feel like I know you. You're all she talks about on Sunday."

Sweet baby in a manger!

124

Camron peers down at me. "I hope it wasn't all bad, Mrs. Spencer."

I roll my eyes toward the family portraits on the adjacent wall, utterly embarrassed she'd ratted me out. Things would be so much more awkward if she knew my calls home left out one major gripe about his penchant for dating women at his office.

"Amari has the same woes as everyone else that has a boss, Camron," she replies sweetly. "Not enough time to date and—"

"O-kay!" I cut in, horrified she'll rattle off the whole list of my complaints. She needs another list. "What's for dinner?"

Brandon plops back in his chair, laughing his ass off after spotting a desperate attempt at distraction when he sees one. I'm not hungry in the least when my fake boyfriend wants an audience with my parents who he promised to leave destitute if I didn't agree to his blackmail scheme. Nope, don't want to eat.

"We're having pot roast, mashed potatoes, green beans, corn on the cob, the red wine Camron bought, thank you very much, and cherry pie a la mode in twenty minutes, which I need to check on. I'll yell when it's time for you to go wash up. Amari, you get to show Camron where yours and Brandon's bathroom is when it's time. Brandon and Mitchum will entertain you both until then." That means the men should get out of me what she hasn't already since she switched topics so easily.

I have a bigger concern however: Camron is still probing the side of my face. Being alone with him after this, I'd pass on if I could. He'll take the first opportunity to cross-examine me about what pieces of his dirty laundry I aired. That would be just about all of them. A fatal mistake, obviously. Going to need a therapist with the benefit of patient confidentiality to vent to after this visit.

My mother leaves the room on black, soft kid leather flats, the second shoe design I completed to her specifications for her forty-seventh birthday. She wears them faithfully. When they wear out, I think she'll give them a proper burial in the backyard.

I ease from under Camron's arm to the rim of the couch, sitting up ramrod straight. He follows me down, perching with me too close. It gets a little warmer. I plan to inch away to a cooler spot, as soon as my brother and father are looking elsewhere.

"Soooo, Camron." Brandon palms his chin, elbow burrowing into his armrest. "How long have you owned Powers Enterprises and loved my sister?" Seriously, three little words shouldn't cause years' worth of mortification as 'loved my sister' does me.

"Mama, is dinner ready yet?" I yell to her stirring something on top of the stove, on the other side of the house.

"No, baby girl."

Brandon sticks his bottom lip out. "Ah, princess, let us hear about your love life. PG 13, of course. You know Dad still has that bad ticker."

My father harrumphs, when he should be intervening in Brandon's tasteless grilling of Camron, who'll get tripped up in a lie sooner rather than later at this point.

Camron hooks my body in the crook of his arm and carts me into his side. "I don't mind telling them how long I've been pining for you, sweetheart. It's a cute story."

Did he say cute?

Yep.

I grit my teeth, smile pleasantly, and then playfully punch his pectoral. It's like hitting a boulder.

"There is no story... *honey*. We just got together yesterday, remember?"

He smirks. "Oh, but there's a story. You just don't know it yet."

Yet!

I should've been the first. "Before you tell it, let's go wash up, and I can show you my old room. We'll be back in time for 'show and tell' before dinner." With our stories synchronized and a muzzle on Camron if I can find one.

126

"Uh oh. Someone's in trouble," Brandon singsongs. Nothing is getting past him.

This social call should've never happened.

I motion with my head for Camron to follow me out of the room before hauling ass off the sofa to the left, past my mother retrieving a pan from the oven, and then down the hallway filled with pictures of Brandon and I from every period of our life that we lived here. At the end is a small alcove with three solid white, closed doors. I veer to the left again, into my bedroom that hasn't changed.

I step back in time as I take in the panoramic view of the room. A pine twin bed posts against the wall, skinny tall boy under the window, along with a small dresser and mirror and pink vanity Princess set with burn marks and a padded stool.

The door closes behind me with a click, snapping me back to why I'm in here. Camron is doing too much and going too far.

I whirl around. "We need to get our stories or rather script down pat first, then cut this visit short, or they're going to chew us up out there. Pretend you're getting an urgent business call in about fifteen minutes."

"No need for any of that, Amari. The truth will do, and I like your family."

"Just not the *whole* truth," I say snidely. "I still have to move back home with them, Camron, when this…" I wave my hands around, trying to pluck an appropriate phrase for what we are out of the air, coming up empty-handed. "…*thing* is over between us. I'd like to not have to dance around too many lies while I'm here, restarting my life."

He circles around me, nestling on the cheetah print and zebra-striped cover of the bed. "Amari, we're not going to lie to them. I said you couldn't tell them about the contract. That's all."

"No, that's not *all*. I also can't tell them we're as good as history when three months are up and I'll be homeless, limping back here with my tail tucked between my legs without so much as a purse in my hand. That. Leaves. Lies. Camron."

"Wrong again, and there is a story behind us."

I've had it with his cryptic statements. "What story?"

"I'll tell you during dinner with everyone else. Once is enough."

"Wrong again, Camron." I back up to the door. "We're not leaving this room until you tell me first. I should know before anyone else since it's my story, too."

"No, it's actually *my* story, sweetheart. You just showed them you don't know it, so your reaction should be genuine when I spill it. Your family will know if you're not hearing it for the first time."

I'll give him this much, he sounds reasonable, but I don't care much for being blindsided, so I hunker down against the barrier behind me.

"We're not going until you spill *right now*, Camron."

He grins. "Are you testing me right now, Amari?"

"Are you seriously pulling rank right now?"

"Yes. If I didn't have the contract over you, I think you'd try beating information out of me."

His torso starts to shake with erupting chuckles, and they're contagious. I wipe a smile from my face, so not in the smiling mood.

"Don't do that, Camron."

"What?"

"Make me laugh. I'm supposed to be wanting to slit my wrists just to get away from your wrecking party of one."

He laughs harder. "Overdramatic much?"

I snigger. "Not from where I stand."

His forehead collapses on itself. "Why?"

"Because I don't want to like you."

"Why?"

"Because you'll break me."

"Never."

"Prove it."

"I always planned to."

And I believe him. Trust him. I'm doomed. Heartache incoming.

Maybe not, but he certainly got your story out of you.

Shit.

Knee deep.

He rises slowly from the bed then stops a snap of a finger away. His exhales warm my face while the rest of the atmosphere stands still. Waiting. Along with me. His hands lift off, framing my face, rotating it sideways. My lips spread, inviting him in without my consent. Instincts forming on his behalf. Self-preservation nowhere to be seen.

His mouth finds mine, rocking me off-balance. My mind doesn't even rebel against the gentle lip lock. Tiny shudders skip through me, hands grasping for stability at his waist.

My thumbs trail the V shape of his abdomen that points to happy-inducing terrain. He vibrates beneath the pads of my fingers, tongue grazing mine. A purr splits the air wide open. I want more reasons to moan like that. Starving for them, and making up for the loss of a man's affections with the enemy no less who's tormenting me with feather-light kisses.

Remember you're just another body in an extensive line of them, Amari. Whatever you do, don't get sucked into his lovemaking. Time with him is temporary.

His mouth retreats. I drop my hands, back away from him mentally, to stare over his shoulder, seeing nothing. Bizarrely, I'm feeling teased. He keeps heating me up then calling a halt to the seduction.

"Amari," he murmurs above me.

"What?" I answer blandly.

"Look at me."

I sigh then obey.

He runs his thumb over my mouth. "Are you upset with me?"

I shake my head. Just disappointed, as I always am when he fails to do any of the things I need him to. Like notice me when I worked for him. I rub at my forehead, which is letting a long-forgotten wish enter it. They're all supposed to be filed away in a cabinet in the back of my mind, with a lock on it.

Not anymore.

"Talk to me, sweetheart, please," he pleads.

"Okay. What's your story?"

He exhales then looks over my shoulder. "That again. You're persistent for sure, but you'll still have to wait."

Why did I expect him to suddenly open up to me? I hardly know anything about what makes him... well, him. Hoping I'll learn is a dangerous game to play with him.

"Fine, Camron. I'll give you first crack at the bathroom next door. Don't bump your head walking inside."

"No. I want to know what's on your mind. You seem so damn far away suddenly, and I know it's my fault."

What hasn't been his fault for the last five years?

"Camron, I came for a story. I didn't get it. Can we go now, or is the king not pleased with his lowly subject?"

Yes, sarcasm is the lowest form of wit, but I'm not feeling all that witty or inclined to be obliging in another moment where I give and he takes.

"We can go, but the only time I'm not pleased with you is when you shut down on me. You do that a lot, Amari... and it's discouraging."

It's second nature to me now after five years around him.

"I only do it when there's no point to being all in my feelings. I can't make you do anything like you can me, remember?"

"Amari—"

"Would like to go now if you don't mind," I interrupt in a bored tone.

He puffs out an agitated breath. "We'll talk about this later."

I wheel around, opening the door and grumbling, "Apparently, we're about to talk about it now with my family, so no need for later."

He walks out. I plant a shoulder in the short wall between the bathroom he's in and the bedroom he left, then cross my feet.

When it's my turn, I rush through washing my hands, as I should have since my mother is waiting outside with Camron when I come out.

"Amari, help me serve. Camron, you can go sit with the men at the table. Take the first two lefts. The dining room is just off the kitchen. Sit anywhere but at the heads of the table."

He ducks his head. "A traditional household then, Mrs. Spencer?"

She shrugs. "Not necessarily. Amari and I are the only ones who don't have two left feet when carrying dishes, and I don't trust you with them either. And I like to see what's happening at all times while I'm eating." Spying.

"Traditional by necessity then," he jokes, but Cecilia Spencer does things in her home herself because she wants them done right.

"That sounds about right, Camron. Now go. I need a private moment alone with my daughter."

He gives me a meaningful glance, moving away only when I nod my head just enough for him to get my subliminal message of 'Quit worrying already'. It's like being stalked by a big cat that's waiting for me to slip up.

Fingers snap together in my face. "Amari, come back, and then come on. Jeez, he isn't going to get lost from here to the dining room. You haven't been acting like yourself since you arrived in his arms and he couldn't be convinced to put you down so you'd sleep more comfortably."

131

She saunters off. I realize I'm frozen, scrutinizing Camron's backside. Get it together, Amari.

I follow her into the kitchen. The men are thirty feet away at an oak six-chair dining room table, with a backdrop of the backyard from a semi-circle of bare, bow windows encompassed by ceiling-mounted ferns. Camron caresses the flute of a wine glass on the left side of my father. Directly in front of Camron, Brandon talks quietly with them both.

"Are you pregnant, Amari?" my mother whispers out of the blue, while transferring the corn to a platter on a granite countertop.

"No, Mama. You need to have sex for that. What do you want me to do first?"

"Come put the roast dish on its heating pad. So, you two aren't sleeping together?"

"No. We just decided to make it official yesterday. There hasn't been time to... sleep together."

You hope so though... and soon.

Alright, yes, I do. Camron has lit too many damn fires under my skin, in my core, and it's only right he douses them before they consume me... or I take what I want from him.

Who's the sexual deviant now?

Oh, shut up.

Cecilia spoons beans into a round bowl. "Amari, I'm going to be honest with you. This whole getting together and bringing him to meet everyone right afterwards feels weird. Nobody does that. And Gabriela saw your car at the gas station yesterday on her way to a doctor's appointment in Candleton. You were definitely on your way here, so what's going on with you two if you're not pregnant too?"

"I had a problem with my credit card that I went back... home to straighten out. Camron... came by. The rest is history. Mama, aren't you supposed to be hanging Camron by a noose with all these questions instead of me?"

Just roll the man under the bus and then ride over him, why don't you?

Why not? He's the reason we're here and I'm telling half-truths.

You're getting good at that too.

She pulls out a drawer, picking out different oversized utensils then passing them on to me. "When my daughter is exhibiting odd behavior after quitting her job, happily I might add, then turns up with the same boss that made her miserable for five years, claiming him as her boyfriend, I'm interviewing everybody in the room. You seemed content in his arms while you slept by the way. Care to tell me how you really feel about him because something is off? I know it. Mitchum knows it. Even Brandon knows it, and he's too silly to notice anything obvious, even less what's off with anybody. Lord knows how he got a woman like Gabriela to marry him. She'll be here in a little while. Spending time with her mother right now. So, what is unsettling about your new relationship that's worrying me?"

If only I could answer her without raising even more questions. My family doesn't deserve to be kept out of the loop when something affects us all. Keeping the lies to a minimum is the best I can do.

"It's been a long time since I've been in a relationship, Mama. You'll get used to it."

"Get used to what?" Camron asks from behind me, tone harder than stone.

I whip around. "Us, Camron. We'll talk more tomorrow about it, Mama."

You don't have your phone, nitwit.

"Oh… ah my phone is… not working properly." Certainly not if I don't have it with me.

She pats my forearm. "Camron said it's at your home when I asked why didn't you call like you were supposed to before showing up. He promised you'd have it by the time you get to his house on Blanchard Row tonight, and it's okay if you call me from his phone if you need anything before you get there. He already gave me his number and his address right after you got here."

Camron has said a lot, and my mother knows more about what'll happen in the next few hours of my life than I do. Both bothers me.

I swirl around on my heels to face off with Camron. "Is there anything else I missed while I was sleep?"

My mother taps me on the shoulder. "Only Brandon's arrival right behind yours, which is probably why you woke up in the first place. Take the beans and roast to the table, baby girl. I'll bring the rest. I need to speak with Camron about something."

I balance the overstuffed dishes on each palm, then breeze angrily by him.

"If you hurt my daughter in any way, Camron, nothing in this world, including your gobs of money will keep me off your ass. You understand?"

Horrified by my mother's threat, I look back and stumble over my own feet into the dining room, giving Brandon something to cackle about.

"Crystal clear, Mrs. Spencer," Camron says equally soft, "and it's a good thing I don't plan on hurting her, doesn't it?

"*Very* good for you, Camron," my mother using her dead serious tone that Brandon and I know better than to talk back to.

"Need help with the food, Mrs. Spencer?" It's as if he's discussing the weather with my mother.

He should be as disturbed as I am by her promise, which he could've avoided if he'd steered clear of Winchester.

"Nope, but thank you, Camron."

He shows up in the dining room while I'm placing the serving ware in the middle of the table. I have to smack Brandon's hand away from the potatoes simmering in the roast casserole. Camron pulls out a chair beside his, waiting for me to sit down. This isn't the Camron I know.

You wanted him to change.

I gave up on that years ago too.

Yeah well, shit doesn't happen when you want it to all the time.

True. But why change now when I need things to hate him for?

You'll have to ask him that.

No freaking way.

Suit yourself.

When he scoots my chair under the table with me in it, the doorbell rings. Gabriela. Maybe everyone will gush over her pregnancy and forget about me and Camron's sham of a relationship. Not likely, but I can hope.

"I got it." Brandon gets up.

I sip water and eyeball my mother taking her seat. Brandon and his wife are back in a matter of seconds. I jet upwards to hug her, with my brother hovering. Nothing I can see has changed in Gabriela's appearance. Her build still slim, skin perfectly tan and unblemished, black, silky straight hair from her Cuban heritage maintained at waist-length after three years of marriage. Yet, she carries the future within her. That changes everybody around her.

We give cheek smooches before I introduce her to Camron standing behind me. She's immediately intrigued. Before she can sink her teeth into him, Brandon escorts her to the empty chair next to his.

She doesn't have to lift a finger to serve herself, being catered to by everyone at the table, including me. Am I jealous? Hell yes. Can't picture Camron giving up his lifestyle for a wife and kids, even after he's married. God, I hope I'm long gone by the time he marries someone else. Don't want to see it.

Don't want to wish it was you.

That too—already been there, done that, and admitted I would never be enough for him before planting my feet firmly in reality.

Yeah, but you were a little in love with him before that.

Ripping the rest of my heart out of my chest, longing for something I'll never have with him, is not something I'd like to be a party to.

****

Camron

I get my first taste of a family more than happy to interact with each other and me too, and it's mind-blowing. Not once am I regulated to outsider looking in. There isn't a subject started that I'm not asked my opinion on. It's almost too noisy as they help themselves to dinner, fuss over, and with, one another with an easy rapport that allows them to say exactly what's on their minds. No one takes offense. Quick to respond with a bark of laughter, cherished memory, or snappy comeback that contradicts the other's point of view, or all three.

Ebbing and flowing as they work together to make sure everyone has enough with their own two hands. No servant or butler needed. Yeah, I know nothing about this. It's almost too damn loud in here, and I'll be damned if I don't wish my life was like this. I'm too old to be adopted but not to adopt their ways, so I absorb their behavior with a fascination that I found only from observing Amari.

She gets extremely quiet after serving her and I, pushing her food around her plate with her fork. Distant again, off in her own world, but present enough in this one to give one-worded replies to every question she's directly asked.

At least I'm not the only one she does that to.

Gabriela, a tiny, twenty-six-year old kindergarten teacher, who looks fresh out of high school and already ready to give birth, sets her gray-eyed sights on Amari. "Sis-n-law, how long have you and Camron been circling each other around the office?"

Maybe I should field Gabriela's curiosity, getting the ball rolling on my secrets... uh, story. "She hasn't been circling me, Mrs. Spencer, but I've been circling her."

Amari kicks the side of my foot under the table without looking up. That's definitely the signal to shut up, or a warning to keep the fibs to a short stack. More than likely both, and I would if I was fibbing.

Gabriela tables her fork and forms an arch with her fingers over her plate. "Yeah, Camron, I don't know if you are talking to me or Cecilia when you say Mrs. Spencer. Call me Gabby. I'll call you Camron. How long?"

"Six years, Gabby." I move my foot out of Amari's range.

Brandon chokes, swallows too fast, and then scrambles for his water glass. Grabby beats him too hard in the back with a fist. Amari's jaw drops into her beans, eyes wide and trained on me. She holds my attention simply by being too damn beautiful to look away from. I've been suffering with that for quite a long time now. Doesn't look like that's ever going to change either, no matter who I'm dating or not, and I don't want it to.

Mrs. Spencer frowns behind Amari's turned head. "You've only known her for five years."

Blindly, I reach for the eight-hundred-dollar wine I brought, then gulp it down. The carefree mood stretches taut like a rubber band. Here goes everything.

"I first saw Amari at her college. A classmate of mine from Stanford teaches there, Professor Sorensen. He requested I speak about the pros and pitfalls of being in business during Amari's human resource class one Friday before summer started. Amari walked out of the building just as I drove up. In the old days, they'd say I was smitten. Hasn't changed. I never found out why she didn't stay for the speech, but I have wondered all these years."

"I had to choose between listening to your speech in a class that I was ace-ing and going to celebrate my roommate's birthday with her," she whispers.

"Now that I know you much better, sweetheart, I understand why you chose the latter. You were and are more beautiful than any horizon I've witnessed from my yacht... but too young back then, so I kept a limited eye on you and your grades, making

138

personally sure you knew there was a job opening at my company when you graduated... and became a woman. You just never became my woman until today."

"*You* called me for the personal assistant job?"

"Yes."

"I didn't know you were outside the school, Camron, or I'd have stayed for sure to hear you speak."

So, she is or *was* attracted to me. I'll be doing my damndest to make 'is' the verb that describes her attraction to me from here on out.

I locate her hand under the table, bringing it up to kiss her knuckles. Gabriela ahhh's beside Brandon, who chews slowly on his meat and potatoes.

"So, you've been stalking my little sister?"

"No, I made regular calls to her Professor, and that's it." I hope Brandon doesn't find it rude I'm not looking him in the eye as I talk. His little sister has me caught in whatever the spell she weaves whenever she looks at me, like always. "I expected her to enjoy college with all that entails."

"In other words, get other men, maybe even women, and partying out her system before becoming yours in every way, huh?"

"Something like that. I wasn't ready to marry anyone then, and don't believe in double standards, but I've always wanted an exclusive relationship with her for as long as it lasts."

"Get women out of her system. Really, Brandon?" Gabriela condescends with a slap to the back of his head.

He ducks too late. "No need for violence, Gabby. People experiment in college. This isn't breaking news to you."

"But you still don't want marriage?" Mr. Spencer speaks for the first time since opening the door.

The 'observant, not going to waste my breath unless I have something to say' type. Amari's fingers strangle mine. For once, it matters what I say and do to someone outside of the office. *I* matter, and have expectations to live up to that exceed growing money and the reach of Powers' influence.

"If Amari would have me, I'd marry her right now."

"Not without my blessing and me walking her down the aisle in a church, you won't."

I nod respectfully in her father's direction. "Duly noted, Mr. Spencer."

He grins. "Call me Mitchum. I don't know if you're talking to me or my son."

Gabriel sniggers nasally. Amari hasn't lost her baffled expression yet, but she blinks finally. Seems to be the only one thrown by my full disclosure.

"Amari is definitely not ready for marriage after only twenty-four hours of being with you, Camron," Mrs. Spencer dictates.

"I'm still not exactly ready either, Mrs. Spencer. Not good enough for her yet, but I'm working on it. I know better than to let a woman like Amari get away from me. All she has to do is tell me what makes her happy and it's hers."

Mrs. Spencer stands up to her full height, knee-high to an apple, and scoops up her half-empty plate. "Well, there's too many Spencer's in here to stand on ceremony, Camron... so call me Cecilia. Amari, give me your plate, love."

Amari doesn't budge. I'm all she sees, the feeling mutual. My image isn't all that's reflecting in the depths of her pupils though. She's wary of my past behavior in the office. Obviously still a roadblock for her, and I'll wait as long as it takes for her to relegate it to ancient history, along with her doubts about me. It's the first time I ever wished I'd been raised with the enforcement of earning others' trust, sparing her from having to worry if she can trust me.

Somehow, I don't think this family forgives trespasses easily against one of its own or extends first-name basis to everyone. As close-knit as they come. I'm monumentally screwed if they ever find out what I've done to Amari today, truly afraid to lose their respect like I have Amari's. It's a privilege to pierce another layer of her world. I appreciate completely why Blake is terrified of losing the Owens and Astrid.

They've become his heartbeat. Losing them would be like losing an essential part of himself that doesn't grow back once gone. Amari has converted to that for me, now that I've finally let her in. The Spencer's have been that for her for as long as she's been alive. I hope she values the bonds between them. Not everyone is so lucky to have them. God willing, they'll last a lifetime for her… and me too.

"*Amari!*" Cecilia calls harshly.

Amari jumps clean out of her skin toward her mother. "Ma'am."

"Give me your plate, baby girl. You're not going to eat your food, and you're not getting your favorite desert either because of it."

Amari sighs and reaches for her plate.

I lift it before she can, giving it to Cecilia, who shakes her head. "Something is definitely off." Which is my fault.

Brandon cosigns with a wobble of his head. "She should've buried her head and her necklace in the main course just to get to the pie."

"I'm sorry, sweetheart," I apologize for the tenth time today. "You're checking out because I hit you with my story publicly. Lesson learned."

"It's fine, Camron. The pie always sticks to my butt anyway."

I thumb her chin up. "I love your butt, Amari."

She grins. I don't know about anyone else's world, but suddenly, everything is good with mine.

"Where is the necklace I gave you by the way, Amari?" Brandon inquires around a mouthful.

Amari's lip forms a large 'o'. "It's broken, Brandon."

He gave it to her? She lied to me. Amari is supposed to be one of the few people who doesn't do that. Not to me.

"Well, where is it, lil sis? I'll have it fixed and give it back to you the next time you come up."

For the first time, Amari looks to me for support, and I'd rather it not be to cover her ass with her family. "It's in the car, and I already promised to get it fixed, Brandon."

I excavate my phone from my pocket and bury my eyes in the bright blue display of Italy's Adriatic Ocean, the place I used to go when being at home with my parents became stifling. I swipe the screen as if there's a message on it.

"Camron, it's—"

"Time to go, Amari." I intercept her, then clear out of my chair in a hurry. The scraping of the legs on the wood floor is like nails on a chalkboard to my raw nerves and with everyone vigilant on my movements. "Blake needs me for something with the resort. The construction crew is getting paid to lay off and be behind schedule."

It's not a total lie, and I'm doing exactly what Amari wants, finding us a way out of here, and I'm not leaving without her, even if I'm so fucking angry with her right now.

She jumps to her feet. "Wait, Camron. I can explain."

"Not here. It's was nice to meet you all. A beautiful family that I wished I met long before now." Maybe they could've saved me. "Say your goodbyes, Amari, while I go get the car."

I shake everyone's hand before almost jogging out the front door. Couldn't breathe in there anymore, smothering under Amari's refusal to be straight with me and my own inability to do the same thing with her until she openly admits she wants me. Deep inside, I know it's not going to happen. Too much water under the bridge for us now.

Blake is right, was always right. Any effort I expend to make my life resemble his is pointless. I've done too many things without consequences, looking for what was never meant to be mine. Taking what Amari wasn't willing to give only adds to my wrongdoings.

Well, the deed is done, the recoil for that making its rounds, and I'll settle for whatever parts of herself that she'll give me access to until the three months are up. At least I've earned loving and then losing her.

The cool night air closes around me. The chill I feel inside is much colder.

I text Ernesto. Almost immediately, the car rounds the cul-de-sac flooded with lamplight from the Spencer's living area. None of it reaches the night I wait in on the driveway. I'm where I'm supposed to be, in the dark, have always been. Only a few yards away from all that's pure, good, and healthy, like Amari. The distance between earth and outer space separates us, and I should stop trying to drag myself into the light where she belongs without me.

Chapter Six
~Amari~

I know Camron's ringtone, personally set the haunting tune by Tim Janis myself, which never sounded off. He'd never turn it down or off and miss the next property deal. If he's faking an emergency, my little white lie has come back for round two of biting me in the ass and he's livid.

Biting you for pissing him off is what he may do when he gets you alone.

If that's the only boomerang effect from my actions, I'll handle it.

I bet you will... happily.

Brandon's head switches from Camron, who's storming out of here like there's hellhounds at his heels, to me who's unsure of what to do. "What just happened, Amari?"

I cup my hip and forehead where the beginnings of a tension headache is starting. "I didn't exactly tell the truth about who gave the necklace to me, and I think I hurt him." I didn't know he could feel any of my attempts at attacking him for hurting me—they were weak.

But you knew lashing out even passive aggressively usually makes a victim out of somebody, and you did it anyway.

If Camron can be made into my prey, then he's capable of hurting alright.

"I'm positive you hurt him, lil sis. Only men in love look at a woman like he does you."

"I don't know about love, but I didn't know he had feelings for me before I even met him." Hell, I didn't know he *had* feelings before now. My ignorance should count for something, but what if he cancels the deal because of it?

It'll be your fault.

"I've got to make this right. I have to go."

You think! You'll be much more broke than you are if you don't... and even sorrier for hurting him.

Too late for that.

"Amari," my father's husky tenor emits like thunder in the house, "Camron may need a little time to cool down. We can take you home tomorrow."

What home?

"No, Daddy. I'm good. Camron's not…He's mad because of me, but he won't hurt me. Thank you for always, always trying to be there for me. All of you. I don't know what I'd do without you all."

I latch onto my father's shoulders, becoming the meat in a group sandwich as everyone hitches on to us one by one.

"Amari, this feels like a permanent goodbye and I don't like it," my mother says behind me.

More like permanent guilt.

"It's not goodbye, Mama. I promise." What's three months away from the ones who'll give their lives for mine, right?

I have to wiggle my way out of the group hug. "Be good, everyone. I'll call you tonight, Mama."

"You better, little girl, or I'm calling you *and* Camron."

"Okay."

My pace is a lot quicker to the door than Camron's. He stands like a watchtower in the darkness, his white shirt billowing in the soft breeze passing over, seeming more alone than a beacon. Lost. With nothing to guide him back to where he should be.

And where is that?

With me… at least for the next eighty-nine days.

"Camron."

I cross the freshly-cut grass, dodging the sidewalk much to my mother's dismay. The limousine brakes in the street where he stands. He opens the rear door then scans the neighborhood as if I never called his name.

He doesn't ever ignore my voice.

Oh, he's more than pissed.

Shit and more shit!

Waist-high in it this time.

I stop in front of the car door, clutching the frame of it. "Camron."

"Get in the car, Amari." He doesn't even look down.

"I'm sorry. I can explain."

"Fine. Get in."

I delay, waiting for him to acknowledge me, with my family looking on from the doorway.

When seconds morph into a full minute, I slink into the closest seat. He climbs in behind me, isolating himself on the other side of the car, head pointed toward the window.

Wasn't that you earlier?

Shut up. Things are bad enough without input that doesn't help.

You two are a lot alike you know. It's going to take something extreme to get his attention like it does yours.

Shut up… please!

I'll think about it.

Yeah, well, *I* can't think if my head is talking back to me, so stop it.

"Camron, look at me… please."

"Why?" Then he grimaces into the glass, as if he hadn't ever intended to respond.

He pushes against a section of black panel under the window near his elbow. A smuggler's pocket pops out. He removes a remote. A two-sided monitor drops down from the ceiling. Spaudau Ballet's *True* flashes across the blue screen. A smooth groove from the eighties trickles out of invisible speakers.

He just totally checked out on you.

146

I set whatever he's feeling in motion, so I can stop it. Or slow it down some.

Don't let 'it' roll right over you first. That probably hurts like hell. Now make him talk to you.

Maybe if I had a bullhorn.

You're a woman. At least I think you're a woman. He's definitely a man. Get naked or… something. Figure it out.

I sit up, yank my shirt over my head. My hands bump the ceiling. Doing stripteases in a car, even a limo, isn't advised. There's not enough headspace. I fling the shirt to the floor. Camron's head rockets around as if he's possessed.

Bingo. Now you have to keep his attention. Good luck.

There's one taboo topic that will guarantee that. "Camron, where's my necklace?"

After adjusting the volume on the music, he dead-eyes me. "You lied to me." Then he looks away.

I unsnap the button of my jeans then arch my back, shoving the clinging material down my thighs.

"I-I didn't exactly lie, Camron. Brandon *is* a man."

Camron side eyes me briefly, then continues taking in the scenery outside the car. "He's not *your* man or an ex. He's your brother. What are you doing?"

I bend to chuck my boots into the floor with my dignity. "Getting your attention. While I have it, let's talk. You're pissed because Brandon's no threat, but I let you assume he was."

"Dammit, yes!" Finally, some emotion from him.

"I'm not fully to blame. You wanted to believe he was, even after I told you he wasn't a boyfriend or ex. You didn't listen because you were intent on being jealous."

"Dammit, yes to that too, Amari!"

He dives across the car. I wasn't trying to get him to come closer, so I don't have enough time to react before he glides over me menacingly. I collapse against the headrest, needing a chasm to divide us. His hands slap the fabric beside my head with both hands.

"Fuck, Amari," he snarls from low in his throat.

Oh yeah, he's a predator that starts to reign brutal kisses on my mouth, grinding my lips into my teeth. I'd be afraid of his ferocity if phantom appendages weren't roving over me, pinching, tweaking, and then caressing and flicking places as if I've told them what to do to me and where. Dampness is slickening the apex of my legs, along with more crushing passes of his lips. Can't bear too many more of those, so I turn my head sideways, eyes shut tight. It's disheartening to see him like this… the way I made him.

"Why are you still mad, Camron? You have me right where you want me."

"*Wanted* you before you lied to me, and you're not where I wanted you to be by a long shot, Amari."

The manner he uses 'wanted' in is like a sledge hammer, battering places within that aren't meant to take those kinds of blows. Lung functioning just up and quits on air. Could've given me some notice so I had time to find something else to breathe. Slowly suffocating, I writhe below him, looking for any sign of forgiveness in his face. There isn't any.

"Then be straight with me again, Camron. What do you want from me now?"

"I wanted you and everything that involves until my dying day. And then, I'd look for you in heaven or hell, wherever I ended up. But those seem like the only two places I might have gotten you to at least look at me with something other than contempt or shock in your face. You won't let me get even remotely close to you here on earth, Amari. I have no hope for your trust here anymore either."

"That's not my fault, Camron!" I yell, lungs suddenly in top form. I found something else to inhale. Rage. "So, you're a hypocrite who gives up on me and the deal the minute I make one little mistake that isn't all that huge if you count up all the wrong judgment calls you've made! You should be relieved my faults aren't as bad as yours, and I'm still here, under you with your fingerprints all over me body! How close do you need to get to me?"

His hand skims over the center of my breasts, idling there. "This close, Amari," his tone suddenly gentle, worming its way into places that should be forbidden to him. "Heart to heart. Mind to mind. Soul to soul. Until you let me in here, we were just spinning wheels, going nowhere fast."

He's already traveled through all those places... without me. Since a return trip together is no longer on any of his flight plans, fuck it, I'll stay grounded.

Hopefully, not permanently again. I like sex.

Curiosity prompts me to ask, "Where do... where did you want to go with me?"

"Everywhere possible. We've been in Hell together for five years, but that left Heaven and parallel universes that only our minds can enter. Hell, I'll settle for an exotic location on the other side of the globe if it'll make you smile... but it's too late for that. I've learned my place and only want your time now."

You did this, Amari.

And I want to scream to the top of my lungs 'I'm sorry,' except it's not what he wants to hear right now. It was always going to be a tug of war between us, where we struggle for control of me who's also stuck in the middle. Well, I'll be damned if I get pulled in every which way but loose without taking something from him too, what I've always wanted. Him.

"You should've just told me you wanted me instead of slapping a challenge on my head, but okay, Camron. Take your clothes off."

His eyebrows meet in the middle of his brow. "What?"

149

"You don't see me anymore as a woman you want to take to all those places. That's okay. I've learned my place too, years ago, on the edge of your world, a potential body in the long line of women you've fucked and thrown away. So fuck me quickly. We'll both get what we've always wanted. Afterwards, *never* cross my path again." Just stop breaking me.

He glides backwards to his knees on the floor. "Quick it is. Lay down beside me, Amari."

Did I secretly want my speech to work reverse psychology on him? Yep, but how many times do things work out as I plan, especially with this man?

Usually, never. Think of him as spilled milk from now on.

Not going to cry over him either.

Humph, you've said that before.

I watch him undress, from my bird's eye view at his feet. He faces the back of the car. It's like I'm not even here, until he drops down on his bare ass to shuck his pants and shoes off. Only then does he glance down at me for a micro-second.

I let my eyes roam over him freely. He's crafted from golden-brown marble, with sleek lines and bulging muscles flexing when he skulks over me. Erotic. My white panther. No, not mine. On loan.

My knees adapt into two banks opening to the river flowing from my womanhood. We're about to use each other, make a mockery of every emotion I ever felt for him, and no part of my body gives a damn. It's going to pull every fantasy I've ever woven around Camron to the front of my head and make them real. Not all of them of course. He'd have to love me for me to get everything it wanted from him.

My heart is another ball game entirely, craving what it can't have, but I'll get through the longing until it stops, even if I have to sneak out from under it on my hands and knees.

Camron walks backwards on all fours, stopping to trail his lips along the flesh on each side of my bent knees before he plunges to eye-level with my southbound mouth. The lapping of his tongue there draws an instant orgasm from me. It's too intense to withstand, so my hips coast upwards, seeking relief from my release.

I'd creep out of my own skin if I could, and I try, by gouging his shoulders with my nails, scooting up the black carpet. Crying out. That only helps with jamming myself between his body and the seat.

Camron slopes over me. Plants a hand on the side of my head. Uses the other to fondle the drenched slit of my sex with the tip of his length. That's too much stimulation for me.

"Wait, Camron."

"No, Amari. You're done running from me."

He drives forward, bottoms out inside me, stretching me to the hilt. The room he can't find in my body he borrows from my soul. That would be all well and good if that area wasn't supposed to be off limits to him. Yet, it seems no barrier is strong enough, line long enough, or wall tall enough to keep him out. Suddenly, I'm starving for oxygen.

"Fuck, baby," he hisses against my temple, planting a light peck there. "Are you okay?"

Well, of course not if I'm hyperventilating. "I'm fine. Give me a little time to get used to your size."

"You are tight, little one."

Won't be when he's done.

"It's…" my voice cracks. "…fine."

"It'll be more than that, Amari."

Promises, promises.

He begins to rock back and forth, in and out. Graceful, unhurried strokes that target my g-spot and dismantle my right mind. I wrap around him like a cocoon, holding on for dear life as he steals other things from my body that I never meant to part with, while transferring overpowering joy into the empty places... and memories. I doubt if they'll ever fade.

Buckling under the overflow of sensations I haven't experienced before, can't tolerate now, I start to tremble beneath him. Water leaks from my eyes bizarrely. Why does Camron have the power to affect me like this? It's not fair when I can't protect myself from him no matter what I do and he can harden his heart at will.

Branches unfurling from his wrists slip into the crooks of my knees and push them backwards until they're aligned with my shoulders. He balances on the backs of my thighs. They're leverage for him to power drive into me, shove himself deeper at a breakneck pace.

"Cum now, Amari," he grunts, the veins and muscles in his neck overworking.

I explode on command, then rocket upwards, paving the way for him into the stars. Earthquakes roll through every fiber of my being, brutalizing nerve-endings not fortified to handle the force of a natural disaster.

Breathless, I scream, "I want it to stop, Camron!"

"Me too, love," he grunts. "Just hold onto me."

He collapses on top of me, chanting my name in a rapid, hushed tune, huffing and puffing into the curve of my neck, and smearing sweat from his body to mine. Filling me up with his seed. I cradle the back of his head, until his breathing quiets. A God in the sack or rather limo that feels like home when he's in my arms.

You should've waited until you got home. Maybe you'd have remembered the condoms in your nightstand drawer.

Oh no no no! Shit and goddammit and even more shit!

It'll be in diapers if you're lucky. You do want a child.

The last thing Camron wants is for me to have his baby.

It'll be your baby too. With the man you've wanted for a long, long time. It's a win-win, and he doesn't have to know.

I've done enough things wrong today.

"Camron."

He hums into the nook of my neck and shoulder that his nose seems quite comfortable in.

"I'm not on birth control. You didn't use a condom."

He rolls over to his back, leaving me feeling deserted, lonely. That's fine. I...Have to search for the strength to continuing lying to myself.

And you were so good at it too.

"I'm clean, Amari. I'll let you look at my medical records when I take you home."

Take me home. The deal is truly done. I've lost it all, even what wasn't mine. How do I tell my parents what I've done? One thing at a time, Amari.

"I... I believe you're clean, Camron, but your medical records won't help with an unwanted pregnancy."

"Right. You don't want my child. We'll take care of that in the morning."

"I didn't say I didn't want your child, Camron, or specify *who* didn't want it. You have to stop putting words in my damn mouth."

He heaves himself up. "Sorry. I'll still take care of it in the morning."

"Take care of what? There's nothing you can do but wait." I'm not even discussing an abortion with him because it's not a selection.

"Then we'll wait."

After getting dressed on the double, he exiles himself on the other side of the car again, gone in mind if not body. I mimic him, bouncing up to relieve the floor of my clothes, strangely vulnerable in my nudity around him. That's never happened to me with any of the three guys I've slept with before… because it's not just my body that's exposed.

Muscles that I didn't know I have protest while I put my clothes on. Camron's eyes bore into my spine until I'm facing him from my seat.

"Camron, we need to talk about my money."

He disperses something from his throat. "What about it?"

"Are you going to put it back in my account?"

"It'll be there by the time I get you home."

"My family's?"

"Where it's always been."

One less thing to worry about, but I'll certainly be warning my mother to move her savings to a much more secure place.

"How long before you drop me off at my apartment?" The stretch of highway we're on has no sign posts or mile markers.

"Not happening. We'll be on Blanchard Row in twenty minutes."

My heart misses a beat. I coddle it with one hand, coaxing it back into a steady rhythm. "I thought—"

"No."

"…the deal was over at this point. I need to go home."

"You will."

I sit up. "To *my* apartment. Not Blanchard Row."

"No."

"Why?"

"Because I said so."

"Then give me one night alone. I need that to prepare myself for the days ahead." To come undone, regroup, and then rebuild the shambles of myself into a whole person again. Have done it a hundred times before after setbacks. I'm never the same, but not falling apart anymore. Can't do that in present company however.

"I'm not prepared for them either, Amari. Why should I give you the same courtesy?"

"Kindness from one human being to another."

His turns his blank eyes to me, and it's heartbreaking to see him this dead inside. "Where was yours, Amari, when you were making me believe you still loved another man? It's not that someone else might have your heart, it's that you lied about it."

Feeling two feet tall, I peep at him from beneath my lashes. "I didn't think it mattered to you, Camron."

"Well, now you know."

"If I had known you had *any* feelings for me—"

"Amari, do I look like a man who would go through all this just to get somebody in my bed?"

"No, but—"

"Then maybe you should've considered that I would have for someone I loved *before* you lied to me."

Who loves without forgiveness?

"If you love me, Camron, you have a funny way of showing it."

"Loved," he declares, cruelly, cutting me deeper than any man ever has.

"I am *sorry* I used the necklace to hurt you, Camron. I just didn't think it through before I let you—"

"It doesn't matter anymore."

"It matters to me. If it didn't to you, you wouldn't be this cold to me."

"Think what you want."

"What if I choose to believe you still love me?" A long shot, but I'm desperate to believe I can salvage whatever damage done to him.

"Believing that is a mistake you'll regret, Amari. At the end of this contract, we're done."

If he wasn't trying to make me love him before, so he could throw it back in my face in the end, he is now.

155

"We can be done now, Camron. Just rip the band-aid off and move on. It'll be easier for us both."

"I'm not interested in making things easy for you anymore."

"You never have, Camron. If this arrangement is all about getting revenge, you should know it's never going to pan out how you want it to. You have dug two graves with vengeance. One for me. One for yourself. Don't think for a second I'll be the only one miserable in this farce, which you probably do, and you are a piece of work for hoping to hurt me back when I never knew that I had the power to hurt you."

His attention slips away to the window again. "I'm not a piece of work, Amari. I'm in pieces. Always have been. I'm sick of living like this. Since you'll have a lot of time on your hands, why don't you fix me?"

"You want me to make you a better man?" I squeal in horror.

For another woman? Never! I can't stomach the thought of it.

"Yes, Amari."

What is it with him issuing all the 'mission impossibles' lately?

"I can't do that for you, Camron." Or to me.

"I guess we're going to find out the hard way if you will or won't, aren't we?" There's dogged determination in his face. He's not going to let this go either, but he needs to be persuaded to.

I'm not equipped to deal with the level of cruelty he's disbursing right now. I sure as hell won't survive taming him, loving him, just to let someone else have what I mold him into.

"You ask too much, Camron. We won't last a month in the same house together. I'm not in your league, wasn't born with a silver-spoon in my mouth, and I attended college in small-town Winchester, not an Ivy League school where tuition fees could fund a small country. I don't buy material possessions for the labels. I wouldn't anyway. I have other expensive tastes, like shampoo, groceries, plant food, and starting my own business to

156

one day pay for my father's surgery, while saving for my retirement."

"That's why I have money, Amari, so you don't want for anything while you're with me." But I won't really be with him.

"I'll still want for what I need the most from you, Camron."

"Which is?" His love… again. It's unjust I never knew had it before it was gone.

"Doesn't matter, Camron. You can't give it to me, so don't trouble yourself about it. We all have our limits."

"Really? I pride myself on rising to any challenge. What are your limits?"

"Anything that hurts me."

"I do believe that's a given for *everyone*," he mocks. "So, try that again."

"I'm much more weak-hearted than some."

"Okay, I'll tell you what your limits are then. You have a serious temper, prone to violence, and you don't tolerate what you perceive as competition well."

I swear to God if he says Bailey's name, I'll hit him for sure.

He shrugs. "I don't like competition either, but it's not a big deal. I'll fight until I find a way to win what I want, but being rigid in your beliefs, lying to cause pain, and hard to make listen is a deal breaker." All the crimes I've committed.

"I'm going to jump down the rabbit hole, Camron, and ask what is so wrong with thinking there's right, there's wrong, hitting back when I've been kicked, or sticking to my guns when I feel strongly about something."

Which sort of makes me small-minded when life is full of unexpected, extensive gray areas that can't be explored with narrowmindedness. He exposes me to more than a few of those areas with just his kisses. But I'm human. Born to make mistakes. Worthy of being forgiven, once at least.

"It doesn't occur to you that there are right reasons for people doing the wrong things, Amari, so you don't want to hear them out when they try to explain."

Can't argue with him there.

But like most people, I don't want to hear about my imperfections. Not for long anyway.

"That's enough, judge and juror."

He arches an eyebrow. "You don't trust easily either, and you're a very imaginative name-caller."

"Enough!"

"Can dish out others' flaws but can't take your own?"

"You know I think the same thing about you often."

"You're deflecting, and we're not all that different then, are we?"

I drop back in the seat. "Throwing my words back at me, huh? Things are going to be so much worse than I thought on Blanchard Row."

"Why?"

"I didn't think you would pull the silver spoon out your butt long enough to look past your own selfishness and snobbish ways to see my faults. Your inability to own your own faults has gotten me through a lot of hard days and lonely nights."

Did I say 'lonely nights' out loud?

Yep.

Damn. He'll totally question me about that.

"Amari, what in the hell does that mean?"

"I'll tell you one day." When I have Alzheimer and have forgotten.

"Are you refusing me?"

"Don't start that shit, Camron. I'll tell you. Your faults gave me the power to deal with you every day. That's it."

If he doesn't have any fatal flaws that I can wield to weaken his hold over me, what's to stop it from growing stronger? Nothing. I end up head over heels in love by myself.

"How do my faults give you power, Amari?"

"I didn't have to worry about lo… liking you more than I should or taking a good look at myself as long as I'm judging you for looking down on others and treating them badly."

"And now?"

"Well, I can't point fingers at you if I'm doing the same thing as you… to you."

He gives me a quick once over from head to toe. "I guess you can't anymore."

But if I don't, the pitiful walls I've built are going to crumble completely and I'll see him as a regular man with faults, needs, and the drive to do better. Approachable. Loveable.

You're already doing it.

"God, help me."

"And you rudely talk to yourself when I'm right here, Amari. Now about those nights. Why were they lonely?"

"I haven't found Mr. Right to make them feel less lonely yet."

"So there really is no Mr. Right for you. There's always Mr. Right Now."

I haven't been looking for him either.

Because you'd already found them both in one.

"No, no Mr. Right. You happen to be Mr. Right Now, which you'll stay because you'll be bored with me when the novelty of me wears off… whatever that is for you. I'm staking my last hundred-dollar bill on us killing each other before our time is up first."

"Amari, being bored with you isn't even possible."

"You say that now, but—"

"I mean it now."

159

It's 'later' that I'm worried about. I need some peace and quiet to mend the fences around my heart that he's already torn down. "So, this conversation is titillating and all, but I'd really like to know when can I have my necklace back? I want to wear it while I'm on Blanchard Row. Something to remind me of what I have to look forward to after we both move on."

He doesn't respond. When my face begins to tingle under his glare and he begins to clench his jaw, I decide that's a resounding 'no' to cushioning my fall into misery while he works at propelling me there. Flipping on my side, I wrap my arms around myself while facing the trunk.

"Anything else, Amari?"

I let my silence speak for me. The Human League's *Human* keeps the quiet from becoming deafening. More eighties pop music that depresses me and induces longings for things that I can't buy or think up: surefire ways to unlove Camron. That should be no problem in the long run as long as he keeps treating me like this. However, I've got to get to the end of the 'long run,' and it might be a good idea to teach him how to be civil towards those that have gotten on his bad side.

Start with stop pissing him off, and then lead by example.

Which means keeping my lips glued shut, my unrequited love to myself, and letting Camron be himself with no complaints from me at his home, where I'll pretend to be completely under his control. I have about as much love for that as Camron does me right now.

Time stretches until I lapse into a troubled sleep. Every swerve of the car wakes me. Every stop fills me with anxiety. When the car mobilizes again, I fall back into another restless doze, getting about thirteen winks instead of forty.

At the next full stop, the door opens. I gravitate towards it, needing fresh air, the bathroom, and Camron to let me go home. Not necessarily in that lineup.

I step onto the curling driveway of his sprawling, gray stone mansion. It needs twin long porches and two-story columns to support the A-line shingled roof and the massive balcony suspended between trios of stacked picture windows that are climbing each level. There's an unending view into a brightly-lit room on the first floor. Strange women lounge on snow-white chaises and a loveseat in next to nothing, clutching glasses of champagne bigger than their outfits.

You were wrong, Amari. He hasn't thrown all his excess ass away. A few of them are here.

My stomach revolts. If it wasn't empty, it would be. There's a goddamn harem in these four walls too, a fatal error to presume it would be just me and Camron living here during my contracted stay. Residing with just one of him who's angry enough to demand I fix him for someone else is going to be bad enough. A team of divas is too much. Getting him to breach his own contract as soon as possible, however I can, becomes priority number one.

He grins down at me. "Welcome to my home, Amari."

"Don't you mean whorehouse? Why am I even here? You have enough pussy here to satisfy three men... unless you're overcompensating for something."

His eyebrows brush the sky. "Nope, never bored with you, and you don't talk like that. Don't start now. You now know for yourself if I need to overcompensate after the car ride. You're here because I want you to be, and jumping to conclusions as usual."

"No jumping involved, Camron. What I see is what I see. Want to explain what these women are doing in your home? Better yet. Don't! You'll just look worse in my eyes."

The car drives away. I want to hail the driver down like a taxi, or mount the hood, and demand he take me with him. Won't do me any good. Camron will find me. At just the thought of him putting me through something worse than today and yesterday, I grab for my roiling abdomen.

161

You knew this wasn't going to be a pleasant stay, Amari. Just be numb, and you can walk into this cage. It's as easy as placing one foot in front of the other when you feel nothing.

"You okay, Amari?"

No. Jealousy is riding me like a backwards cowgirl, and I despise him for it. Again. But that loathing is going to save me from him again, as long as I let him do him.

"I'm fine."

He points toward the double-front doors. I precede him, consider plotting a course in any direction but forward, which is futile. The black wrought-iron gate surrounding the property is unsurmountable at ten feet without a ladder. I'm no climber. Nor will the women inside the house not condemn me as a competitor for Camron. They'll soon learn that he is theirs to do with as they want. There's no fixing him for me, and he'll damn sure have to be reprogrammed when it comes to needing other women around.

He unlocks one door, places a hand on the small of my back, and ushers me inside the white onyx foyer... into a ring of crystal vases with long-stemmed red roses. The bouquets follow the curves of the walls, out of a small opening at the backside of the entry. It expands into the central part of the first level where a massive chandelier is suspended from an oval skylight.

I'd follow the path the bouquets are generating up a spiral staircase to my left if Camron wasn't guiding me out of them to the immediate right, into the diva's domain. When their chatter floats to us over hardwood floors, I freeze in my tracks. The repulsive odor of cattiness pumps out of the opened tearoom draped in women wearing bikinis.

So, there's a pool here. If not, I'm coloring each and every one of these wenches as pathetic for waiting for him to come home in swimwear.

Camron strolls pass me. "Come on, Amari. I want you to meet your guests before you start tracking the flowers you're so passionate about like they're bread crumbs."

"My guests! Those people are *your* guests, and I'll pass."

He comes back for me and murmurs low enough for only me to hear, "Are you refusing me?"

"I'm afraid I'm going to have to, Camron. Packing a bunch of ovaries in one room with only two testicles is worse than adding gasoline to a forest fire. Something or someone is bound to get blown to smithereens. That won't be you... *or* me." I thumb over my shoulder. "Because I'm going that way to track the flowers. They're beautiful."

"Amari, you can do that later because it'll take you a while. There are two arrangements for every birthday of yours that I missed, which is all of them. I also have a spare contract in my office that states you'll be here for half a year instead of a fourth of it if you don't do as I ask. Now, make me use it."

Fifty-four vases of red roses for me—a small fortune spent on my birthdays past. Stunned, I can't even speak to thank him. The shock doesn't last long though. There's something worse than everything I've gone through at his hands: the doubling of my sentence here. That trumps the astonishing thought he put into the gifts. It had to be him—what woman in his life would go through this much trouble for me unless he put her up to it?

A soft rumbling emanates from my nostrils. "Thank you for the flowers. No one has ever done something like for me, but if I was a bear with claws right now—"

"You're welcome, and violence will not be tolerated here, Amari."

"You can't outlaw violence with this many vaginas in your house while threatening to make me stay here longer than I already agreed. I sure as hell didn't agree to stay here with *them*."

"I can outlaw violence because you are above it. Now follow me, or I will activate the new agreement." I'm so not above it.

He walks off. Behind him, I vibrate with contradicting emotions, animosity and wanting to kiss him senseless for the flowers. A stupid romantic at heart maybe, but I'm not stupid. Distance between us at all times is the best tactic I can employ until I get to move out. For now, we invade the threshold of the extra-large entryway into the tearoom, the women instantly quieting down.

"Ladies, I want you to meet Amari Spencer, the woman I had you all moving heaven and earth for yesterday and today. Introduce yourselves, girls."

A vibe that can be only be labeled as cliquish swamps the atmosphere. I'm out before they even let me in their clique. That's cool with me. I didn't want in it.

"How long is flower-girl going to be here?" A dark, exotic beauty with an accent indigenous to Jamaica inquires from under a mop of tight spiral curls cascading over plump breasts that are overflowing shiny, gold triangles.

Her shapely legs cross on a slim body that is sunk into a chaise lounge. I can't tell if she has on bottoms or not. Don't want to be here when she gets up. She begins to eye Camron as if we're in a drought and he's the last drop of water for miles around.

"As long as I say, Sasha," Camron replies coolly, as if he's bored already.

"But Camron," a pale, too thin Barbie doll complains in a Texan twang with a pretty pout of her glossy lips. Golden-haired, blue eyed, and a curvaceous whiner.

Camron twirls his neck, a sure sign of his irritation. "What, Layla?"

"I still want the room across from yours." She bats her eyelash extensions.

I wonder does that actually work for her when she wants something, or someone.

"You know it's Amari's room, Layla. Why even ask?" he drones.

I decide it'll be a bad move to get between her and Camron's bedroom door, and that I'm not going to. "Layla, is it? Hi, you can have the room. I can bunk down here on the couch. Have no luggage anyway. Don't need much space."

Camron's jaw locks.

Layla screws up her face as if she smells something vile. "I wasn't talking to you."

I point my forehead toward the vaulted ceiling, and silently pray for heavenly strength and patience. I've already run out of the earthly kind. "Ladies, you're welcomed to pretend I don't exist. I won't be getting in your way."

"Oh, honey, you're not a threat to anyone in that getup. Ever heard of Prada, Louis, Manolos?" The third woman speaks up at last, her intonation mirroring Camron's Italian lilt.

"Oh honey," I mimic her. "Even if you were wearing all three designer labels, you would still be classless." But maybe not. She's just as attractive as Sasha and Layla, with a flawless skin tone symbolic of mixed black and white heritage, in a white swimsuit trimmed in gold and a mass of tight brown and blonde tendrils.

"That's enough, ladies," Camron referees. "You all know why you're here."

She who has yet to be named clambers to the edge of the loveseat, slams a bottle of the bubbly down on the white surface of an egg-shaped table with a fish aquarium in the base, and yells, "Camron, are you going to let that bitch talk to us like that while we're visiting you?" Volatile. Much more venomous than the others. I even go so far as to dub her territorial. Must be the leader of the crew. Great. I'm living with the mean girls.

"That's. Enough. Everyone," he growls. Is that all he has to say?

Looks like I'm on my own here then. Fine.

"Is 'bitch' the best insult you can come up with for me with all that head you're carrying on those linebacker shoulders? Must've inherited them from your father. You could make a lot of money with those playing professional football, you know? I'm sure money is what you're all about anyway, gold digger."

She hops to her feet in a huff. I envision drawing an imaginary line in the floor with the tip of my shoe, daring the snobbish socialite to cross it. Right now, I need something to exorcise the stress creeping up my spine and neck. She never progresses further than the immediate circle of furniture and her friends though. It's disappointing to me, even though I'm not your everyday brawler. Maybe I should be glad she's talking smack from a distance. She does have backup that I don't.

"Bailey," Camron says dryly, "her name is Amari, and she's talking to you in the same way you're talking to her. As you can see, she's very skilled at throwing rail for rail, even when no one's thrown the first rail. If you can't take it…" I tune him out.

So, this is Bailey, who's pointing an accusing finger at me with her lips moving under matted, black lipstick soundlessly. She stops talking, tilts her head to the side, to give Camron a onceover that lasts for… well, she's still looking. The tip of her tongue peeks out the corner of her mouth like she's suddenly hungry and Camron is to be her next meal. Damn trollop.

When he looks down at me, I reset the sound barrier.

"…and you're not helping, Amari." He's chastising me, when it's the witch squad who started the lip battling without knowing me from a turkey sandwich.

I should've left him on mute. "And neither were you helping, Camron, when you bought me here with the octopuses ready to tentacle my eyes out for a man not worth all of this trouble. No man is, and you don't put women in the same room as the man they've all slept with or want to sleep with. You sure as hell don't offer them all accommodations at the same time. But you know what's worse, I never understood why women attack the woman being unknowingly added to the chaos but not the man who's doing the adding. I guess this makes me the peanut butter selection of your 31 ice cream flavors. How many women are you actually sleeping with right now, by the way? I'm sure we all want to know."

"I said that's *enough*, Amari."

"You're right, and I'm out of here." I rotate around.

Have no clue where I'm going. If I end up in a closet, it'll be better than being in this one.

"Dammit! Get back here, Amari."

I pitch my middle finger over my shoulder as farewell. Someone squeaks in outrage.

"Six months!" he bellows.

Ninety more days here isn't an alternative, so I stop.

"Turn around and come back now, Amari."

I retrace my steps to his side, and inspect a spot on the bare wall behind the women.

"She obviously doesn't want to be here, Camron, so why is she?" Scorn mars Bailey's face like bacteria on rotten meat, and it's in her voice. On her shoulders that's hiked up to her ears, which are really big too for such a slender woman.

If the intense dislike for me swamping her features is any indication, she'll make my time here a complete agony, but only if I don't forge an exit out of the Faustian pact with the devil soon.

"Again, she's here because I want her here, Bailey," Camron retorts. "Just like you all are, but you're all welcomed to leave."

I raise a finger in the air and bow my head in gratitude. "That's my cue."

Camron's head slants downward like a whip in my direction. "Not you, Amari."

You tried it even when you knew better.

"Why don't I have the same privileges as them?" If he won't enlighten them about the reason for my staycation here, I will surely hint at it. Fending off attacks from these women isn't my idea of a good time.

"That's enough, Amari," he hisses.

You're cutting it close to the terms of the deal.

But not close enough.

"Camron, do you see the identical look on their faces? That's pure disdain for the new girl that is absolutely baseless. Tell them the facts. You aren't catnip for every feline in heat." That excludes the four women in this house, but what they don't know about me won't hurt anyone.

"So you've said, Amari. Now follow me to your room."

"I'm fine right here. I can wait for the... *ladies* to retire to their bedrooms. Layla is still welcome to mine. The sofa looks absolutely comfortable enough. Plush and clean." Vacant of asses.

"Fol-low. Me." he repeats slowly, as if he's talking to a foreigner.

I'm still a pet that must perform tricks. Nothing's changed there at least.

"Alright, Camron, but you should stop gritting your teeth like that. You'll have nubs by the time you're fifty."

"Stop giving me reasons to, Amari."

"Hey, I'm not your problem," I chirp back under the chandelier. "Cruella and the two Dalmatians in the tearoom are."

He whirls around on me. I nearly crash into his chest, rocking backwards on my heels to prevent the collision. We clash enough as is.

By lassoing my shoulders with both hands, he stabilizes me. "Amari, the only woman I've slept with in here is you." Then why are they here?

That's not your business, Amari. Getting out of the contract is.

"You don't have to limit yourself for me, Camron. All it'll do is cramp your style during my prison term."

"You're not listening again."

"Oh, I heard you, and you're very much welcome to sleep with any of them for the first time while I'm here and after I've gotten out for good behavior." My midsection begins doing its usual acrobatics when imagining him with others.

"What does that *mean*?"

"Just what it sounds like, *Camron*."

"There is no getting out for good behavior, *Amari*."

"Sure there is, if I have anything to do with it. Do you know what kind of pit you've dragged me into with those women here? A viper pit."

He has the grace to look apologetic. "That wasn't my intention."

"Are you telling me you can't recognize when a woman wants you? All three are so open with their attraction to you, a blind man could see it."

Four.

Shut up.

"I'm sorry, Amari. Shit! I'm always apologizing to you. Look, I should've gave you the option of their company before we got here. Bailey Rossi's a longtime family friend from Italy. She's like family to me. Layla Jensen and Sasha Higgins are her friends from NYU. I thought you'd welcome the company when I'm gone. I thought they'd embrace you with open arms. That's the impression Bailey gave me when she was helping me get ready for your stay."

How many things did he do in the name of 'thinking of me' before I got here tonight? If he makes that a habit, I'm done for.

169

"Thanks, Camron, but no thanks to the company. I'm a big girl. Don't be sorry. Just let me go home."

"No. I can't." His thumbs skim over my collar bones. "I want to but I can't."

I shiver. "You can, but you won't."

"Yes. I'll send them home."

Good. Perfect setup to christen every inch of this house with no onlookers.

Oh no, we won't.

"Don't send them away, Camron." They'll keep me alert, judgment sound. "You wanted them here for a reason. They can keep *you* company when you're here." And out of my bed.

Sleeping with him is like quicksand. Will suck me into him until I don't want a way out. Have to refrain from that at all costs, even if I have to cope with claws and minor skirmishes with the in-house wildlife in lipstick and hair extensions.

I feel icky just thinking about it. "You can show me where my room is now if you don't mind. I need a bath... and a computer of some kind. I don't have a change of clothes and need to order some."

"No, there's..." A loud bang at the front of the house interrupts him.

Linking his hand with mine, he tugs me along to the doors. "I think that's Blake and Astrid."

"Allies. I need a few of those at the moment. How long are they staying?"

"They're not staying, and I am your ally, Amari."

"You're not, Camron. I've made an enemy of you just as I did those women in there, but I wished I'd told you the truth about the necklace. Maybe things would've have turned out differently if we'd both been straight with each other."

At the door, his chin drops into his chest, as if he's dog-tired. Then he blows his breath out. "We'll talk about it later, Amari.

There's too damn many people here right now and I need to play host." He wrenches open a door to Blake and Astrid. "Hey, guys."

Once inside, Astrid crushes me against her sheriff's uniform. "The flowers are so beautiful. They must be for you, and happy belated birthday."

"Thank you." I hug her one-armed, appreciating her so much for the friendliness. The beasties in the other room are probably going to be my only contact with civilization, and there's nothing civilized about them.

Blake rocks baby BJ behind her, frowning as if someone peed in his cereal this morning. "Hey guys right back to you two. I need to speak with you in private, Camron. A.S.A.P.!"

"We can do it here, Blake. I'm not hiding anything else from Amari, and I know what you're pissed about."

"Oh, you do? Then why is there a meat market in your damn tearoom while Amari is here too? I told you to keep your women away from her."

Has Camron been going to Blake for advice? Did Camron stop dating for me?

I think you know the answers already.

I look at him from an unfamiliar perspective, as someone I can trust with my heart.

"They're not meat I've been with, Blake," Camron defends with a stranglehold on my hand. "They're company for Amari when I'm gone on business trips and at work. This house is big and it'll be lonely for her until she's comfortable here alone."

Sounds like I'm never moving back out if he has his way.

Would that be so bad?

I no longer know.

Astrid releases me to relieve Blake of the sailor short-suited baby who's gnawing on his miniature fist beneath a slick crop of jet black hair. "Blake, before you two start, Amari and I are—"

"We're not staying long enough to need to fix the baby a bottle, Astrid." Blake collars the nape of her neck with a huge hand. "And neither is Amari. I'm not letting any of you be tainted any further by the stupid shit Camron's done."

Without all the facts, I think Blake might just fireman-carry me out of here. He's a sweet, overprotective loose cannon that may unload on all the Spencers with friendly fire if I don't speak up.

"It's okay, Blake. I told Camron that Layla, Sasha, and Bailey…" I throw up a little in my mouth. "…can stay here with me."

Then I side eye Camron, signaling for him to amen with me before Blake gets any more heated. He doesn't hesitate.

"The woman of the house has spoken, Blake, so she's not going anywhere. Stay for dinner so we *all* can talk."

I'm not sure I did the right thing covering for Camron, but the smile unfurling on his lips is almost a reward in itself. Panty-freaking-dropping! Should be licensed as lethal. He kisses my knuckles, making matters worse. I begin to fan myself. Astrid grins.

Blake steps to Camron. "I want to know exactly what you've done to get Amari here. She wanted nothing to do with you twenty-four hours ago."

An ex-cop and a practicing martial artist stand toe to toe. Both over six feet tall. Neither backing down. Carmon pulls on my hand, relocating me behind him. That's definitely protecting me from incoming blows. Everything is going downhill fast. Nothing good is going to come of the truth at this point.

Then do something… like lie.

I swat at Camron's forearm, resume my spot beside him. "Stop it, you two. Blake, I'm fine. Here of my own free will. Thank you for your concern though."

Astrid jerks on Blake's blue, long-sleeved dress shirt over black slacks. "Blake, let it go. I don't think Amari's being held hostage exactly."

"Maybe not, baby, but Camron's already admitted to doing something illegal to get her here. It's just a matter of time before I find out what it is. Then I'll be back, Camron. And it won't be with handcuffs, cousin. You're not getting off that easy. If anything happens to Amari while she's—"

"Blake, it's okay." I couldn't let him finish. Don't want to be an ear or eye witness nor the source that tears the cousins apart. "If anything happens here I can't handle, I'll call Astrid. I have her number."

Lot of good that's going to do you when you don't have your phone.

Blake doesn't know that, but he does an appraisal of me from head to foot. "If she gets one scratch on her—"

"I *hear* you, Blake," discharges from Camron like a firearm blasting off.

"Good. Because I'll be the next set of consequences and repercussions you suffer through because of Amari."

"What consequences and repercussions did I cause, Camron?" I'm the one still reeling from those stemming from quitting my job. Haven't had time to cause trouble for anyone else. Not much anyway.

Camron peers down at me. "Nothing hurts worse than hurting you and being without you, Amari. I would've done anything to be good enough for you."

That's how he feels? Jaw hitting the floor now.

I slam it right back shut. "You're good enough, Camron."

"No, I'm not, Amari." He comes across with so much conviction, I have to believe that he believes it, then he cuts to Blake and Astrid again. "Are you two staying for dinner?"

I wonder if he came after me for the sole purpose of me making him a better man for *me*. And if he did…

Tallying up how much I've royally fucked up with him gives me a bad case of the vapors. I paw at the inside of Camron's elbow with my free hand, needing an anchor to this moment. It's look like I'm fawning all over him. That's better than appearing to be about to faint for ruining more chances than I knew I had with him. A bitter pill to swallow, and my throat refuses to.

Chapter Seven
~Camron~

Blake shakes his head. His disapproval is a living, breathing being in the entrance hall with us. No doubt a setback in reforming the full bond we developed then lost as children. To get it back, I'd transport New York to Timbuktu piece by piece, but I won't chalk Amari up to the girl that got away to pacify Blake and anyone else.

I need this time with her before I let her move on to a man who deserves her. I'll take on high water and Blake combined to keep her here for the time being. If he wants to know what I've done to ensure Amari is mine for however long it takes her to realize I have nothing of hers, not even her heart, he'll have to stay for dinner.

Amari lays her head on my arm, an Oscar-winning performance of the doting girlfriend. "I need to go to my room and take care of some things, Blake and Astrid. Will you come back tomorrow?"

I glance down at her, not liking how she sounds distant and down suddenly. I wrap my arm around her. She nuzzles the side of my chest with her nose then stills, with her eyes closed, neck working overtime as if she's trying to get something down that just won't go.

Astrid nods. "We can do that, Amari. Blake, we need to get to the hotel now if you're not staying here to make BJ a bottle. If he starts crying, he becomes just your son until he isn't."

Blake smooches Astrid's cheek, while evil-eying me. "Okay, baby. Let's go. I'm taking your jet home the day after tomorrow, Camron, and keeping it in case Amari needs us to get back here quickly."

"Consider it a wedding present, Blake. If you need me to run interference with Ashley tomorrow, let me know."

Amari and I disconnect so I can walk them out. In the foyer alone, she looks as if she's been forsaken. Sad. Maybe Astrid can come visit more. I'll certainly suggest it after Blake has cooled down. Once he and Astrid are in the car with Ernesto, who'll drop them off at the Ritz-Carlton before going home himself, I lock the door. Amari windmills inside the circle of Tiffany vases, instinctively following them ascending the stairs. She doesn't really need an escort. They lead right to her room, and I think she's aware of that.

She stoops over to finger the petals, completely disengaged at this point. There's a faraway look in her expression, as if she's here in only body. Well, we know how much I hate that, but maybe everything I've had moved in her room will reconnect her to the living. To me. Because everything I say and do pushes her further away.

At the top of the staircase, the vases veer into the west wing where our separate bedrooms are behind two sets of double doors. Bailey and crew are thankfully entrenched in the east wing.

Amari reaches her room at the end of the wide, empty hallway. This is one time I'm not going to open her doors for her. She turns the knobs slowly, allowing the lyrics to Maxwell's *Pretty Wings* to be carried into the corridor on a soft breeze blowing in from her balcony.

"Good Lord," she utters then walks inside. Shocked. Good. "This room is the size of two apartments in my building."

I wouldn't be amazed if she expected me to stick her in a broom closet after her first meeting with Layla, Sasha, and Bailey. A total catastrophe, but they followed my instructions to the letter for the quick makeover for Amari's homecoming thankfully. It would've been my breaking point if they hadn't. And maybe Amari's too.

"I should give you a tour of the house before you..." Shut me out even more for the night. "...go to sleep. If the lingering paint fumes are too much, you can stay in my room tonight. I can camp in my office. There's a couch in there."

I can't be sure if she's heard a thing I said while surveying the mahogany, California King canopy bed at the back wall, freshly painted in eggplant copied from the floral comforter. Potted palm trees are scattered about the room. Creeping ivy snakes out of their pots on the giant nightstands to tease the mosquito netting crowning the bedposts and throw pillows in every shade of purple.

Then she sniffs the air, and it's too damn cute.

"I don't smell anything. Just tell me where the light switch is and describe the rest of the house for me."

I never know what she's going to do or say next. Don't want to miss a thing, good or bad, so I lean against the wall between the opened bedroom doors and the oversized dresser. These moments will have to carry me into the next lifetime.

"The dials for the lights is on a pad behind me. The first is for the overhead light."

She points upwards. "That's not a light. That's a humongous chandelier that would spotlight the whole property."

"Good, you won't need your glasses when reading or making shoe designs."

She whirls around on me. "How do you—"

"I know most of what I need to know about you, Amari, and you tend to doodle when you're bored on the jet. The middle dial is for the lamps beside the bed, third for the ones on the wall above your lounging area. Fourth for the heated hardwood floors. The remote controls for the stereo and TV in the armoire are in the nightstand."

She heads toward the couch and loveseat in front of the French doors. On each side are immovable glass panes for the live plants hooked to chains strung from the ceiling. She changes course, gliding across the room to the farthest nightstand. It's like she walks on water when she moves. Graceful. Serene. Angelic. And probably upset if she's discovered what I think she has. Nothing I do for her is right. Whatever she does next is going to be entertaining, frustrating, and might lead to another one of those times Blake has warned me about; giving her space to sort through her feelings and let my fuck-ups become foggy to her.

She picks up a ceramic elephant, pushes the ivy stems aside, to trace the rim of the planter. "This is the same planter I nicked with a trowel. *This* is my plant. Are all of them mine?"

"Yes. I didn't want them to die because you're too stubborn to have someone water them."

Yeah, that's going to rub her the wrong way.

Should've just nodded my head. "I thought you'd be happy I had them brought here, along with some of your other things. Your furniture and breakables are in storage."

"Is this why you told me not to take anything with me? So you could empty out my apartment?"

"Yes. I've been thoroughly reprimanded by Blake for letting you carry the basket during our trip in Arrow. I was trained to let a woman be her own woman, until she asks for help, but I've decided you can't even tote keys when I'm around. I just don't want to hear Blake's mouth. It's like listening to wolves baying at the damn moon."

She laughs with her whole body. "Camron, first of all, thank you. These plants are like my children. At this rate, I'll probably never have any. And second, it's the heavy-lifting Blake was talking about. Not things like keys or purses... or phones. You could've told me this from the start instead of letting me think my things were going to be a part of a free-for-all for crooks."

Will I ever get tired of hearing her say 'thank you?' Nope. If she's happy, then I am too. I get more comfortable in my position, crossing my feet and arms.

"I probably should have, still learning, so forgive me. Your purse is in the closet with your other things. The girls hung just about everything up, but you can put what you want in the dresser and tallboy with your underthings."

She sobers up. The temperature drops. I rub at the fine hair raising up on the back of my neck. Shouldn't have mentioned the other women.

She puts the plant back, jeans outlining her ass, triggering flashbacks of being imprisoned in her body that's wall-to-wall tight. Too warm. Almost too wet. Exactly right for quickies. Not so much for when I'll want to make love to her all night. My cock is at full mast, demanding I fuck her for however long it lasts. Haven't gotten nearly enough of her—powerless to resist her striptease in the car. Supposed to have taken it slow with her. If she so much as twitches now, I'll be on her again.

"Do you want kids, Amari?" I'd have asked in the car, but I was already inside her raw before I thought about it, needing to punish her for lying to me.

Hurting me.

I ended up punishing myself with her heat and snugness of her body that she forced me to endure every time her tunnel closed around me.

"Yes, I do want kids, Camron. Very much."

Wrong answer. She'll have the first in nine months if I stay here any longer.

"I should go." I straighten up to walk out.

Amari props her hands on her hips. "Tell the witches I said thank you for supervising the placement of my underwear. Although, I'm sure they're not up to their standards, I'll still piss them off." Firecracker. The roof isn't going to last long with all of them here. And I don't want to blow up with it.

"Amari, I couldn't give a shit what they think about anything. I just couldn't be in two places at one time. Would rather be with you than anywhere else. I called Bailey for decorating advice yesterday, and she volunteered her and her henchwomen services. I answered her call at your apartment because I needed a moving company on short notice and to get you to your parents' house for dinner at a reasonable time. Yes, I get I should've called a professional now, but Bailey was available to delegate to at the eleventh hour, had a designer on speed dial who she promised could perform miracles, and she could be here to keep you company when I can't. Contrary to popular belief, I don't deal with women in plural unless I'm at a fundraiser, and I had no idea they'd act as children when we arrived. You're welcomed to kick them out when you get ready. Just let me know when."

I swipe a hand down my face, utterly worn out from trying to appease Amari, yet still thinking of more ways to make her want me even after we're both six feet under. Apparently, I don't know when to quit striving for something once I put my mind to it.

"Camron, stop stressing. I'm not blaming you for their behavior. That's on them as grown women whether you slept with them or not. This suite is beautiful by the way, but don't do that to me again."

For a moment, everything is still. No music plays from the wall CD player over the bed. The draft from the French door dies down. The air condenses. It's as if everything is hiding from something that's coming any minute now. It is, my three thousand four hundred and fifty third failure with Amari in one day. Might as well get it over with.

"Don't do what exactly this time, sweetheart?"

"That! You switch up on me. Ice cold one minute, and then you're so fucking sweet that my teeth ache. Just be the monster to me so I'm not stuck in love with you after you throw me away in… eighty-nine days."

She's counting too.

Just not high enough, and she doesn't know how to take me. Huh.

I grin. "Stop protecting yourself from me, Amari."

It'll be so much easier to fall in love with me if she just lets her shields down. Tony Toni Tone begins to croon *That's All I Ask of You* from the system in the four corners of the room, as if the chart-topping guy group knew I needed cosigners.

"I can't stop protecting myself from you now, Camron." Now? When has she not?

"You can, and I can wait until you do."

"Shit, you're patient *too*?"

"Yes, baby."

"Well, that plus the smile on your face frightens the hell out of me." At least she's being honest.

I'll do her the same service. "I should scare you, woman. I'll find you in the morning for breakfast. Night, Amari."

You should've stayed and fucked her, dummy.

True, but it's not solving anything, and I need to plan my next attack.

She's given me the element of surprise, and doesn't know it. Despite what I promised her in the car—to let her go—it's not a choice anymore. There's a distinct possibility that I can give my dying campaign for her heart new life. I have one-hundred-seventy-nine days to win her. Hopefully, there won't be blood or tears shed on either side before.

****

~Amari~

"Night, Camron."

He closes the doors quietly behind him, and what am I doing? Smiling like a goddamn lunatic. If ever I've saw a man about to go to all-out war for something he wants, Camron is it. And he's coming for me... again. Soon. I can feel it. I'm not leaving anything to chance though, which means my family still needs to be counselled about their financials. I'll have to let them in on my secret then swear them all to secrecy. Camron's not a man to be trifled with when he's on a mission, or his back is up.

"I need my phone."

He didn't stick around long enough to designate which shut doors located catty- corner to each other are the closet. The first one yields a bathroom right out of a spa. Oh, my damn!

Sections of small mosaic blocks surround the standalone octagon shower, sunken jacuzzi, and expensive bath products neatly lined on his and her sinks, along with a makeup line that matches my skin tone perfectly. It's unavailable at the market on the corner of my block, so I didn't buy them.

Fortunately, my hygienic things were relocated to under the 'her' side of the cabinet. Postponing a hot soak in lavender in the jacuzzi with jets makes me a little irritable, but there's only one more door. Get to it, Amari.

Walk-in doesn't do the closet justice. I explore the vast space with a vanity set for an adult in the back corner, padded benches in the center, and wall-shelving for shoes and purses.

"I could move all my furniture in here and... damn, Amari, you don't have anywhere to call your own anymore."

Regret seeps in—I gave up so much willingly in order not to lose everything, but what's gone defined me. My home. My independence. My...

A tag peeking from between two shirts on environmental-friendly bamboo hangers catches my eye. I don't own anything I haven't worn.

"*Vera Wang!* I buy Faded Glory and Levi's." Then I single out more tags.

Twelve-hundred dollar Versace shredded jeans. Three-thousand-dollar peep-toe Manolo winged-heels. Five-hundred-dollar Gucci purse.

"Bitch! Layla moved her stuff in here anyway!"

Somebody's about to get it.

I break for the door. Behind it, the purse I left in my apartment squats humbly in a slot, light reflecting off the set of keys in front of it. Oh, I bet those witches went through it. My car key is missing, but there's a BMW key in its place. In the same second I spread my fingers toward the bag, my phone vibrates in it.

"Hey, Mama. Just listen to…"

"Amari, you better be fine, girl."

"Mama! I am. Don't interrupt me. You, Brandon, Grandpa and Ma Ma need to move your money to a hole in the backyard. I'm being blackmailed into being Camron's girlfriend, and you can't say anything, or even let on that you know. He'll ruin us all. He's already taken all my money out of the bank… and probably put it back… and he's the reason my credit card wasn't working. But he's probably fixed that too, while threatening to take it all back and everyone else's financial stability if he even suspects you know. He had me sign a three-month agreement to live with him, but he'll let me go at the end of it. You can't tell Daddy or anyone else, now or ever. I know it's a lot to ask of you, or anyone, but you have to let me deal with this my way while I live on Blanchard Row, on his dime. The only money I can spend is his. He's replaced my car with a BMW and our first date was…" Things start to smell fishy. "…at *your* house."

Camron's giving more than he's taken, and definitely not isolating me. What if the new things in the closet are mine too?

"Jesus Christ, Amari! I know you're beautiful, but did he have to go this far for a damn date? Who the hell takes their prisoner on a first date to their prisoner's family home anyway?"

Despite my fear of Camron finding out that I've already broken his terms, I giggle. She's outraged at the weirdest of things about the whole situation; Camron not following the blackmailer's protocol. If there is one.

"I tell you I'm being forced into a relationship and you want to know why he brought me to my family's home instead of keeping me locked up. Well, he was adamant that he meets my family as my boyfriend, which makes not a damn bit of sense."

"Amari, any idiot can see that man cares for you, and yes, he's going over and beyond to get you to feel the same. There was something so sweet in the way he held you while you were sleeping. He wasn't being a blackmailer then, but a protector, so he's not as bad as I want to think he is after making you sign a damn contract, or you *would* be in a dungeon somewhere. I'm sure you told him no to dating before he took a twisted shot at making you date him. Granted, money can twist people, but we can call his bluff. Money and material things isn't worth the damage he can do to you, sweetheart. We'll get through whatever fallout there is and have him arrested for this. If that doesn't work, there's a patch of land in the backyard that just won't grow no matter what I do to it. I hear dead bodies infuse the soil with nitrates and can make just about anything sprout out of it. All you have to do is tell me to come get you."

"Good God, Mama, no! This is a mess for sure, but it's my mess. I can fix it without one of us going to jail or hell. He hasn't done anything I can't handle so far. Nor did he just ask me to go out on a date with him, which is weird. I would've said yes. Well, I would've five years ago, and three months here is nothing compared to five years."

"Three months feels like a lifetime when you're unhappy, baby girl, but I'm not sure you are since you're trying to make light of the situation you're in. You would only do that if it's not terribly troubling to you like it would be to me... unless it was Mitchum that had me locked in some shit like this. Want to tell me how you really feel about Camron now?" No, not really, but the cat's already out of the bag. It needs a leash at this point.

Where to begin?

Not the ass-end that's for sure.

"I was heavily attracted to him during my first few weeks at his company. Then he started going through woman like a Haitian with a machete in the jungle. I settled for getting through the days at work after that. Daddy needs that operation, and I knew I'd need capital to start my own business. I got tired of feeling like a voyeur and invisible to Camron, and got up the nerve to quit. He came after me literally. Now, I'm stuck as his girlfriend with no identity, which he took. That's nothing compared to what we'll lose if you snitch on me to anyone. I'm even breaking my NDA right now, so he doesn't have to take everything from me. He can sue me for it, and win. I'm just trying to make him tired of me way before the contract's up."

"How do you know he's gone through women like a Haitian with a machete?"

"He dated them right in front of me at the office."

She whistles low, or tries to. "This guy has layers."

"Like an onion."

"He reminds me of your father."

"How? Daddy's a good man."

"And can be thickheaded and determined when he wants to be, like you. But he also dated someone else, or rather someone else's before we got together like a normal couple. He's a lot like

185

Camron actually... stubborn to a fault, without the gobs of money."

Ew, you have the same taste in men as your mother.

"I thought you and daddy were love at first sight."

"I didn't tell you exactly how I met your father, Amari."

"Yes, you did, after a college football game at our old alma mater that Daddy coached football at before he got sick."

"There's a little bit more to it than that."

"*Obviously,*" I shriek.

"I met him twice, Amari. The first was during a bet that led to a one-night stand, which produced our first born that isn't Brandon."

"So, you had a miscarriage?" How could I not know this?

Because she didn't tell you, idiot. You're certainly not psychic.

"Yes, I had *three* kids, not two. After the game, Mitchum's friends and mine met up at a bar. My friends got drunk enough that night to gamble away my lips to the only other sober person there besides me, the man I'd been crushing on for weeks. Mitchum and his buddies were happy to egg the bet on, swearing I was afraid of him. I was, but I wasn't going to let them all be right, and it was a chance to kiss the guy I wanted more than any other, so I kissed him to shut everybody up. Even more because I wanted to, then we performed our designated driver duties. I found Mitchum waiting on the apartment steps I shared with a roommate. I guess I drove slower than he did.

Things... the obvious of course happened that night between us. We didn't talk anymore afterwards. How could we when we didn't exchange numbers the next morning before I found him gone? It broke my heart. I thought I was just a... *dare* that let him get more from me than he should've. Of course, I was too afraid to approach him again, let alone tell him that I was pregnant during our junior year. I quit as soon as I found out. I was glad to after that mistake, and got a real job to support my child. The baby came five months too early.

I still couldn't face Mitchum. Nataria Long spilled the beans to him in another bar after we all were dating someone else and they'd graduated. She was good and alcoholic by then, but her habit saved me from my own insecurities and permanently losing the man I loved. He found me. Asked was it true about the baby even though he was getting ready to marry someone else all because he thought I didn't want him either.

I had plenty of chances to say something to him after our night together too, but I didn't, or I'd have known he'd left his number on my nightstand before he left for cafeteria duty. The paper got blown under the bed by Nataria bursting into my room after Mitchum left. She was hungover and looking for aspirin. I guess it's only fair she didn't find sobriety until she'd righted what she'd unintentionally sent sideways. He promised he'd never let me go again, and he hasn't. Whatever goes sideways between us now, he finds a way to fix even if I don't want him to at that moment."

I feel a lecture coming on. "What are you saying, Mama?"

"Tell Camron how you really feel about him before this contract thing goes too far… or I kill him for it, so yeah, no I'm not moving anybody's money. It'll be justified homicide, but I can't help but feel he's doing this to you to save himself from something. Maybe a life without you in it. And no one has *ever* wished they'd met us sooner. Brandon's been ruining my dinner parties since he was in diapers, but everyone in New York has heard about the Powers. Camron didn't come from a good family, Amari."

"Trust me when I say I know that, Mama."

"But he's endangering both of your hearts. You'll only know the truth of how he feels if you're truthful with him. Put it out there, baby girl."

"Mama—"

"Amari, I can see your hardheadness through the phone. Now *you* just listen. There are some things people cannot come back from, sweetheart. This thing with the contract is one. Letting first love die a premature death is another. It'll be Hell for Camron if he breaks your heart."

Too late for that, and I don't want a second helping. "I can't do it, Mama."

"You can, sweetheart. You are fearless when it comes to everything else. This part of your life is no different from going to Candleton by yourself to live and work. Sure, rejection can make and break you, but only if you let it. If you aren't meant to be, then you'll have another chance at finding real love with the right someone. And you'll be glad you've done all you can before moving on. Camron *needs* to hear this from you if you ever want a relationship with him that can be fulfilling. Won't happen unless you're both truly honest with each other, and I'll get those grandkids that I want, not grand baby as in one."

Should've known it would be something in it for her.

"I'll think about it."

"Do it soon, Amari, because my first instinct is to bring Hell to Blanchard Row tonight, but I'm compromising because it's your life and your decision to stay there. Neither am I going to just sit back for three months while he takes moments from you that you'll never get back. I'm not concerned about the money. Don't think Camron will go as far to take anything from your family either. He'd have already taken it when he took yours. He's playing the long game for your attention."

"He's got it for however long it takes me to dig us out of this mess, even if it takes the whole ninety days."

"It won't be the whole ninety days. That's a fact. I'll have rearranged the houses on Blanchard Row with my bare hands before then. Camron had better love your dirty underwear after this shit. Brandon and Mitchum will know about this in a week tops,

188

love. You better get to talking now. Camron better profess his undying love right afterwards. One week, Amari. That's all you've got."

Another time limit with an ultimatum, and my mother *will* act a fool, unless Camron and I find what she thinks is good sense. Who gets themselves into these types of dilemmas?

That's a stupid question.

"Okay, Mama, just move everyone's money like I asked please for my sanity. Whatever penalties you have to pay, I'll reimburse as soon as I can. Maybe Camron will see my feelings as more than he bargained for and kicks me out of here."

"I doubt that if he feels for you like I think he does, but we can hope he doesn't if you want to. One week, Amari."

"Got it, Mama."

"Things will work out just how they're supposed to."

"I hope you know what you're talking about."

"I wish I didn't, baby girl, but I do."

"Okay. Bye."

"Bye, love."

Camron steps around the doorway in only black silk pajama bottoms. "Who do you hope knows what they're talking about?"

My first reaction to his sudden appearance is to pitch the phone across the room, watch it crash into a pair of Giuseppe gladiator sandals, and then tumble to the floor. I look so guilty right now, and feel it.

"What have you done, Amari?" His forehead has so many wrinkles it's going to take an iron to get them all out.

"Nothing, Camron."

"You're lying to me again."

He really hates that. Stop it.

Shut up.

"Okay, it's true. I'm lying, but I… ah…" I just can't tell him or stop myself from ogling his chest. Arms. Bare feet. The bulge at his crotch. Too gorgeous for his own damn good. And mine.

"You told your mother, didn't you?"

My head snaps up, giving me whiplash. He already knows what I've done, just looking for confirmation. I do what anyone else would do when caught red-handed, give him attitude while gripping both hips.

"Yes. I broke my word to you, Camron. I did the wrong thing for the right reasons. I had to. You have to understand why I did it because they're my family who have worked their asses off for that money. They need it. You know my father is sick, my grandparents too old to work. You can ruin me again. I don't care—"

"Good. Six months," he says too quietly.

"I…" Wasn't expecting him to be this calm about it. "You should be much angrier than this with me."

"Well, I'm not angry at all, because I get something out of your breaking the contract in the same day. A new one. Nobody has ever done that to me. You will pay for it. We sign the new agreement in the morning."

Immense relief crowds my chest—I'd saved everyone's livelihood.

But yours.

Right, but the price I'll pay is worth it. Now, why is he in here in the first place?

"Is wanting to know who I was talking to on the phone all you wanted?"

"No, I came to ask were you hungry. I overheard you on the phone. There's cold cuts in the fridge, water, and wine if you want it."

"No, but thank you."

He pirouettes to leave.

"Camron, wait."

He turns sideways in the doorway.

"Layla's stuff is in here and in my... *the* bathroom."

"It's *all* yours."

"No, it's... you delegated again, didn't you?"

"Yes. As much as I'd like to learn more about your world, I already know too much about mine where most people are label whores. You've already gotten a taste of that, much to my embarrassment, and I don't want you constantly defending your right to wear what you want or to drive. I love what you wear, not so much your car, so you get to choose what you want to wear, and your new car is in the garage."

Thinking of me again. Another wall is poof. Gone.

"Where's my old car?"

"In the garage."

"But I can't drive it?"

"Not yet."

Not. Yet.

"O... okay. Thank you." At this point, I need to stop fighting and survive Camron's attacks because he doesn't play fair. Blindsiding me at every turn. Hitting me in the chest where I feel the most.

"You're welcome, Amari. Night again."

He departs as quietly as he came. Bath time comes and passes, the lavender soak a bust. Shouldn't have left me keyed up as if I chugged back a caffeinated drink. Sleep is going to be hard to come by tonight, although I didn't get anywhere near the amount I should've in the limo.

Under the ultra-soft bed cover, my head sinks into the feather-filled pillows. Maybe, they'll communicate that it's night-time to my body. The neon red numbers on the clock countdown thirty minutes that have raced by at a turtle's pace. I flip over on my back. Consider counting sheep. Um, no, but fresh air may work.

The notes to Monica's *Without You* flits above me in the air, reminding me that I'm the only one in here.

That's what's wrong you.

Whatever.

I crack the bedroom doors. Camron's is shut. I catch myself staring at them for too long then shake my head. "Get it together, Amari, open the French doors, and lay your ass down."

I try the fetal position while facing the moonlight sneaking in, then kick the covers off. The open-air flutters over my skin like pricks from tiny needles, as irritating as the white sheer gown I found in the closet. It's like being trapped in between two cheese graters balled around me like a python.

I tug at the rough material. "Which witch picked this out? This damn thing was not meant for sleeping in."

"Take it off then, Amari," Camron whispers behind me, chuckling.

I scream bloody murder and leap off the bed on the other side. His silhouette emerges out of the pitch-black near the tall boy beside the closet.

"Are you trying to give me a heart attack, Camron?"

"No, but I could hear you tossing and turning all the way in my bedroom."

"Sorry."

"Don't be. Just tell me what you need to sleep."

Don't lie.

Shut up.

I brace myself for rejection. "You, Camron. I need you."

"At your service. Lay down. I'll give you a massage."

That was easy.

Almost too easy. I pluck the hem of the gown over my head then knee the bed to get on it. On my stomach with my head angled away from him, I begin doubting myself. What if I can't let him touch me without wanting to touch him back? What if I'm a single-mother afterwards?

Camron straddles my backside. His cock nuzzles the slit of my ass then establishes itself at home—he'd taken his pants off. I stiffen, wondering why the hell I laid on my front instead of my back. A budding nymphomaniac. He starts to knead my shoulders tucked up to my ears.

"Get out your head, Amari. Forget about the past, present, and the future. Just be in the moment with me."

"Trust me. I'm in it… and I have questions."

"Shoot." His laidback demeanor relaxes me faster than his hands never will.

Skin to skin contact with him is vicious on my senses, causes physical aches in my nether region, and rouses my blood to boiling point in no time. I start gulping air. Focus, Amari.

"What were you looking for in the other women?"

He's slow to answer. "What I was looking for in them, Amari… was you." 'Was' makes my eyes burn.

Don't you dare cry, Amari.

"I'm sorry."

"Not as much as I am. I found you only to lose you in six months."

"Camron…" I choke on my mother's advice. Just doesn't feel like the time to say, 'I've loved you all this time'.

Admit it, you want him to love you back first.

Yes.

"I'm right here. Right now, Camron."

"Not really. Your heart is still your own." That remains to be seen, and I'm going stir-crazy with his fingers working the twin indents in my lower back.

I shift underneath him. He rocks to the side, so I can turn over, then he kneels over my thighs.

"You're driving me insane with the massage, Camron."

He bends. His lips scrape mine. I walk my fingers up his outstretched arms sheltering his weight from me, stopping at his neck to knit my hands around it. My thumbs propel his chin downward, opening his mouth so I can slip inside. When his tongue dances with mine, my lady parts hit their flashpoint. I begin to fidget and whine.

"Camron."

"I know, baby, but we're taking our time tonight."

He plants a butterfly kiss on my shoulder, and then one on the other. Holy hell. I get a little closer to becoming a parent, but not if that isn't what he wants too.

"What about—"

"You getting pregnant?" His lips start a trail of soft pecks down my stomach. "I hope so. You can't forget me." A kiss. "If you have a someone." Another. "With my DNA running around." Another one. "Now can you?"

"*You* want children?"

"Yes, very much." His response is almost inaudible, but loud enough to blow my mind.

"We could already be facing that after the limo ride, and the last thing you are is forgettable."

He lifts his head and smiles. "What's the first thing about me?"

"Fishing for compliments?"

"From you? Yes. You don't give them as easily as you do insults."

"Well, I should start. You're beautiful."

"That category belongs to you, sweetheart."

"No one has the monopoly on being beautiful, Camron."

"You do, Amari. Now hush, love. I want to talk to your body. I can't if we're talking."

True to his word, his mouth gets conversant with every inch of me. Pure divine torture, and I wouldn't trade the torment he's putting me through for all the money in the world, but it's my turn. Squashing his ribcage between my knees as he nips at my breast, I roll us over. Camron ends up spread-eagle in the middle of the bed, eyes as wide as saucers.

"Shit, Amari, that was hot."

"Somebody likes being dominated in the bedroom." Crouching over his chest, I reach between my thighs to palm his velvet-steel length.

His body jolts, and he groans, "If you're doing the dominating, the bedroom isn't the only place."

"Careful. My ego will swell. I'll get possessive and grow claws like Bailey."

"Are you going to scratch me with them?"

"Probably."

"Good."

"Kinky."

I stretch out between his legs to slurp, lick, and deepthroat him, intending to cause him as much distress as possible. I run my fingertips through the black curls a shade lighter than the strands on his head. His pelvic gyrates to the unhurried tempo of J. Holiday's *Bed.* I think, *this white boy can dance*, and then I'm being plucked up and plopped down chest to chest with him.

"Ride me."

"Just demand sex, huh? No kiss? Dinner? Date?"

"Been there. Did that earlier and I didn't get enough of either. I want inside of you."

"Well, since you're acting like you're starving, Cam." I spread my legs on each side of him.

Chris Brown's *4 Seconds* melody enhances the ambience created from Camron's presence with soulful, erotic harmony.

Camron frisks the globes of my ass. "Cam, huh? I like it, and you've got 4 seconds to put me inside you, Amari, or I'm going to fuck you like you stole something." Bossy.

I take my time adjusting my hips and tipping his rod up so I can guide it him inside my soaked opening. I moan low and long, while immersing my body in an ocean of bliss slowly. Going under.

"How many seconds... Shit! Was that, Cam?" I pant, clutching his chest as if it's a life raft.

Being a smartass and full to the hilt with him isn't cohesive to proper breathing.

"Too long," he replies hoarsely then springs up, and gathers my feet behind him. With two handfuls of my ass, he pounds up into me, topping from the bottom. "Now, I'm going to make you call me your God."

Arrogant as hell this one, and he has every right to be when he's spearing through white hot spots high in my body. I meet him swing for swing, while weak-kneed and quivering under the bombardment of sensations he's sparking. The floodgates to my climax blows open.

"Oh, you're definitely my God, Cam!"

He shoulders my legs then blitzes me with rapid pumps until I can't tell up from down or if the climax is ever going to stop. A magical lover. I cling to his neck until he rotates us and fills me from the behind.

"Jesus, you're tight! My fucking Goddess!"

It's all downhill from there. I lose consciousness. When I wake, the bedroom doors stand wide open, and he's gone. I can't remember much else other than being called his goddess. Must've fried my damn brains.

Déjà vu rears its head. To decide if it's ugly or not, I check the nightstand then lean over the bed. Searching under the mattress for anything he'd left behind for me, a sign that we'd graduated from... I still don't have a name for what we are, but whatever it is, we're still that. The surfaces are whistle-clean.

"Damn. I thought we'd hit a milestone last night. Guess not." But I'll leave the walls down around my heart until I find out why not.

Maybe, I should feel used after finding him missing in action. Yeah, well, I don't, just thoroughly made love to. What does that say about me?

"What are you looking for under there?"

I jerk up to Bailey in the doorway, barefoot in a navy-blue mini-dress. If she bends over...

Don't even want to think about it.

I bound upwards and cloak my body with the crumpled sheets. "What is it with people just walking into my room?"

"Yours? Pfff. The doors were open. Who else has been in here?"

I peek at the clock. "It's too damn early for conflict at seven thirty a.m., Bailey. Get out."

She throws her hand ups. "Camron told me to tell you that breakfast is in thirty minutes. He wants to eat at eight sharp... and *I'm* sorry about last night."

"Why?" The last thing this bitch wants is peace between us.

Why didn't Camron tell me about breakfast himself? Not asking her that though. The other last thing she needs is ammunition to shoot at me with later.

"Because I shouldn't have spoken to you like that. I was raised better, but sometimes the alcohol does the talking." My money's on her hormones doing the talking.

"It only says what you want to, Bailey."

"I know I was..." She shifts her weight to one foot, ill at ease. "Look, Camron doesn't have to make anyone be here. Why are you if you don't want to be?"

She isn't apologizing but prying about another woman possibly poaching on her territory.

"Listen, Baily. I'm going to be honest with you. You don't like me. I sure as hell don't like you. Don't walk into my room anymore with permission even if the doors are open. Let Camron do his own dirty work. If you want to know the exact reasons I'm here, ask him."

Bailey frowns, and hugs herself. "He's on a call."

"Well, he's not on a call in *here*, Bailey."

She twirls away, giving me a glimpse of her red thong and butt cheeks. They're not bad looking, and I didn't ever want to know that. Now, I'm pissed.

I charge to the doors, to engage the lock. There isn't one on my side. I find a singular keyhole on the outside though.

"Son of a bitch! He'd given me this room for a reason. He could lock me *in* it."

His bedroom doors open across the hall, while I stand between mine. When he steps out in a raven-black, double-breasted suit and smiles, I close my doors and sequester myself in the bathroom, which can be locked from the inside. Someone tries the knob immediately, gets no entrance, and starts beating on the door.

"Open the door, Amari."

"After I bathe, Camron. Then we'll discuss why my doors have a lock on the outside and not the inside."

First the contract. Then Bailey. Now, this. How much am I supposed to endure here?

"I never intended to lock you in anywhere, and I'll give you the key if it bothers you. Now, open the door."

"I'll gladly take that key. Slide it under the door then go away. I need to bathe." I turn on the shower to remove Camron from all over me. I don't think Bailey is above sniffing me for his essence, and I don't want her knowing anymore about me. Information in the wrong hands is power, and she shouldn't ever have that over me.

"You're being childish, Amari!"

198

"No, that's what your witch squad is! I'm being private and locked away! Now, let me be that, please!"

"Open up before I break it down!" Camron's tone could strip paint from the walls.

"Hey, it's your door," I quip, and then the barrier between us starts breathing. "Camron, stop!"

He doesn't. It crashes to the floor. He tramples it, rushing toward me. Damn, he's strong.

"Is this what you want, Amari? Me chasing you and tearing down my doors! Fine! You got it!" He towers over me, chest laboring for air. Intimidating. All bark, but very little bite, and I've seen him naked, how he looks when he's climaxing. Yeah, he's still a beast, but he's not that scary anymore.

"Don't put this on me, Camron. I didn't tell you to tear down anything to get into my room. Privacy is a right amongst adults, not a privilege. If you don't want me locking the door, take it off the damn hinges. Oh, but you already have in a tantrum worthy of a two-year-old. Congratulations. Now, grow up and learn some respect for the people and inanimate objects around you. I only wanted some privacy to bathe, nitwit."

"So, I'm back to being Camron now?"

"You are when you're tearing up shit to get to me." What won't he do to knock down hurdles that separate us?

You don't want to know.

Actually, I do.

"What is going on in here?" Bailey asks sweetly, while violating the room, and wearing troublemaker like armor. I want to wrap Camron in the sheet with me and howl *Mine!*

I don't. "You all need to leave. My shower is *not* a group activity." But I must be lying again because no one budges, even Layla and Sasha are still spectating from the doorway.

"Get out, Bailey," Camron demands, while fixated on me.

"Camron," she starts.

He sneers, "I said leave, Bailey."

She poses behind him, with her arms crossed, one knee bent. "No, Camron, I'm not leaving. You don't act like this. It's *her* making you like this, isn't it?"

'Yes, bitch, it is' trips to the tip of my tongue. There's underlying nervousness in her tone, and she's a woman that doesn't know how to get a clue. I can see the thirst she has for Camron a mile away, but she can't get from him what he doesn't want her to have. I'm undressed. Until I'm not, she needs to go be clueless and thirsty somewhere else.

"Please leave, *everyone*," I urge.

Camron just moves closer. "We need to talk, Amari."

I tamper with the buttons at his abdomen. "I know, Cam, but I think you need to talk to Bailey more. She definitely has something to get off her chest. You need to deal with it and her, and I need to bathe." My wishes are disregarded again, or everyone is hard of hearing. "Fine, I'll go to a less busy area."

I step.

Camron snags my elbow gently. "Bathe. I'll see you in the dining room. Everyone out or I'll carry you out. Amari, breakfast is at eight sharp."

"So I've heard."

The room clears without Camron having to handle anyone. I shower quickly. Blast through brushing my teeth and combing my hair. Even quicker, I dress in a two-tone, white and black halter jumpsuit that is damn near priceless if the tag I snatch off it is right, and eighty-dollar black flats. I didn't know who was coming through any of my doors at any moment, didn't want to be nude when they did. A glimpse at my phone on the bench in the closet catapults a greater need to check on my finances and family than be on time for breakfast that includes the witches.

Chapter Eight
~Amari~

Missed texts from Sheryl inquiring about what happened at work yesterday, why wasn't I there, and did I have to skip our date last night at the bar is ignored. I don't know what to tell her, but I'll see if I can make it up to her tonight... after I run it by Master Camron. That irks me, but at least I can delay that for the time being with my priorities. Calling my mother first gets me her voicemail. I leave a message to call me when she can. After I enter my information into the automated system for the credit card, I wait for it to spit out my credit limit for today. Unlimited is the golden number, and... that's not a number.

I look at my phone as if it's I'm listening to another language. "What the hell?" I press 2 for a repeat of my limit.

"Unlimited." That's not right.

"Customer representative," I gurgle into the line.

Elevator music cuts in instantly. Shortly afterwards, a too damn chirper female. "This is Operator Lindsey. How may I help you, Ms. Spencer?"

"I need to close my account... please!"

"Are you sure, Ms. Spencer?" Now, she's worried. Well, so am I.

"Absolutely!"

"Well, we just upgraded your account to unlimited—"

"Why would you do that?"

"You have a co-creditor whose income bumped up your eligibility for a much larger credit line."

Camron.

"Shut it down."

"You should take advantage, ma'am. Paying the balance off in the same month raises your credit score significantly."

"My credit is just fine, or it will be after I close this account. You've allowed it to be mismanaged twice in a matter of days. That's after you let someone make changes to my account and report that I'm not me before you snatched my credit limit and threatened to prosecute me. Then you let the same impostor tell you to give me all the credit available. I have no faith in your company anymore. Closed. The. Account."

"Okay, Ms. Spencer. I'm doing it now, but I wish you'd reconsider."

"I'm giving you're the same consideration I was given two days ago by a representative who I pleaded with to restore my account after it was flagged for fraudulent activity. None. Your need to set more guidelines and firewalls for hackers and people that can just enter my information in your system and alter my account when they feel like it."

"I'm very sorry, Ms. Spencer. I can have you express your concerns to a supervisor. I'm sure any one of them can implement the changes you require to protect your account more efficiently if you would just—"

"I'm not changing my mind. No need for the scripted plea. Mail my final bill to my…" Damn. "To this address." I rattle off my mother's."

"It's closed now, Ms. Spencer. I apologize for—"

I hang up then dial the bank. "Available balance for checking is one million, three hundred—."

"Jesus Christ Almighty Camron!"

"Your selection is invalid."

"Oh, screw you, machine!" I disconnect the call two minutes before eight.

Camron hasn't stop executing his will over my finances. Adding money to my accounts almost makes me feel bought, but he's just being generous. Too generous. Nothing unusual for him now that I've taken off my rose-tinted glasses that blurred his true nature. I haven't earned the excess money, so I don't want it. Can't close my bank accounts without being there in person to carry my money to another institution. Don't have a mattress to stash it under either.

Camron is going to have to withdraw his funds, but this isn't a request I'll issue in front of the witch squad. They're too privy to my business as it is with doors that don't lock or even stand to keep them out.

Downstairs, I follow the aroma of breakfast under the chandelier into a stainless steel and oak kitchen fit for the chef busying himself with turning slices of bacon in one skillet, flipping egg in another on an eight-aisle stove in the center of the room. I cross the threshold and stop a few yards away from the wide island he's working at.

"Hello." I catch him by surprise, hand in midair over a loaf of bread on the counter.

"Hey," he says with blue eyes wide enough to see into the future, pointing to an opened doorway to his left. "The others are in the dining room. Down the steps, to the right of the wall right there with water flowing over it, then another right. Left takes you to the pool and sunroom."

"Okay. Thank you. Need any help?"

He frowns as if I've asked him strip. "Ah… I'm good." A blond lock of unruly hair falls across his forehead, escaping an intentional bedhead hairstyle. He sweeps it away with the back of his hand.

"I don't mind helping. I'm not exactly thrilled to sit in there with *them*."

He consults the loaf of bread before wobbling his head and thrusting the bag over the stove. "You can brown these for me. There's a toaster to your left on the counter under the low hanging cabinets. Just drop the slices on the platter in front of the toaster. They don't eat butter or fruit spreads here. So yeah, that's it."

While accepting the bread, I pinch a barstool from the other side of the island. "I'm Amari Spencer, a regular girl who eats butter, fruit spreads, pork, and salt, though I know shouldn't."

"I'm Tommy Listern. I appreciate your help and anything eaten in moderation is healthy."

"Tell that to my figure. It stores every bit of fat like I'm in permanent starvation mode."

His heart-shaped face splits wide around the pinkish lips over a muscular build well-concealed by the chef jacket, until I'm only inches away from him. I stick four slices in the toaster before side saddling the stool. It's not hard to learn anything about him. Looks much younger than twenty-eight. Have been Camron's chef since he graduated college. Hopes to open a restaurant in Paris one day. Family genes trace back to the Rockefellers. His two older sisters are attorneys who own a prestigious law firm in New York City. They are not happy about him choosing to be a chef.

"A blue blood, huh?" I drop more toast on the pile I've amassed.

Nobody's probably going to eat a tenth of it, but I brown more bread to prolong connecting with someone that's not conceited.

"My sisters are blue bloods. I'm just a chef, the equivalent to being a part of domestic help to them."

"Well, I'm just a nobody. I don't even have a job."

He transfers the eggs to a dish. "That doesn't mean you're a nobody."

"We know that, but you can't tell the people in the dining room that."

"Well, Amari Spencer, you're the first body to acknowledge I'm human here, so you're somebody to me." A kindred spirit.

"Right back at you, Tommy."

Camron materializes in front of the waterfall across from the steps. He mounts them in a hurry, blowing into the room with the strength and thunderous look of a hurricane. "You're late, Amari." I know that.

I click my tongue. "See, Tommy. No hello. How are you doing? Did you sleep well? Did you get lost? Just come where I tell you, puppy, or you'll be punished."

I drop off the platter of toast on the island on my way out. "Nice to meet you, Tommy, the only other human being who's like me in the house. Normal."

His advanced directions put me where I'm supposed to be, the dining room, with Camron bringing up the rear. "Your place is at the other end of the table, Amari."

Bailey and Sasha snicker while holding court on the far side of the twenty-four-chair, purposely distressed light wood table with double bases. Layla's opposite them, tittering under her breath. Camron and I unquestionably did not have a breakthrough last night. Just really great, *great* sex.

And now you're banished to No Man's Land.

Yeah, well, I won't be entirely by myself. I'll have a goblet of water and juice on an empty placemat and plate to mingle with. Utensils to jab the witches with if they get out of hand. This is pitiful.

"Might as well get used to the loneliness now, oh girl," I gripe, heading to what feels like the other side of the house. "Six months is a long way away."

When I pass a china cabinet and hutch mate to the table, Camron asks, "What did you say, Amari?"

"I'm headed to No Man's Land, Camron. What do you think I said?"

I park in a cushioned-back, armed chair, prop my chin on a fist, and drum on the tabletop lightly, surrounded by elegant, black and gold, damask-designed wallpaper. I'd admire the beauty of the room, but it's purgatory as long as the witches are here too. Laughter erupts from the women. Camron pins them with a hostile glare I'm grateful to not be on the wrong end of. And then, it's on me.

"That's not No Man's Land, Amari. It's your place as one of the heads of this household."

Oh. He's replicating my parents' seating arrangement. I'd have got that if he'd accounted for the length of the table, and that the women would flock to his end like crows who are suddenly targeting me with their black stares, coveting my place. Heavy is the head that wears the crown, I adjust an imaginary tiara and grin just to ruffle the women's feathers.

"Your intentions were good, Cam. That's all that counts. Thank you."

When we don't have so many eyes and ears in attendance, I'll point out that he pretty much isolated me from everyone, almost giving the women more bullets to fire at me. For now, I let him heckle to himself while taking his seat. One-upping the witches is becoming a game that I like to play.

Petty.

Am not. I can't beat them, too many witches, so I've joined them with Camron as an unaware supporter instead of opponent. Or maybe he knows. Who cares as long as the witches are mad?

Tommy enters, spies me, and cocks his head with a puzzled expression as he delivers the platters to the tabletop before them. "Stay there, Amari. I'll serve you in a minute."

More interested in filling their plates than maintaining the stare off, the women send sporadic, hostile glances down the tabletop. Camron simply focuses on me, face devoid of his previous humor. I'm not fooled by his mask. Somehow, I've offended everybody but Tommy. When he returns with a single plate with sausage links, scrambled cheese eggs with chunks of ham, buttered toast, and sliced strawberries, I've grown self-conscious under Camron's observation.

I don't have to be encouraged to look elsewhere. "Thank you, Tommy."

He alternates the dishes. "This is half of my breakfast, but you are welcomed to it, Amari." He's about six two, and is going to go hungry for me.

"You don't have to do that, Tommy. I can—"

"Yes, I did. I found a friend and it's my job to feed you. Now, eat. See you at lunchtime." God bless Tommy.

He returns from whence he came. I inhale the heavenly smell from the food. My stomach rumbles, not understanding why I'm filling my senses and not it. I fork the cheesy eggs up before Tommy comes back for them. Orgasmic explosions detonate on my taste buds. He's not getting these back.

"I swear to God I'm kissing the cook after this."

"What did you just say, Amari?" Camron asks, eyes narrowed.

In trouble again.

"These eggs." I kiss my fingertips. "Tommy really should be in Paris, but I'm glad he's here."

"Who's Tommy?" Layla looks thoroughly confused, not the sharpest socialite at the table.

"Tommy is the chef, Layla," Camron says impatiently. "And you'll be doing what to him, Amari?"

I swallow hard, knowing a tempest of jealously is coming, but he doesn't like when I fib, so he's asked for it. "I said I was going to kiss the cook. You know show your appreciation for someone's hard work and talents."

Carmon rocks back, haven't eaten a thing. Content to watch me eat. I'm happy to let him, until the last bite. It comes too soon.

I close my eyes and savor it. "Tommy, you stuck your foot in this!"

He shouts back, "I sure did for you, Amari!"

Layla coughs out chewed up toast into her plate then chucks the remains in her hand across the table. It skids under Bailey's plate. who's horrified instantly. Layla scrubs at her tongue furiously with a napkin. Try as I might to keep my sniggers contained, some burst free until they're all absconding like criminals during a jailbreak.

Camron sprouts up to his full height, chair tipping over behind him. "What the hell are you doing, Layla?"

"He said he put his *foot* on it, Camron!" she cries, still swiping residue from her mouth.

Camron retrieves his chair then her toast, hurling it on her plate. "*In* it, Layla, meaning his cooking is excellent!"

"Oh." Layla gives her tongue a much needed break.

I'm sure she's had much worse on it. Needless to say, I'm laughing my ass off, and I've changed my mind. Six months here will be a walk in the park.

Camron plunks down in his seat. "Are you done yet, Amari? I have some news for you."

One last laugh flares up, and then I gain enough control to sip some juice. "What's the news?"

"Bailey, Layla, and Sasha are leaving after dinner. That's the earliest flight they could get to the Bahamas. I have to go into the office this Sunday morning because the owner of the Dubai property I was buying didn't like me pulling out of the deal at the last minute. Threatened to sue me since he declined the other offers that almost matched mine to accept mine, so I'm going to work to see if I can finish the deal from there and avoid going *to* Dubai. Don't know how long that's going to take, but Astrid and Blake are going to stop by for a while today. You're welcome to invite you family to stay with you if you get lonely or scared. It's a big house."

So, he's put the witches out?

Just when they were beginning to be entertaining, but they should've never been here in the first place.

Territorial much?

Shut up. I have bigger problems.

I'm having withdrawals. He's already leaving me to my own devices, and I should be more ecstatic about it. I'm not. It didn't take long for me to get used to his body next to mine in bed.

Bailey reverts her eyes in my direction with a crook to her lips, enjoying my and Camron's impending parting before it even happens. Yet, she's not sniping about being evicted from the house. Devious bitch. If it's not one petty thing, it's another with her. I can't wait to see the back of her for the last time.

Camron bites his lip. Dammit, he's sexy.

"Amari, are you going to be fine here by yourself?"

"Yep."

He squints. "Talk to me."

"That's what saying 'yep' is, Cam. Talking."

"You look like you have something else on your mind." Quite a few things, but I'm not offloading in front of company.

"I'm fine. If I have any problems, I'll call you." Everyday. Definitely at night. Maybe in the afternoons.

You're whipped.

So.

"Everybody out," dispels from him abruptly.

The witches' heads twist toward Camron. Sasha's fork clatters in her plate. Layla gasps. Bailey slings her napkin down and pushes back her chair. They aren't appreciating being dismissed one bit. Me either, but I'm the only one who has to obey, so they're getting off easy.

Camron tilts his head. "Not you, Amari."

How did you not see that coming?

I retake my seat.

While emptying the room, Bailey rolls her eyes heavenward. I have a mind to pluck them out. She's getting on my last nerve.

Camron rises. His fingertips cleave to the wood grain of the table leading him right to me. "You were ten minutes late when I

209

specifically said eight sharp for breakfast for a reason. Now, how do I punish you for it?"

The arrangement is still in play, but what did I expect? That he'd suddenly want me to be more than a body in his bed after last night? I did, and it sucks.

"Not sure, Cam. What reason? What do you have in mind for me to do? Wash dishes? Mop floors? Go to my room?" What else can he do to me?

He slides my dirty dishes along the surface a few feet away. "I wanted to introduce you to our staff before breakfast, not find you as Tommy's friendly sous chef."

"Was I supposed to ignore him? Oh, I get it. I'm supposed to treat him like the help, like you and Bailey and Layla and Sasha do. Well, I'm not you or Layla or Sasha and certainly not Bailey."

He smiles, and it's irritatingly mesmerizing. "Now, you're being feisty, Amari. Lay on the table."

I stand. "Cam, I'm not doing that. I have to *eat* on this side of the table, remember?"

"Now, you're breaking the agreement again, Amari. You're supposed to move when I say move, no matter where. Not disagree. We haven't even signed the six-months contract after your last infraction, and you're working on another one already. Keep standing, and I might demand you stay here for a year."

"You're enjoying this, aren't you?"

He slants his head. "Very much, and we're speeding into 'you living here for one year if you don't lay down' territory."

I hitch a knee on the tabletop that I'm not dining at again. Anything is better than a year here. Barely going to allow half of that.

"No need for climbing, sweetheart." He clutches my elevated thigh, feeding arousing vibrations to my core. My body eats it up like a glutton, and it's not pleased when I cut off its supply by removing my leg from his grip.

Camron contorts an eyebrow. "Face down, sweetheart."

It rankles, but I bend cheek to varnish. Slowly.

"I'm going to do you a favor and warn you about something, Amari."

My thighs are pressed into from behind by much more hard and toned ones, the split of my ass pierced by a rigid pole that fits neatly between them. Jesus! He's turned on.

"This is what you do to me every time you fight me. I love your feistiness. Damn near get off on it. Keep it up and I'll never let you go." But never love me again either.

That more than sucks. It's painful.

I lash out in the only way I know how, from my mouth. "You don't want me to check out on you. You don't want me to fight you. You want a Stepford wife. Is that it? Because if it is, you're out of luck. You get nothing or my feistiness. Now, pick."

"Feisty it is then," he mutters.

What did you just do, Amari?

He clinches my hips, draws back, aligns his length with my womanhood, and thrusts into me, repeatedly. The fucker dry-humps me until my panties are moist, I think I have on too many clothes, and I'm stifling moans. He could take me right here and I wouldn't argue. This point goes to him.

"I'll be good, Camron."

He stops grinding on me. "I like your nickname for me better."

"Earn it."

"I thought I had already."

"You lost it, prick."

He chuckles and squeezes my ass. "Fuck, Amari, you have no idea how much of a prick I can be. Apparently, I need to prove to you that you're quite capable of bringing out the worst in me without even trying."

"No need to prove it. We agree."

"Not good enough. I need you to believe it and fear it. One year is on the table now."

"No," I croak.

He sweeps my hair to one side, unfastens the button at my nape, squats, and licks up the length of my bare spine. My back bows as a firestorm breaks loose under my skin. Abdomen muscles contracting until it hurts.

Counterattacks, that's what he does every single time I defy him. Deny him. Get smart with him. Frustrate him. Fall a little deeper in love with him. Hell, even when I breathe, he gets even by inciting my body into betraying me, craving him.

He's going to stamp out all my defenses like that. Turn me out. It'll be a slow process, but eventually, I'll crack, surrendering to him without his love, and I literally signed up for it.

"Camron, I'm going home."

"No deal."

He hauls me up by my forearms then swings me up into his. I enfold his neck with my hands, for steadiness, but I'm still clinging to him, his counterattack successful. Then he lays me out on the table gently, as if I'm a damn buffet.

Ripping my loose top down, he suckles my nipple. I feel it tighten while encased in his mouth that's excruciatingly hot. Feasting on me. I backbend toward him, nails skewering over his scalp. He groans and laves the valley between my breasts with his tongue before tenderly kissing the underside of my chin.

Animalistic lust slams into me like an eighteen-wheeler. The tender things he does are what fucks with my head and heart the most, initiating a greed that my body is compelled to satisfy. I have to get Camron out of my system or him inside me. One of them will keep me from going insane. Both require the same outlet; him.

"Fine, Amari," he says out of the blue.

He's letting me go. I won. It doesn't feel like, but I wait for him to move away.

He doesn't. "Six months. You can talk to Tommy, even help him cook, but you stay here, and we make love tonight."

"What does this have to do with Tommy?" An epiphany knocks me sideways. "This isn't about me being late for breakfast. You're jealous again. Have you been holding it in the whole time since you found me cooking toast on the *other* side of the kitchen?"

"Yes," he deadpans.

"Why?"

His throat works to swallow, as if he's consuming the first words to hit his tongue. "Because I am. You're mine." Not a real explanation.

"Don't hold your feelings in, Camron. Talk to me, or it's no deal."

"Then Tommy doesn't work anywhere ever again. Here or Paris."

Not only is he using my family to keep me in line, now the people I genuinely like. "Jesus, Camron. When does this stop?"

"When you accept you're *my* Goddess." The ferocity in his tenor should be staggering. Frightening. But he's adamant about me being *his* Goddess. Something about that nickname that does it for me, probably because he has me on a pedestal at the moment, so forgive me for being off kilter mentally.

You're just as crazy as he is.

Probably.

"Do we have a deal, Amari?"

I nod stupidly.

"Tommy!" he yells.

Why is he calling Tommy? I cover my breasts just the chef appears, wiping his hands on a dishtowel.

"Yes, Mr. Powers."

"Do you see this beautiful woman on the table in this dining room apart of this house? Everything I just mentioned is mine,

213

Tommy. You can't take it with you when you leave. You can't have it in any way when you're here. Do you understand me?"

"Don't touch the merchandise, Mr. Powers," Tommy states plainly.

"Correct. You may leave."

By the time Tommy nods, I've buttoned my top with shame and humiliation burning in my face, no longer on the pedestal, more like under Camron's feet.

I dive upwards. "What the hell, Camron? You might as well pee on me or bite my damn neck. You can't make people feel like meat. It's not alright."

Tommy chuckles low in his throat. "Looks like your merchandise has a mind of its own, Mr. Powers. Good for you, Amari."

Tommy goes back the way he came, while I try stabbing holes in Camron with just my eyes.

He crooks one side of his mouth. "Sorry about that, love, but I reverted back for a moment so you could see how bad I can be."

"Reverted back to what? A jackass?"

"To the old Camron. The one I was taught to be."

I grind my teeth. "Point made. Your parents should be tarred and feathered."

He roars with laughter. "It didn't take you long to figure out I didn't have the best role models growing up."

"You're laughing, but I'm serious. They ruined a potentially much more powerful man than they tried to raise. Being a good person would've increased not just your family's power but your inspiration on more people to strive."

"So, make me what they didn't."

"You have to do that for yourself, Cam. No one can make you into what you don't want to be. Yes, you should've been exposed to the good in people long ago, but you're an adult with self-control who can easily follow the golden rule."

"Which is?"

I dangle my feet over the edge. "Do unto others as you would have them do unto you. Would you like me dry-humping you on the dining room table?" Then I scratch my head. "Hell, I liked being dry-humped on the dining room table. How am I going to expect you not to? So that's a bad example." He barks laughter.

"Okay, try this, Cam. Don't make people feel like food. It's degrading and hurts their feelings. Makes them feel as if they don't matter."

"Amari, you are food… for my soul. I wasn't sure I had one until I met you. You're all that matters to me right now, and when I get home tonight, I'm most certainly going to eat you… out. You're going to cum in my mouth. Then I'll fuck you until you don't know where you are anymore. You'll want me to hold you until you come back to your sense, and then while you sleep in my arms. I'll hate to get up to go shower for work, but you need a roof over your head and whatever else you can think of. I'm going to provide that for as long as you're with me."

He's no longer the beast, and sweet Jesus, it's like a sauna in here. I tug on the strap crossing my neck to let cooler air underneath it.

"What I need starts with you taking your money out of my account, Camron."

He responds with a firm, "No."

The biggest threat I can come up with is, "I'm going to spend it."

"So, Goddess."

I melt inside, all because of a name. Goddess. What would I do if he said the 'L' word in present tense? Whatever I do is going to be pathetic for sure.

"I'm serious, Cam." And pitiful at threatening people.

"What are you waiting for?"

"I didn't earn that money."

He smiles. It's the kind that gives affection without needing physical contact. Kind is what he is when he's not being inflexible, and I need his heart to crack open just a little. I'll figure how to get inside it from there.

"You earned everything I have six years ago, Amari."

What about your love? Nope, still not ready to bring up that topic. He was adamant he didn't love me anymore, and I believe him. Sort of. Need proof he was lying.

"Cam, take the money out of my account by in the morning or I'm donating it to an abused women's shelter."

"Good. Get a receipt. Now, kiss me."

Yeah, no I wasn't expecting that response from him. He doesn't have a philanthropic side, or he didn't. Maybe he's just indulging me who wishes she could give back. All I know is he's growing. I can't ask anymore of him, and it's almost illegal how fast I cover his lips with mine.

A moan emits between us. I'm not sure if it's his or mine. I sway backwards under a sudden head rush. His arms are enfolding me before I collide with the table. Too afraid to tell him I'm crashing and burning in my mind. Invisible strings unfurl from my chest, writhing and reaching, as if they're alive and determined to connect to a man who can't bring himself to love me again or let me go. Stupid, stupid heart. How am I supposed to get out from under this?

And then, I'm floating. Being crushed into a hard chest. I have no idea where I am right now. Tonight, I'll probably float into space, happily as long as I'm tethered to the caring side of him. We start to incline. My weight resting heavily on him. Not once does he breathe hard.

A door clicks, snapping me out of my haze. We're in an unfamiliar room. Bare, custom-built bookshelves are the walls closing in on a massive, black lacquer desk with a large computer monitor, floor lamp, and throne-back chair. A gold scrolled mirror reflects his backside to me and the unguarded, adoring look on my face.

Camron sets me down on my feet. "We're in your office on the second floor. Take a left instead of a right at the stairs into the east wing. First door on the right. The rest are bedrooms."

My office? The six months I hadn't signed up for yet reassert themselves. I spiral low—needing him to want me without a piece of paper between us.

"The contract," I mention.

He steps back. "Your clothes, Amari. I want them off. I trust you'll stick to this new agreement without your John Hancock."

I do a double-take. "What?"

He trusts you, dummy.

It's more faith than he had in me yesterday. Progress.

He shrugs out of his jacket. "I'm going to fuck you against that door, while you watch yourself in that mirror. Can't do that if you're dressed."

He's giving me what he doesn't even know I want. The freedom to love him on my terms. The spiraling stops. I undo the button behind my neck. The top flops around my waist. I grab the stitched border of the jumpsuit, and rock my hips out of it. Another striptease. Much better than the first because there's more room, less clothes.

He unfastens his pants and yank out his iron gray shirttails, never breaking eye contact. When my clothes pool in the floor, he crowds me. Lifts me. Lines my vertebrae with the door. I wrap my legs around him, opening myself up in too many more ways than just my body to him. Can't do a damn thing about what my heart's doing. Then he's inside me. Lips on mine. Pinning me against the door by his clamp on the base of my ass, I can't meet his rapid long strokes or slow down how fast he slingshots me into oblivion. Too fast. I'm lost in the inky black behind my eyelids in no time, just feeling. Taking whatever and how much of himself he gives.

"Open your eyes for me, Amari."

I drink him in. His face swims with more emotions that I've ever seen him let show. I wonder if it's the mirror he really wanted me to look in instead of his black orbs that are devouring me. Probably not. Always misdirection with him. Sleight of hand. But that mirror is definitely recording us. I won't enter this room again without it replaying these moments. That's what he wanted. And he's got it.

****

~Camron~

Amari's body is a punishment, gripping me, about to knock me down to my knees. Trying to teach her she's mine no matter what or who's around, by fucking her with our clothes on in the dining room, has backfired on me beautifully, as everything I do to bring to her heel. She won't break, but I'm bending, becoming a slave to her. She's the teacher. I'm relearning that just being in her presence slaughters my strength and will to deny her anything. As bad as I need to be at work, I can't leave without being inside her. The ribs in her tunnel are strangling my cock. I'm prime to empty inside her at any second. The struggle is real, and she's going to have to cum now.

"Unwrap your legs from around me, Amari."

It's almost a letdown to lose their encirclement of my waist and how quick she submits to me. She has to under the deal, but her bucking my commands is a natural high for me. That's possibly due to how swift other women caved into me with a single word, but I can plummet down then up into her, grazing her clitoris. Her eyes close again.

"Shit, Cam!" Her breathless rendition of my name, *her* name for me, is almost better than making love to her.

She starts to shake, pinioning my ears to the side of my head with her hands, heading right where I want her to go.

I have to see her moans instead of hearing them, and there's something so erotic about that. When my balls and the base of my spine starts to tingle, the journey into her is almost over. Too soon. I do regret that.

No more dry-humping, Cam. Your endurance level is low as shit with her as it is.

My climax hits full force. I almost lose my grip on reality, along with Amari. Tiny lights circle my heads, dizzy, but I don't think she'd appreciate hitting the floor. I move in closer, supporting her with my thigh. Then I let go.

"Fuck, Goddess! You're going to be the death of me, woman! Wrap your legs around me now!"

She giggles and gathers me close, fingers stroking my spine, making me shiver and harden again. "Death of you, Cam? What about me?"

"*You* have me by the balls, Amari." I nuzzle her cheek. "And you don't even know it."

"You didn't tell me," she whispers right next to my ear, giving me goosebumps on every inch of me.

"I didn't think you were ready to know."

She nips at my earlobe. "I've been ready."

What? Since when?

"How long, Amari?" I woof into her shoulder.

Yep, I'm furious. Have been through the wringer to make her feel something for me, anything other than scorn. And now, she tells me this.

"Since the day I met you, Cam... and I'm going to tell you one more time to stop doing that to me." She captures two handfuls of my hair and jerks my head back.

God, it hurts so good to see her this irrationally angry, just like me. Matching my moods fire for fire. Desperate for her, I am, will take any emotion from her except indifference.

My eye sockets flame under her bruising grasp on my hair. "What did I do now, love?"

"I told you if you're going to throw me away in six months, don't do and say things that make me want you more than I already do, dammit!"

I have to snatch her hands down and pin them in my chest, or she'll probably murder me with them. "You know, Amari... you are too small to be so damn violent."

Her small nostrils flare. "You haven't seen violent yet, Cam, if you don't stop playing with my damn heart. You've been doing it for years." Her version of my name clinches it for me.

No more games. No more contracts. No more hiding behind any of it, while taking shots in the dark at the bullseye on her heart.

"Then give me your heart, Amari."

"It's always been yours, jackass!"

"And you're the air I breathe. My heartbeat. My only reason to be on this earth." Unless I've impregnated her, then she'll become one of two reasons to live.

Her eyes water. Well damn, I made her cry.

I catch the first tear with my thumb and then drink the salty essence of her. "Don't cry, sweetheart. I'm sorry."

"Don't be, Cam. I needed those words from you."

"And you'll get more, after I come from work. Hate to go in on Sunday, but somebody quit as my PA, so I have to do my own typing on the weekends, and you've made me late for the first time since I started my business. I'm happy you're the reason, but somebody has to pay the bills until your business is off the ground."

"What business?"

"Your shoe business. It's your dream, right? That's what this office and the money in your account is for or whatever you want to do with it. I don't care."

"How do you…" She trails off, wide-eyed and floored.

I like that I'm the one who's rocked her, maybe too much. "Six years, Amari, to know almost everything I need to know about you… along with background checks. And I'm still learning, so don't give up on me."

"Not in this lifetime, Cam," she's murmurs breathlessly, but it feels as she shouted at me.

Finally, she's mine, and I wish I hadn't ever started my own business. Could stay right here until eternity. And then, I'd still need another day with her.

"I need a favor, Cam."

Nose to nose with her, I ask, "What is it?"

"I need to check on my family. My mother didn't answer her phone when I called this morning, and I stood Sheryl up at the bar last night. I forgot about our date, but she wants to know what happened. I want to make it up to her tonight."

"I want to go, too."

She shifts her head downward. "I'm not going to tell her anything about us."

"I hope you do and I want to go because I want to spend time with you and your friends. There's more to you than just being my girl. I want to know everything about you."

She looks up, a soft smile encompassing her mouth. "Okay."

"What time?"

"I'll have to run it by her first. I'll text you the time and place."

"I'll meet you after work. Here or there. Doesn't matter."

I know why her mother hasn't answered her phone too, but I don't want to be the one to tell her, so I stay mum about the good news coming her way, kissing her goodbye, which will lead to making love to her again at a more unhurried pace if I don't stop.

I carry her back to her room so she can shower. Rather be squirreling her away in my room for safekeeping, but we've come so far already in one day. I don't want to seem as if I'm pushing for more than she's ready for.

In the hallway, Bailey exits her quarters in the east wing with three more bedrooms. Layla and Sasha have the good sense to stay in theirs. I shouldn't have let Bailey talk me into keeping Amari company here. Bailey and crew have been nothing but headaches.

"Camron, I need to talk to you."

I descend the first step, finding it a little creepy that she was waiting for me. "Got to get to work, Bailey. Shouldn't you be packing?"

"Layla and Sasha are doing it for me so I can walk you to the garage."

"What is it?"

She trails a step behind. "Camron, you don't have to bring women who don't want to be here to take care of your needs. I can. We come from the same world. I know what you need. If you need a little extra on the side, I have no problems with adding Layla and Sasha to the bedroom." Basically, Layla and Sasha aren't a concern. Amari is.

Bailey sees much more than I give her credit for, and willing to compromise too much. I don't like the anxiety in her voice. Desperate women do desperate things.

"Stop right there, Bailey. You knew the deal when I called you for—"

She grapples my arm, bringing me to a standstill at the bottom of the staircase, in contact with her frantic expression. "I know the deal, but—"

I peel my arm out of her talons. "But nothing, Bailey. You got access to my house and money within reason for three months for Amari. That didn't include me at any time."

"She should have her own friends."

"You mean entourage. There's a difference."

"Whatever!" she snipes. "You said we were like family when we were little. Well, you're letting Amari come in between that."

"How is she coming between us? If you really thought of me as family, you'd think of her as that too for me. Family tolerates significant others for each other. I'm not seeing that quality in you."

She clenches her fists at the edges of her too short skirt. Hers always are for attention-seeking purposes, but I don't use the bathroom where I eat. She's too close to my real family.

"You're supposed to be mine, Camron."

Now, the conversation is interesting. "Who told you that? I thought we were just family."

"Your mother told me that, and to be indispensable to you until you saw me as an advantage to your life in time. I have to right background, know my way around fundraisers, dinner parties, the rich and famous who can skyrocket your business."

Make the rich even richer, the only aim in life people like Bailey have. I'm not the only one ruined by my parents. She also has a predatory nature that's only gotten worse with time. I'd have known this if I'd gone home for longer than the family business conferences.

"I know how to skyrocket my own business, Bailey. I don't need you for that." I guess my parents gave me some knowledge worthwhile after all.

"A man in your league needs a wife who can help him increase his power, take care of his needs in the bedroom." So her mother, my mother, Blake's mother, and every other parent in our circle says.

"Amari took care of my business for six years, and every other person at my company. And now she takes care of my needs in the bedroom. I'm satisfied."

"You won't have to give me a salary though, Camron, and I'll fill the void in your bedroom a hell of a lot better."

"No, you'll just bleed me dry because that's what women in your league do, Bailey. You're all leeches, looking for someone to suck on... literally, therefore the need for connections that keep you in your lifestyle. I'm not one of those for you. Never was, or I'd have married someone like you long ago. As far as my mother is concerned, she runs nothing but her mouth when it comes to who'll be in my bed, so stop breathing in the hot air coming out of her. I'd appreciate if you and your buddies left my house in the next half hour and not to bother Amari. I've watched you try to best her at every turn, and then you openly gloat when you think I've put her in her place. Well know this, her place is exactly where you'll never be, and when she's ready to take that seat as my wife, I'll send you an invitation."

"You're damaged too, Camron. Do you think we don't know you're forcing Amari to be here? We're not stupid. Do you think Amari will ever love you after this?"

"You're right, Bailey. I brought Amari here because I was desperate to keep her when all she wanted from me was to let her go. There's a reason why people like us are never truly happy. We have no idea what self-worth is because we chip away at each other's, sell ourselves to the highest bidder, and haven't learned to earn what we want the most from others. By the time we take it, it's in pieces from everyone trying to hold on to it, and no good. But if you knew what I was doing, why did you stay?"

She shrugs. "Because it would've been fun to play with Amari. Make her feel like exactly what she is. Nothing. You were supposed to fuck her, not fall in love with her. If I'd known you were going to do that, I wouldn't have help with the makeover to her bedroom. I helped decorate it for a target to toss darts at, not your future wife."

"Do you know how thoughtless you are to admit to me how you were going to treat the woman I've been love with since—"

"Oh my God! You're really in love with her!"

"...before I even got within fifty feet of her, six years ago, Bailey. A long time to be too stupid and arrogant to know it, and you and my mother sure as hell don't decide who I'm supposed to have in my bedroom or life."

"You don't need her, Camron. You have me. She could never be one of us."

"You're right. She's better than us, has a good heart, a kind soul, a loving family that she'll give up everything for. I know because I made her do it, and all she wanted was for me to not play games with her. Playing games with lives and money and comparing bank accounts and power is the biggest thrill in our world. Well, I want something more, and Amari is it. Do us all a favor and leave here and go find what I've found in Amari, Bailey. I'll be having Tommy check the house after I've left to make sure you're gone in the next half hour."

I continue through the entrance hall into the kitchen, where Tommy is cleaning and preparing for Amari's lunch. He looks up briefly.

"Add two more places to the lunch menu besides Amari, Tommy. Blake and Astrid will be here sometime today. Bailey and her crew are leaving *now*."

He smiles and nod, probably heard everything said between Bailey and me. I hope he reports every word back to Amari, then I open the garage access in the top corner of the kitchen and descend the steps into the dimly-lit carport.

"Camron, I love you," Bailey tosses after me.

Sunshine pouring into the portholes on the door barely making a dent in the dark, I pass the rear end of Amari's Hyundai and a collection of other cars bought for their pedigree. Wasted money when there are people like Amari's father who need an extension of life.

"You don't love me, Bailey, or yourself. Or you wouldn't be throwing yourself at me. You have no idea what those words means, so don't ever use them where I can hear you again."

"Fine, but I'm not letting you go this easy. She'll never cut it in our circle."

"God, I hope not. I don't want Amari to ever become less than what she is."

226

Bailey stomps off like a petulant child. I open the driver's door to the Ferrari parked next to Amari's blood red BMW, driving onto the street as fast the black devil on chrome wheels will go.

"Dial, Blake," I command the car.

"What, Camron?" he answers gruffly.

"No time for your attitude, Blake, or your 'I told you so'. You were right about having Bailey stay over. She's on a rampage. Shouldn't have agreed to her and her crew living with Amari and I. Bailey's gone so far as to tell me she loves me. I should've never let her convince me she'd get along with Amari. I'm headed to Power Enterprises. Have some business trouble of my own that needs to be sorted out today if I can. If you're still in town, come by the house as fast you can, and make sure Bailey and her friends leave it. Amari's in the shower, but she won't be for long. I don't want her upset but about any of this, or Bailey seizing the opportunity to start drama while I'm gone. Just don't let Amari know that I'm sending in a certified bodyguard. She'll be pissed."

"That I can do for you, cousin. Astrid!" He hangs up.

Hopefully, Amari never finds out she's being guarded from my own mistakes, and then considers me one.

Chapter Ten
~Amari~

"Sheryl, I swear I'll be there tonight, and I'll pay because I shouldn't have forgot. I just... had a lot going on." More than my fair share of complications.

"What did you have going on, Amari, besides quitting your job? I need details if I'm going to forgive you and keep my promise to pay."

"I... this will have to be done in person. It's too long a story to tell over the phone and I need to track my parents down. Neither one of them are answering their phones."

I quickly dress in my usual garb: skinny brown jeans, white high-low shirt, and peep-toe heels that buckle around my ankles. The only thing missing is my necklace.

And the turmoil it bought.

It's brewing in a different form. Bailey.

"Okay, Amari, eight at Gianni's tonight, or I'm tracking you down. I've been worried about you too. It doesn't seem right to work without you *and* Mr. Powers. I didn't get an answer from him either when I called him this morning."

"That's because he was with me, Sheryl."

She screams, "Tell me everything!"

If I want to save my hearing, I'm going to have to cut this call short.

"Sheryl, I'll be there tonight on time to explain. Tell Desmond I said hello. Bye, love."

It's possible she didn't hear me. She's still screaming, "I want to know right now, Amari!" when I disconnect the call, and redial my mother. No answer. A quick trip to my parents' home should produce some results... unless my father is at the hospital for tests in Candleton. That's normal with his condition, and the cell service there is spotty at best without the personnel demanding you shut

228

your phones completely off. I ring Candleton General Hospital just to be on the safe side, and ask if Mitchum Spencer has been scheduled for tests.

"Your mother said you'd track them down, Ms. Spencer. Your father's tests are already completed. His surgery will be performed at eight tonight. He's only allowed one guest today, to keep down infection. Regular visits begin in the morning."

I fist the wood of the bedroom doors. "No one told me anything about he needs surgery. How bad has his condition worsened?" I cannot lose my father after all I've been through.

"His condition is stable, but his surgery was scheduled last minute, and he had to be here within the hour of the call placed just last night after his grant had been approved for his hospital stay. It takes twenty-four hours for the round of antibiotics to enter his system and the tests results to come back."

"Grant? What grant? From what organization?" I sink down to the bed. "He's been there all night?"

"Yes. It's a private donor funding the experimental surgery."

"Experimental? We can't afford that procedure yet."

"The grant covers all costs, and it's common for any patient that'll have a new procedure like this to have to leave home right then to be prepped for surgery. This technique is so much more advanced than most I'm surprised he didn't have to be here all week before the surgeons gave the okay, but the survival rate is ninety-eight percent."

"It's the two percent that worries me."

"Your father's in good health, Ms. Spencer, so he should be more than fine when it's over. It's not as invasive or hard to recover from as the older procedures are. You'll be wasting your time coming here today. Your mother won't be able to come of his room until tomorrow or she won't be able to go back in. She's had to scrub free of germs before she could even go in. That takes twenty minutes and she's not going to want to do it again. They're both being well taken care of. Someone is certainly looking out for your family, Ms. Spencer."

There's only one 'someone' I know who can pull strings this fast and afford to just give away one, no, *two* million dollars. Camron, who wouldn't have told me just because this is who he is, secretive until the last moment. And maybe he just doesn't want me to feel as if I owe him anything. If my father survives, I'll owe him everything.

"Thank you. I'll check in again tonight on my father if that's alright."

"It's surely is, Ms. Spencer. Have a good day."

I send out text after text, telling off my family, including Camron...

Oh damn, I'm already thinking of him as family who didn't let me in on my father's upcoming surgery and isn't here to distract me from my worries.

Brandon calls back. I give him an earful about keeping me in the dark about our father's approval for the surgery.

"Slow down, Amari! I didn't know either!"

"What do you mean you didn't know either, Brandon? You live and work as a graphic designer for the same city as Mama and Daddy."

"Doesn't mean I'm more prone to know their business any faster you are, and maybe they just didn't want us to worry. We'd have told the other, like we're doing. If they wanted us to know, they'd have told us."

"Why aren't you mad? He could die."

"It's just like you, Amari, to look at the glass half empty instead of half full, and I know you need a hug right now while you imagine the worst."

"Yes, I do, and I am, and you can give me a hug at Gianni's tonight at eight. I expect you and Gabby there with bells on. Non-negotiable."

He laughs. "That's better than when you used to demand I hug you right then, even when I was in college and you were still at home."

"I could still demand you come right now, Brandon."

"That's my cue to end this call right now. Bye, lil sis."

"Bye."

I toss the phone on the unmade bed when I don't see a text back from Camron or anyone else, and start to pace, until there's a knock on the door. I open it to Tommy and a maid, then get out of her way so she can clean it. Tommy reminds me that Astrid and Blake are supposed to be dropping by soon, as well as the witches will be jetting away in the same time frame, before he abandons me to finish fixing lunch. I don't do worrying-while-alone well, so I wonder into the other wing of the house where the witches are, not expecting them to roll a ridiculous number of designer luggage out of their bedrooms.

Aw shit!

At a dead stop, I wait for them to pass. Layla ignores me. Sasha gives me a once-over that communicates her distaste for me without breaking her stride. Or maybe she doesn't approve of my outfit. I can't tell which put a bigger stick up her butt. Probably both. Who cares?

Bailey is the only one to pause beside me. "You can't have him. You're not good enough for him."

"I already have him. You should move on in every way possible."

"We'll see about that, gutter rat. I promise you won't keep him."

A few insults to her name rise in my throat, but I swallow them all. She's already dead to me. She just doesn't know when to lay down.

"You're not even worth the energy it takes to respond. Girl, bye."

I continue down the hall towards the bedrooms they vacated, nosing in the well-designed rooms a third the size of mine. No wonder Layla was complaining about exchanging bedrooms. She had to have been cramped in hers with what looked like all her belongings. While returning to the east wing, Tommy appears at the top of the staircase.

"Astrid and Blake are downstairs."

"They're early."

"What do you want me to do? I can tell them to come back."

"No, I need the company."

I spend more time cooing to BJ than talking to Astrid and Blake, who issues an invitation plus two to their engagement party for the coming weekend. Then he starts grilling me about Camron and me. I answer him evasively or counter with inquiries about the resort's grand opening that's been pushed back indefinitely. Tired of that after an hour, I offer my babysitting services to them. Both have fatigue leaking off them like a faulty spigot. Astrid hauls Blake up to his feet by his arm, then toward the front door without even a thank you. Caring for BJ, a new life, and watching him sleep is the only thing that calms my nerves. At seven thirty, they pick him up so I can get to Gianni's on time.

In my closet, I check my phone while grabbing my purse and keys. Camron has finally texted back, hours ago, promising to explain why he hid his part in my father getting a new lease on life. I text him back that I already know why and he can make it up to me by giving me a hug when he gets off. Hopefully, no news from my mother is good news. The two-door BMW is a smooth animal on wheels. With fifteen minutes to spare, I get to Gianni's, a two-story bar and grill packed to the gills on the ground floor with bodies dancing to August Alsina's "I Love This."

Sweating after simply walking through the crowd, I splurge on a VIP section upstairs, with instructions to direct any guest who asked for me up there. Have barely sat on the red velvet wraparound bench when Camron is standing at the ropes cordoning off my section. Unbuttoning his jacket is all he accomplishes before I bomb rush him. Completely needy. By the deep grin encased in faint dimples on his face, he doesn't seem to mind.

"God, I've missed you, Amari."

"Same here, Cam. Thank you."

"Oh, you missed you too, huh? And you're welcome."

I slap his chest playfully before he tows me into his chest to kiss me. That's how Sheryl and Desmond find us.

"It's about time," she chirps. "Girl, I thought you'd have cobwebs between your thighs forever."

We drift a part, only for Camron to twine our fingers together. Gabby and Brandon show up right afterwards dressed similarly to me. Gabby vows to wear every midriff top and then some while she still can. Most of the chitchat revolves around her pregnancy and Camron whispering sweet nothings that mean everything in my ear, the music too loud to hold a real conversation over. That doesn't stop Brandon from revealing more of my faults to Camron, and Sheryl rubberstamping each and every one, but even that can't stomp my joy, content to just be in good company.

Time flies by and the bar is closing too soon. It's the most time I've spent near Camron without wanting to kill him or hide from him, and I wasn't the third wheel to Sheryl and Desmond wearing matching navy-blue business suits. At our cars, Camron and I wait for the others to leave safely before I trail him home where there's no talking. We fall in the house from the garage kissing, and then into my bed.

Do I wonder what does his bedroom looks like? Shit yeah! When he tells me that he'll might have to fly to Dubai because Sheik Ahlam is being a hard ass about agreeing on a price for the land, I figure I'll get a glance at Camron's space when that time comes. As in a glance that involves rolling in his bed, holding his pillow while breathing in his scent, and then stealing his shirts to sleep in. All the questions in my head about us, I save for a time when we don't have a business trip looming like a bad storm and our relationship isn't so fresh.

You're scared.

Yes, but I won't be when I'm more comfortable in Camron's feelings for me. Some part of me just doesn't want to believe we're really together.

A routine quickly develops. Camron goes to work after practicing martial arts on the balcony under the low embers of sunlight. I call my mother about my father's health every few hours when I'm not visiting the hospital, sketching shoe designs, building my brand, tumbling deeper into love with Camron, or babysitting BJ while Astrid and Blake finalize party plans with his mother. Sometimes, they just use the time to reconnect with each other before taking the jet home to Colorado. My mother spares my father the details of Camron's contract in favor of his health inclining instead of declining. I have no idea why she hasn't told Brandon, just glad she hasn't.

Dodging Blake's third degree about Camron's actions to push us together is the new normal too. Apparently, Camron is too busy to divulge his secrets and refuses to over the phone. The Dubai deal is keeping him tied up at the office to late nights. I'm convinced the contract between us is Camron's story to tell.

Tommy feeds me, and holds small talk over whichever meal I don't eat at my desk. The date for Blake's and Astrid's engagement party arrives. Camron and I ride in a stretch hummer with Brandon and Gabby to the venue, a beautiful vineyard just outside of New York City, crammed with people from all over the world and the states and round tables adorned with silver and gray flower arrangements small enough to be elegant and allow the patrons to socialize.

Malisa in white, off the shoulder organza and carrying her little girl Salon, along with Astrid with BJ greet us at the front entrance. In plain white onesies and socks, the babies babble happily under the extended black awning shading the brown and gray stone sidewalk. Only a damn good mother would keep her kid cool and comfortable at a black-tie event.

People laugh and chatter over the elevator music from inside while I introduce them to Brandon and Gabby and bob my head to a violin's solo.

Astrid grimaces. "The music isn't my idea. My future mother-in-law's."

"It's just one party, Astrid." I hug her, and then Malisa before kidnapping Salon against my black dress, with an opened back and crisscrossing wide straps. She's the chubby, spitting image of her mother with a curly top. I reach across Astrid to tickle BJ's chin. Couldn't help asking about Malisa's boys, Savion and Sebastion the oldest, who are inside, being passed between the Owens and Apollo's mother, Sienna. Camron hugs both women before questioning Astrid about Blake.

She gives him a sly smile. "Inside. I'll take you to him."

Camron winks.

"What are you two up?" I ask her.

"Nothing. We have a bet about the fireworks I expect when it becomes real for Ashley that her son and I are really getting married. She's been on her best behavior though, so maybe she's really changed. I'll take you to your table. Dinner's about to be served and I don't want you to miss Blake's proposal to me during it."

Damn, she even knows when it's going to happen. Sympathetically, I stroke her shoulder under a long, body hugging, sleeveless, sheer black gown. White beadwork outlines her neck, hips, and the train.

"I am sorry about the future mother-in-law, Astrid. It's not so romantic when you have to schedule a defining moment of your life, is it?"

"No, the drama between his mother and I spoiled the surprise it would've been for me, but I love him, so who needs romance?"

The Powers family is just about the pits.

"If it's any consolation, I'm sure I'll still ruin my makeup crying all over the place after Blake proposes."

She giggles. "That makes two of us, Amari."

"Me too," Gabby adds.

Inside the ballroom, Brandon's head roll toward the ceiling. "I'm banning tears from this moment on."

Camron shakes his head. "Yeah, that's probably not going to work, Brandon. There's Blake. Let's go see what he's up to and get the ladies some wine while they figure out our seating arrangements."

They disappear in the crowd filled with people who wear stuck-up like a cape. Their noses scrunch up even higher every time Malisa's uncle, Tommy Owens, makes someone laugh at his table. God forbid the wealthier of the gathering enjoy themselves. I think they're not supposed to do that in mixed company. The vineyard becomes shark-infested waters to me, and I'm the diver treading them. Like Astrid, if I want Camron, I'm going to have to get used to the constant unnatural atmosphere harden by other's self-importance and rigidness.

Good with the bad.

Nothing's perfect.

Close to stage with a red curtains and microphone stand, Astrid stops. "Your table is here, Amari and Gabby. You're with the Owens and Apollo's mother, Sienna. Malisa and I are next to you with my immediate family and Blake's parents. Yay for me," she mocks.

I laugh, drawing the attention of Saleera and Christophe in a one-piece, silk ensemble dress and penguin suit.

Malisa snickers. "Trouble at two o'clock, Uncle Tommy."

I breathe out then in heavily and give the baby back to Malisa, preparing for the showdown incoming.

"What is she doing here?" Christophe asks with a deep frown, loud enough for everyone in the immediate area to crane their necks his way. "I know she's not with *my* son in that dress."

I wonder if I was supposed to come bare ass.

"I don't know, sweetheart, but we should certainly go find out," Saleera sneers before they swivel together, as if joined at the hip.

Their arrival at the table coincides with Brandon's and Camron's carting glasses of wine in both hands, setting them quickly down in front of our name cards before moving to stand beside us.

Camron loops his arm through mine. "Mother. Father."

The tip of Christophe's nostrils skydives for the roof. "What are you doing here with her?"

"She's my date and my girlfriend, father."

"Girlfriend!" he howls. "She's your PA!"

All eyes are on us now.

"Not anymore for a couple weeks now, Father."

Tommy Owens sidles up to the table. "Here we go again with the beefing. For the Powers to be so uppity, you always starting some shit. The older family members are like thugs. Can't take your hostile asses nowhere. Not the hospital. Not weddings. And now, not engagement parties either. I myself enjoy the hell out of a cookout though. Saw a really expensive gas grill outside. Plenty of yard out back. Anybody game?"

Christophe's withered, freckled hands, much like his face, chops through the air in front of him. "Saleera, I can't. You handle this."

She twitches her slight weight from one clunky heel to the other that looks as if they're two different shades of off-white, but it could be the low lighting. At least if a good wind comes through, her shoes will hold her down. "Camron, you know this is unacceptable."

"This," I speak, "has a name. You know it well, Mrs. and Mr. Powers. Use it or I can start calling you Thing One and Thing Two!"

Uncle Tommy spits wine back in his glass. "Yeah, Malisa, Amari doesn't need defending either."

Saleera, heavily made up in too light a shade of makeup and caking-up red lipstick, clutches the triple string of pearls at her neck folding in on itself like crepe paper. Christophe flushes red.

Camron smiles. "You both can respect Amari, or I can watch her disrespect you both all night. Doesn't matter to me what you decide."

I adore the hell out this man for taking my side, but I don't want to ruin Astrid's and Blake's big day. I knew Camron's parents wouldn't accept me, but to solidify my position as outcast in their family fold before a precious moment in someone's life is just plain nasty. Yeah, I want nothing to do with these people.

I tuck my clutch under my arm and kiss Astrid's cheek. "Astrid, do me a favor and have a beautiful engagement party without me."

"No." She switches BJ from one arm to the other. "You're not going anywhere, Amari."

"And I can't stay."

"Well, it was nice while it lasted, Astrid and Blake," Camron says politely.

"No, Camron." I pet his arm. "You stay. You should be a part of Blake's moment. You did so much to make it a reality. I'm going to Uber home, change clothes, then go sit with *my* father."

"*We'll* sit with your father, sweetheart. If you're not wanted here, neither am I, and this is where my parents learn they don't decide who I'm in a relationship with."

Astrid sidesteps between Saleera and me. "The only people leaving will be Saleera and Christophe. This is my party, and I and Blake dictate who shouldn't be here."

Blake enters the fray. "You got that damn right, baby. Saleera and Christophe, this way please. We say goodbye now."

Christophe forms fists at the seam of his pants legs. "Blake, you don't choose other people over your aunt and uncle."

"I just did, Christophe. Let's go."

"Wait!" Saleera yells.

"No waiting, Mother. You've chosen your prejudice over me and Amari and we're out. Let's go, sweetheart."

I twist at the waist.

Uncle Tommy reaches out and twists me right back. "Nuh huh. These people don't get to run off the good people off while I'm around, and I have some things I'd like to say to them."

He turns to Christophe and Saleera. "There's nothing more classless than the people who think they're better than others. Unless, you can walk on water, and I'm damn sure that stick up your butts is more like tree trunks that will sink you like the Titanic, you'll still be judged like the rest of us when you leave this earth. If you can't see how your son feels about this woman, you're as blind as two bats, and you probably are, 'cause lady, your shoes are two different shades. For real, only thugs by the same type of shoe in different colors. If you and your husband got your noses out of the air, you both would've seen the different colored shoes before you got here. The question is why didn't some of the people you two think are your equals tell you that you're wearing mismatched shoes? They've all been joking about both of your colorblindness since you got here."

Ashley breezes up and extracts BJ from Blake's arms. "You two haven't learned why you're all here yet, have you, Christophe and Saleera? It's not our social circle that holds us down in troubled times. Our children do, and they are finding people to love that we don't approve of, people like me from a hardworking family that doesn't sacrifice the little time they have with their children for a buck and a favor from an outsider for when times get rough. We can't do a damn thing about who they love. You should be thanking Amari for sticking with Camron through thick and thin because I know all your histories and I've never seen him happier. But don't listen to me and lose him like I did Blake to people who'll give him things you aren't capable of because you don't want to be. That's the chance you're taking right now. He may not give you a second chance to get it right. Amari will be the only one to convince him that he should, and she might not because you're making an enemy of her."

Blake's father surfaces out of nowhere to tickle his grandson's stomach, and I see the resemblance between him and Camron, who looks nothing like his parents. I'm not one to gossip though.

Uncle Tommy blinks, then looks down in his cup. "You rich people drugged me because I'm hearing shit that isn't possible: Ashley Powers does not admit she's from a poor family in the back of the beyond Spindle, Colorado or defend those that don't live in mansions." He walks off toward the bar. "I want that wine bottle because I'm suing, and then I'll have my business plus forty acres, a mule, *and* a mansion. And I want it all, dammit!"

I start sniggling despite Christophe's scowl ending at his nose that looks more like a beak, his tightly pursed lips, and the dropping temperature.

Saleera wipes her hands clean of something and murmurs, "I'm sorry, Amari and Camron."

Blake cups his ear. "What, Aunt Saleera? They didn't hear you."

She looks directly at Camron and me. "I'm sorry, Amari and Camron. I truly don't want to experience what Ashley has gone through to reconnect with Blake and be a part of his son's life. I can see you two are happy with each other. Camron's never smiled so much in his life. So, if you do that for my son, Amari, I won't stand in your way… but I want my own grandchildren. I'm owed that after listening to Ashley the snobbiest of us all preach."

Ashley hugs her sister-in-law. Malisa cackles beside Apollo, who's materialized with his carbon copies in onesies and cradled in each of his arms. There's nothing of Malisa in Savion and Sebastion, identical twins that let Salon tag along in the womb because their mother would need someone to dote on too.

Christophe throws his hands up in the air. "So be it if my son doesn't want to be with someone with status or a part of this family. I'm not condoning this relationship."

"Father, Amari has all the status that counts. She's human, breathing, and wants what's best for me. Something I can't ever accuse you of, so you should definitely go. The exit is that way." Camron points behind his parents at the neon green sign above a side door with a picturesque view of the vineyards.

I look up at him who chose me, but I have the right to be accepted for who I am. Can't do a thing about Christophe's bias or him clamping off toward the exit like an idiot in a penguin suit.

Saleera glances back at him, her movement making her plain, white dress flare out around her. "I'm going to go too. I need to talk to Christophe about how badly he wants to keep his status and his son in his life. He married into *my* family and took my name… and I need to change my shoes, but I'll be back."

She kisses my cheek and hugs Camron tightly. As she departs, he pulls out my chair, and the party restarts with a few side glances here and there from the elite blessing the room with the presences. If only they knew how much the regular people didn't want them here. Since most of the time before dinner is wasted on

Christophe's tantrum, dinner is served only minutes before Blake is supposed to take the microphone to propose to Astrid. She steps onto the stage first, after depositing BJ in the back room converted into a nursery for the babies.

The noise dies a swift death when she clears her throat. "Blake, sweetheart, I know this is supposed to be your moment. Well, I've stolen it to tell you something. Life wouldn't be nearly as sweet without your love. BJ wouldn't be the man he's going to be without your essence steeling him from a life ahead that has no guarantees for any of us. Your love makes the dark moments bearable, the days brighter, and the world a little easier to tolerate. Without you, I'm nowhere near the woman I want to be for me, for BJ, for you." She removes her hand from behind her back and opens a ring box. "Will you marry me and continue a life-long journey into the unknown at my side?"

He gasps and climbs the stage in a single leap to kiss her for a very long, long time.

Uncle Tommy has to clink his glass with a fork over the catcalls to get them to stop. "Blake, some of us would like to eat. Get a room or something. But first give her your answer, which we already know, just need it for the camera pointed at you from the back."

Even the snobbery heckles at Uncle Tommy's wisecracks. Of course, Blake's answer is yes. They exchange rings. The party is more extravagant with the good people in attendance who live to love and laugh and cry with each other. Astrid crosses the room to high-five Camron.

Blake's mouth drops beside her. "You knew what she was going to do, Camron, and didn't tell me?"

"He's very good at secrets," I interject while admiring the sparkling seven carats on Astrid's white gold band.

Camron grins devilishly. "I kept your secret, Blake, until you told it. It's only fair Astrid gets to drag me into her surprises for you too."

"No, it's not fair. You're my blood first, my cousin. We're supposed to watch each other's backs."

"You have a fiancée now, don't you, Blake?"

"Yeah, *but*—"

"I watched your back then, cousin."

"Smartass."

"Thank you. First compliment you've given me in never."

Blake chuckles into his wineglass, with the diamonds on his wedding band catching the light and tossing it back. "You know I'm going to return this favor, right?"

Saleera returns without Christophe. His absence doesn't dampen our spirits. She partakes in the wine and kisses Camron's cheeks a little too much for his liking. She also steals dances with Uncle Tommy, who looks around for help with his head cradled to Saleera's chest by her hand, a glass of alcohol in her other. No one rescues him. If they did, Malisa's father swore to deal with them afterwards. Uncle Tommy may be one of the few who's very, very glad when the party is over.

At Camron's home, our pattern recommences until the day before his trip to Dubai and my father is discharged with a clean bill of health. The latter is overshadowed by the former when day breaks. There's a bad feeling in my gut. Suffice it to say, Camron didn't get any sleep last night, and neither did I. If not making love, we're making eye contact.

With sunlight caressing the back of my hand on his head, I plead with him not to go. Doesn't occur to me to go with him. He doesn't suggest it. I'm able to get my own company off the ground for once, and I couldn't just put it down to follow my heart. Besides, I trust him. He'll come back to me. He has to. I'm living in his house for God's sakes.

I pack along with him for a night in Winchester. After dropping Camron off at the airport to catch a business flight, I drive slowly to my parents', longing for my lover, to be more than his lover. Cooking for my family, along with Brandon's silliness and Gabby's retribution for his bad acts, keeps me from getting too far down in the dumps and checking my phone too often. Only when Camron calls do I finally drift off to sleep in the wee hours of the morning. I wake up missing home, Camron's home, and him.

Mama and Daddy send me off with their love and Tupperware bursting with the last of dinner—I'd cooked too much. On Blanchard Row, a manila folder is on my bed. I siphon a crystal-clear black and white image of Camron and Bailey kissing on a beach under the overhang of shore side eatery. Grasping at each other's clothes in broad daylight.

"What the motherfuck!"

One day gone, and he's already with Bailey. My God, was the Dubai trip an excuse to meet her? Was I really not enough for him? A passing fancy for him that he he's gotten out of his system? Does he have women stashed in every port like a fucking sailor?

The picture burns my fingertips. It floats to the floor. My stomach heaves. Doubts about the coincidence of them being in the same place with me here accompanies me to the bathroom to puke then pack independent Amari Spencer's shit. The things that belong to the girl who loved Camron completely, enough to receive anything from him happily, is staying here with him. And so is the girl, but my fury at her gullible ass and his cheating one sticks its hooks into my soul.

Why did I let myself drop all the way in love when I knew the outcome with Camron? Have seen it happen up close and personal at Power Enterprises to every other woman who he was with, time and time again. He doesn't love. He takes. Hasn't changed but became a chameleon, exactly what he thought I wanted him to be.

I should've saw this moment coming the second he announced his trip, but I thought I was safe in the honeymoon phase of our relationship, where confessing everlasting love to one another isn't a requirement yet. It doesn't exist for him if he can do this to me only weeks into being together. He's gotten his revenge. I can't look at the photo without getting ill, so I examine his feelings for me.

"Well, he can't have that many if this is already happening behind my back. No wonder he didn't ask if I wanted to go to Dubai with him. I'd have screwed up his arrangements with her. How could you not see it, Amari? Bailey promised you wouldn't keep him."

But if I didn't have trust in Camron to stay faithful while out of my eyesight, we wouldn't have had a fulfilling relationship like my parents anyway. In my office, I save my work to a USB stick, then raid his bedroom twice as large as mine for the key to the Hyundai. It's nowhere to be seen in his desk, nightstand, closets, or his drawers. I tear his space apart looking for it, until everything lays on the ground. Computer, mattress, clothes, shoes, files bought home from work, my tears. The only ones I'm going to cry.

Today.

Yeah, well, I'll worry about tomorrow's tears tomorrow.

Looks like a part of the Amari I never want to see again has to come with me if I want to get away from here. I palm the BMW keys. With a paper towel from the kitchen and Tommy hot on my heels asking, 'What is wrong?' I stuff the photo in its envelope, a reminder of who Camron really is.

And to rile your loathing for him up until it kills the love for him dead inside you.

That too.

Tommy helps me carry my suitcases to the car. On the way to my parents' house, I take out my frustrations on the vehicle. Driving too fast. Braking too hard. Peeling the tires when taking

245

off. Not slowing down for ruts in the road. All abuse that I want to do to Camron. I hate this machine and him. And me. I'd been fooled, and I volunteered to be.

I beat the steering wheel outside my parents' house. "So ridiculous to think it was real, Amari."

My mother opens the front door. The phone in my purse rings. Tommy's number blinks on the display. "I made it, Tommy."

"It's not Tommy. It's Blake. Astrid and I popped by to see if you could babysit, but it seems all hell has broken loose. What happened, Amari?"

"Your goddamn cousin happened, Blake, and I don't want to talk about it. Just keep him away from me."

"I'll handle him, Amari."

"Do that, Blake!"

I sling the phone out the window. A passing car mows it down. I open my door just as my mother opens the passenger's.

"Amari! Jesus, what did you just do to your phone? And you just left. What could've happened that fast that you're back here with..." she peeks in the backseat. "...with what looks like all of your stuff?"

"Look in the folder on the passenger seat, Mama, while I take my stuff inside the house. I'll get an apartment..."

She bends down, seizing the envelope. "Stop! You stay here as long as you...Oh my God! Who is this kissing Camron?"

I hurdle out of the car. "Bailey Rossi, a certified bi... *witch* who promised I wouldn't keep Camron. But she was wrong. I never had him."

"I don't think that's true, Amari. That man loves you."

Not interested in arguing about it, I push the driver's seat upwards with too much force. It bounces off the steering wheel back at me. With a little less strength, I slap it up again and snatch the bag sitting on top of the clothes that are laying across the backseat on hangers.

The contents of a carry-on, which I overstuffed with products then underwear and couldn't zip, spills into the street. Underwear go everywhere. Falling to my knees, I sling it all back inside.

My father squeezes my shoulders from above me. "Baby girl, calm down. It's going to be alright. You don't have to go back to Camron, but let him explain his side for your own piece of mind. Now, go inside the house while I move your stuff in."

"No, Daddy. You just had surgery."

"I'm not lifting a house, Amari. Just clothes on hangers… and shoes strewn all over your car. It's like a hoarder's paradise in here. At least your underwear is in a bag, which you'll be carrying. I love you, but not that much to handle your adult underoos while you're not sick."

I snicker unwillingly, get to my feet quickly before my father tries to help me and risks pulling something in his chest. Backhanding tears from my eyes, I cuddle the bag with my underoos to my chest, stumbling toward the house with my mother attached at the waist by one arm. Her hug just isn't cutting it this time. I was breaking apart and one arm or one hand couldn't hold me together. Maybe not even duct tape or glue. In my room, I fall face down on the bed.

"Amari—"

"Just give me a few minutes, Mama, then we'll talk, okay?"

"Okay." She lays the manila beside me.

I knock it away. It flutters to the carpet.

"Tell Daddy to just dump my clothes in the floor. I'll get them up later."

"Okay." Her presence wanes. I slip into depression.

Two days into being truly heartbroken, Camron's voice manifests outside my door. "Sweetheart, talk to me please. That picture isn't what you think it is."

Each word out his mouth takes potshots at the fragments of my heart drifting around my chest.

247

"It never is what I think it is with you, Camron."

How did he get in the house?

"Not true, Amari. I love you more than anything."

"You know what? I don't believe you, but I loved you too, Camron, more than my own good judgment. Loved! Past tense! Stay away from me!"

I dig deeper into the covers and bury my head under the pillow. He goes away, so does reality. Exactly how I wanted it to. Two more days into my self-imposed exile, my bedroom door opens. Someone whistles low.

"Jeez, lil sis, bath and clean up already."

"Get out, Brandon," I say hoarsely.

"I will, right after I tell you what Blake and I did."

I crack an eye, getting an eyeful of the wall. "What did you do?"

"Beat your boy's ass."

I shift to a sitting position. "What boy?"

"Camron. He told us everything."

I fling the covers back. "Who is us?"

The light from the hall punches me in the eyeballs.

"'Us' is Blake and me."

I scratch at the bird's nest on my head. "I'm sorry. My ears are hallucinating. I thought I heard you say you beat Camron's ass. That's not possible."

"It is when it's two against one."

I jump to my feet and stick the landing in the middle of a neat pile of folded jeans. Pretty good for someone's that thunderstruck and wobbly as hell mentally.

"You jumped him!"

He smiles proudly. "Yep. He fucked over my sister. We worked him over."

"Oh no, no no! Is he alright?"

"Nope. He's laid up at home."

"*You hurt him bad?*" I screech.

"As bad as he's hurt you."

Shit he's almost dying then.

Why do you care if he's dying or not?

Because I do. If I could stop caring about Camron, God knows I would. And I'd stopped crying. And moping. And sleeping around the clock. Worrying my parents who leave food at my door that I leave untouched.

Go see if he's okay already.

I turn in frantic circles, looking for… something. Everything. My brother is going to jail for this.

"Where are you going, lil sis?"

"To see if you're going down for murder or just aggravated assault, nut! Where do you think I'm going? You better hope I can talk him out of having you two arrested."

"I don't care if you can't. No one fucks with mine."

He bends over and scoops the manila folder off the floor. No point in stopping him from looking at it.

"Yep," he drawls out of the blue.

"Yep what, Brandon?" I unearth the carry-on bag from beneath my dresses carefully laid out on the other side of the bed.

"She set up him."

"Who set who up?" I drag a pair of stonewashed jeans from the middle of the heap I pounded under my feet getting out of the bed.

"Bailey. She set Camron up. I didn't want to believe him, but she did."

"What are you talking about, Brandon?" A wrinkled midriff, high-neck shirt is nabbed from another mound.

"Did you take a really good look at this photo, Amari?"

"Yes."

"You sure because—"

"Are you saying it's photoshopped?"

"No. Camron said the photo is definitely real, taken after she took him by surprise."

I snort. "Surprised! Is that the best a marital artist can do? Isn't he supposed to be able to kick ass and take names later when someone surprises him?"

"Amari, even kungfu masters can't go around just hitting people."

"Really, because it sounds exactly like what you and Blake have done."

He continues studying the photograph. "Is Bailey as tall as Camron?"

"No." I rescue the first pair of shoes I see, leather sandals sticking halfway out from under the bed. "Why?"

"Because they're standing lip to lip. That isn't possible if he's taller than her. He said she was standing in a chair when she whipped him around and grabbed him by the collar to hold him still for the photo that ah... Layla, I think he said her name was, took."

"Layla's involved too?"

I start to have doubts again. What if Bailey kept her damn word to steal Camron from me? What if when I wouldn't hear him out, I played right into her hands? What if I refused to see the gray areas in the black and white photo?

Like you always do?

Shut up.

Brandon points at the snapshot. "He said he pushed her off, just not before Layla snapped the photo. His hands..."

I snatch the photo from him, inspecting every detail down to his fingers splayed out from her arms like he's... Oh no.

"He's not holding her. He's pushing her away, and you whooped his *ass Brandon*!"

He grins. "I whooped his ass because of the lovers' contract he made you sign. He understood."

I cover my mouth when it drops wide open in shock and refuses to shut again. "He… he understood?"

"Yep. A good guy, but he has some fucked ways about him."

I pop him one on the arm. "His parents taught them to him. That's not an excuse though. He was trying to do better for me. Oh God, Brandon, I wouldn't let him explain. I was the one who wasn't willing to change… for him."

The world gets this watery film to it.

Brandon leans back, as if I'm holding something that's slimy and wiggling, and begging him to touch it. "Well, don't cry about it. Go fix it. I'm still not sorry I whooped his ass though. But if he needs some chicken soup until his teeth can be fixed, I'll—"

"His teeth!" I yell. "Brandon—"

"And Blake. Don't forget Blake took part in it too."

"You two! Dammit! Camron probably hates me."

"You won't know unless you go see him."

I rush for the door then swirl back around, pointing. "I'm blaming you if I've lost him for good, Brandon."

"And Blake."

"And Blake!"

I whack him in the chest with the photo and stagger from the room. A quick bath, brushing my teeth in the shower, dressing, and a ponytail takes too damn long to achieve. Candleton seems a million miles away even with no traffic. I park in front of the house, leaving the car idling and driver's door standing wide open. Should've done the politically correct thing and called before coming. Ah, no, that would've given Camron the opportunity to turn me around.

I beat the front doors until Tommy answers with the maid behind him, her eyes dilated. I shove past them. "Where's Camron?"

"He's in the pool. Hey to you, too, Amari."

"The pool? Brandon said he was laid up, with no teeth, needing chicken soup."

The maid glances up at Tommy then goes about her businesses, muttering to herself, probably thinking I'm certifiable. I kind of am right now.

Tommy raises both eyebrows under the bedhead cut tumbling into his eyes. "The last time I saw Mr. Powers, he'd just half-eaten a steak and potatoes, as if my cooking is subpar, and then he dove into the pool in a perfect swan dive. He's fine."

"Brandon lied."

Extreme measures to get your attention, remember?

I pinch my hips. "That damn brother of *mine*."

"Yeah, he lied. Mr. Powers looks just like you do, lost. A little bruised however. Go find him. I have a meal to cook."

I shadow Tommy to the kitchen then veer to the right, then left of the waterfall into the sunroom, a screened-in porch that extends from the house. It opens to the concrete deck and chairs surrounding the Olympic-sized figure eight pool.

Camron swims to the ladder and climbs out of the pool, a God in board shorts, toned limbs, and valleys and indentations in his gold flesh that my mind wouldn't let me erase from it. There's also a purplish ring around his eye and bruise traipsing across his upper torso. He shouldn't have any damage to him with self-defense training. He wouldn't if I'd just let him tell his side.

My fingers lift to trace the discoloration around his eye, but I restrain them right back to my side. Hadn't earned the right to touch him yet. If ever again.

"You have a black eye, Camron," I sob, dry-eyed. Couldn't cry anymore.

"Your brother punched me in it. Blake bruised my ribs with the toe of his boot."

Yeah, they whooped his ass!

252

"They double-teamed you, Camron, and you didn't karate chop somebody? Or spin kick their asses into next Wednesday? You're a martial artist for God's sake! Bailey should be suing you for kicking the chair from under her."

He grins with one side of his mouth. "Don't be mad, sweetheart. I didn't fight back because I deserved the blows and so much more. Besides, there were only four licks. Brandon's. Blake's. Then the ground's in front of the house, which *I* hit first, then it hit back. Blake called me and told me what happened. I got home the next morning, looking for you at your parents. They let me in the house only because they thought me being there would get you out the bed. I came home and met Brandon's fast fist and Blake's furious foot. I'm sorry I was so stupid to think you'd care for me, Amari, if I had you on my territory long enough."

"Yeah, you were stupid... I cared for you by the time my interview for your PA was over, dummy."

He reaches out, then pulls his hand back. We're both chickens. I'm the bigger one, but I do step closer.

"Why didn't you tell me, Amari?"

"You were my boss, and I had just got the job. I didn't want to be fired that quickly, but I wanted you to notice me. You never showed any interest in me by the end of my first month, so I bottled up my feelings, and then I quit. Too chicken shit to say how I felt."

"That might've been the smartest thing you've ever done, Amari. I wasn't the man I should've been for you when I hired you, and I knew it. Wouldn't have treasured you like I should have. And I'm still not good enough for you."

"You were, and you are. Anyone that sees there's room for improvement in themselves and works at it is a man good enough. Everybody gets a clean slate if they want it after their lives have gone in whatever direction life has took it. Doing better today than you did yesterday is all I ever needed from you... and fidelity.

Most people don't deserve the good things that happen to them, like Bailey, just like most people don't deserve the bad shit that happens, like abused women. But it all happens, and you have to be thankful for all of it. It all has its purpose."

"Yeah, well, I've been cheating myself and you for years. By the time you finally pushed the issue of the other women being in your territory, I was already sick of them and couldn't wait anymore for you to say anything that indicated I had a chance with you, so I took it." He points to his face. "This is what I have to show for that dumb decision."

"*My* territory?"

"I was always yours, Amari. We both just had to accept it. I came to that conclusion a hell of lot faster than you did though, and then I tried to force it on you. Stupidest shit I've ever done."

I brace for rejection before placing a palm over his heart. "If you hadn't, we wouldn't be together right now, Camron. I had accepted I'd never have you, and it took a lot to turn me around. *You* did that with your crazy contract. It would've taken something that crazy after I thought I could never be all you wanted in a woman after you told me you loved me, not love in present tense. It stuck with me and created doubts, so when I saw the pictures of you and Bailey, I ran, but I'm back… if you want me."

Chapter Eleven
~Camron~

Want her? Want is too damn domesticated a word for how much I need her who looks dazed.

"Saying I *loved* you was me trying to convince myself I could let you go, Amari. As soon as I showed you to your bedroom, I was right on track of convincing you to love me. So, does this mean we're...?" I falter, almost unable to string more consonant and vowels together with her setting my skin on fire with her absent-minded caresses. "Are you sure you want me? I'm not letting you go again, Amari."

She nods shyly. "Yep. Why do you think I'm here? Well, besides checking on you. I got a visit from Brandon. He's somewhat remorseful for what they did to you. I guess that's because you didn't really cheat on me, which he figured out first. And he thinks you deserve a second chance at doing this right. *Us, right?*"

Us. Sweetest combination of the alphabet.

"What about you, Amari?"

Her nails stroke my chest, firing up my manhood. "I do too."

"Well, I don't deserve it, but I'm sure as hell taking you up on your offer. Every day, I'll remember to remind you that you've always been enough, more than enough for me. The only woman to touch me where it matters the most... the heart. I need to be honest with you about why I dated the other women before you. One, I was too senseless to see I should've just approached you and told you what was in my heart. But more than that, I was afraid you would never want me. Childishly, I wanted you to put your foot down and tell me how you felt so I could open the door to you being mine. You quit and mentioned we didn't have an employment contract. I created one for love, and made you signed it, hoping to work on your heart while we were body to body.

Before you, I had a void where love should've been from my parents. After I met you, I needed someone to fill the void *you* made. I finally figured out only you could fill both. I'm only human. Born to make mistakes."

"Born to right them too."

"And no damn one can take your place, woman."

She snickers then deposits her other hand on the other pectoral that's quivering beneath her fingers. "Seriously, you're quoting a song to me right now, Cam?"

Fuck, I love how she says Cam.

"I'm shocked you know anything about The Human League, Amari. You just jumped out of the cradle."

"Well, you robbed it and played the damn song for me on the drive from my parents' house, and you're only five years older than me."

"Damn straight I robbed the cradle for you, and I'll do it again if it's you in it."

Her eye drift downward. "Camron, I have something to tell you."

"What?"

"Bailey promised she wouldn't let me keep you but I didn't listen to her. Didn't think she'd try something like this. I think I was afraid if I entertained the idea that she would, I'd have to admit that I could lose you to her. I wanted so much to believe that she'd just go away. It just never occurred to me that she'd have a photo taken of forcing you to kiss her and send to me."

I pull her into my arms. She exhales so profoundly she could be causing a tornado in China right now. "Do you feel like you're at home too, Amari?"

She nods. Thank God.

"Me too. Right here is where you belong and you're not the only one that Bailey warned. She used subterfuge with you but she outright told me she wasn't going to let you have me and that she loved me before I went to work Sunday. I ignored her too. Didn't think she'd find me in Dubai and set me up. I was turning to leave the bar I was getting lunch at when she stepped up into the chair and pulled that stunt."

"We're both stubborn."

"Yes, but it's not a deal breaker for me."

She lifts her head. "Me either."

"I love you, Goddess, and it's real and true and not going anywhere."

"I love you to, Cam, and it's real and true and won't go anywhere. I tried to make it for years. It just hid inside me, waiting for your contract."

"That contract is real sweetheart. The terms have changed. There's only one. Our hearts are to always be connected in a place where no skilled surgeon or scheming bitch can reach."

"I'll sign that."

An honest to goodness smile lights her mouth that presses against mine curving upwards in the corners. In the pool, is where I relieve the pressure created from her absence in my life and her touch. I'll hear 'Cam' in every octave her voice is capable of before I carry her inside to my bed, where she's belonged since I first saw her.

Epilogue
Five years later
~Camron~

Blake moans from a deck chair during the annual family gathering that transferred to my and Amari's home. "For the love of God, Camron, make Castiel put his damn shorts back on. I have my baby girl in my arms, and Salon can see his pecker. Jeez!"

"I swear to the God, Castiel, I'm going to put your wiener on the grill if you don't put it up," Uncle Tommy yells, coming out the sunroom with an aluminum pan of ribs. "You had to have got that shit from your daddy, because your mama ain't capable of whipping something like that out. And if she can, somebody's been keeping secrets."

The children, which seem to grow by one every year, wade in the shallow end of the pool. Grandmothers and grandfathers, including my father, hover like helicopters over them, fixing floaties every few seconds it seems. It'll take Amari announcing she's pregnant at Blake and Astrid's wedding as surprise to me for Christophe to come around. There have been no more emotionless meetings in boardrooms for the Powers. For five years, we've been wrangling kids back into waterproof diapers and swimsuits, one more than the others, while Malisa's Uncle Tommy cracks horrible jokes around the grill he mans.

Cookouts, that's what he suggested for our first family reunion. More like smorgasbords with meat, vegetables, gourmet meals for the uppity that can't come down far enough to bite a drumstick with Uncle Tommy's homemade, finger-licking BBQ sauce. The Owens, Nordic-Fords, Spencers, and even a few of the Powers are glad. It's more food for them.

"Castiel, put your clothes on, baby boy, since you're offending everyone," Amari shouts through peals of laughter from her

258

canopied deck chair on the other side of the pool, amongst her friends, Astrid and Malisa, and her family members.

Only then does Castiel locate his shorts at the bottom of the pool and swims up, wearing them. Six months pregnant again with our baby girl, Camia, Amari grins without moving an inch, except to run the pads of her fingers over the diamond-covered charm at her neck on a considerably thicker and wider gold chain, with a stronger clasp. As far as she's concerned, Castiel is at home, and who doesn't like his pecker being out can leave, but we invited the family here for the first annual family reunion like idiots, and they've been showing up at the same time every year since. So, manners are necessary right now, and she's the only one who can make Castiel put his pecker, wiener, whatever somebody's calling it at the time he's freeing it of his clothes up.

Her gray areas have increased since our son's birth exactly nine months after our first date at her parents' house, but I don't want her to change too much. Her black and white view of the world is so fun to corrupt in the bedroom when it's just her and I.

Human League's *Human* peals from her cell phone on the stand beside her, the ringtone for her line connected to the local police department. Someone needs a place to stay in Amari's old building that I bought from under her to renovate into a shoe factory. She chose to remodel the apartments for those in need of immediate housing after domestic violence has left them with no place to go. When she's not shelling out keys and managing the household like a well-oiled machine, she manages Blake's resort so he and Astrid can have time off, to keep their relationship fresh after the birth of their children BJ and Arionne.

I couldn't have picked a more giving woman to love, and every day, I remind her that I don't deserve her, but I'm never letting go.

The End

Dear Reader,

I hoped you enjoyed the Owens, Nordic-Ford, Spencer, and Powers tales as much as I enjoyed penning them. If you got an extra kick out of Uncle Tommy as much as everyone else did, then Falon Gold's job is done. Almost. I think Uncle Tommy needs a story, too. Next year. Keep up to date with the additions to Undisclosed Desire series by visiting my like page. https://www.facebook.com/falongold/

Thank for supporting this series and reading to the end with me.

With love,
Falon Gold

www.ingramcontent.com/pod-product-compliance
Lightning Source LLC
Chambersburg PA
CBHW071139170626
46809CB00002B/688